The Jeeptown Sock Hop

a novel

2nd edition

JJ Harrigan

Copyright © 2025 John J Harrigan
Published by Salty Books Publishing, LLC (1870 Foothill Trl, Shakopee, MN)
All rights reserved.
ISBN: 978-1964354088
Library of Congress Catalog Card Number: 2025922409

Book design, Michael David MacBride
Cover design, Susan Stradiotto

Publication history: A prior version of this book was independently published by John J. Harrigan in 2012 under the same title.

FOR

Every survivor of child sex abuse.

NOTE TO READER

This revision of *The Jeeptown Sock Hop* is the exact same story as I wrote it a decade ago. However, some typos have been corrected. Some edits have also been made to make this version more reader friendly and to accommodate the changes in language over time.

CHAPTER 1

When you drive cross country to relax for a few days with your sister, you don't expect a blind date with an old friend. Certainly not with an old friend whose life you had once shattered. However, as I pulled my shiny new Lexus into the driveway of Mollie's house, there she was standing with Mollie on the Victorian front porch in the cool September afternoon. She wore a sleek paisley dress with a white cardigan sweater draped over her shoulders, looking trim, flat stomached, and much younger than her years. I marched up the porch steps, making no effort to hide the limp that had embarrassed me so much when we were young. With the happiest smile I'd flashed in weeks, I clasped the hand she extended.

"You look stunning, Clarice. Just like the young Diana Ross. Only much more elegant."

She grinned, and she still had those little bumps above her cheeks that pushed up when she smiled. "Still the charmer, I see. And getting along okay, according to your sister. Running a big hedge fund in

New York."

"A small hedge fund," I responded, smiling. "All that hustling we learned as kids finally paid off. But, Clarice, it's so good to see you! How long has it been?"

"Too long," snapped Mollie. She led us to her living room, poured three glasses of Pinot Noir, and seated us in overstuffed chairs by the unlit fireplace with a polished oak mantel. "Half the time we speak, Charlie, you ask about Clarice. So I talked her into coming here today. And I don't want either of you to stop talking until you get across that gap between you that you should have bridged a long time ago."

She sounded and looked like the social worker she had become, shifting her blue eyes back and forth between us, her red hair bobbing each time she turned her head.

"Charlie," said Clarice. "I want to know what happened that night. That's why I'm here."

"You already know," I said. "We talked about it that day at the art museum."

"But you never told me WHY you did those things that ended up so horribly, and that's what I want to know now. What you refused to tell me then."

"I didn't refuse to tell you; I was too ashamed to tell you. Or tell anybody for that matter."

She took a sip of wine and paused, crossing her right leg over her left knee and dangling her shoe on the toe as she waited for me to continue. When I hesitated to go on talking, she smiled warmly.

"I figured that out a long time ago. But we were kids then, and the things that troubled us so much as children are usually less shameful as adults. So, there shouldn't be any shame in telling me now. Just trust me, Charlie, the way you used to before that night happened. Just give me some answers to questions I still wonder about."

I stiffened. Not that I was any longer ashamed to talk about it. But even after all these years, I'd never completely reconciled myself with the rage that had consumed me that year and driven me to do what I did. Clarice had paid the price for it, and she deserved to have her questions answered. I swirled the dark liquid in my wineglass and switched my eyes back and forth between the two women.

"You are right, Clarice. It would be good to clear the air between us. You already know most of what happened, especially from your side of the neighborhood. But you had no way to know about some of the things on my side. And what happened that night didn't just pop out of the blue. There were several months leading up to it."

I took a sip of my wine and leaned forward before going on. "But it's a very long story and could keep us here the rest of the afternoon."

"I've got the whole day free." She smiled once more and leaned toward me again so that our foreheads were very close together. "And half the night, if needs be."

"Just let me tell it at my own pace," I replied. "Let me start at the beginning. The day we met that summer."

Nodding her agreement, she curled her feet under her and eased back in the chair. My eyes took in this trim elegant woman in front of me, but my mind slowly drifted back all those years and started to picture her as the girl I once knew. It was as though Clarice and Mollie weren't there. I tried to recall the world as we saw it when we were only fifteen.

Jeeptown seemed bigger in those days—and much more prosperous. The elm trees had not yet died, and the houses had fresher paint. The jeep factory worked overtime cranking out vehicles for the war in Korea, which meant work for Dad at the Spark Plug Company and other kids' dads at plants that made glass and brakes and headlights and starter motors and all sorts of things. The movie house on Dorr Street had lines of people on the weekends. The noise from the taverns spilled out through their doors that were open on hot summer nights. The stores overflowed with shoppers, the bakeries had huge jelly balls you could buy for a nickel, and the buses gave off trails of smelly exhaust as they lumbered down the streets.

A cool breeze from Lake Erie sometimes drifted through the Old North End. But even when the breeze died out, and our sweaty tee shirts stuck to our backs, we loved the summer, because we had no school, and we rode our bicycles all over town.

It was a day like that when I got the oddest suggestion I had ever received. If I had just said no, things might have ended better. But I mulled it over as James and I pedaled our bicycles beneath the canopy of leaves formed by the giant elm trees and oak trees along the street. We must have looked strange to anyone coming in the other direction, because we were each dwarfed by a gray cloth sack stuffed with tightly folded newspapers. We had each perched our sack atop a wire basket above the front wheel and wrapped a strap around the handlebars to anchor the sack in place. All that could be seen from the front was a brown face and a white face peering over the tops of our sacks as we squinted in the sunlight that shone through the gaps in the leaves.

"A band?" I asked.

"Yeah," said James. "We're both going to be in our high school bands in another year, and this'll give us some experience. We'll play at parties and dances."

I didn't say aloud the thought in the back of my mind. Start a band? With a colored kid? It might be fun, but never had I heard of an integrated party or dance.

"Think it over, Charlie," he said. "Bring your horn over to my house after supper, and we'll see how good we can play together."

"I can't. I have to babysit my sister while my parents go to the party at the VFW. How about doing it before supper, right after we finish our papers?"

We passed by a police car parked along the curb. We slowed down to look through the open window at the officer with a fat face, aviator sunglasses, and sweaty armpits in his blue shirt, as he sat taking a break in the shade of the huge trees. He took off the sunglasses and stared back with mean eyes. They shifted from James to me and back again, and the cop shook his head slightly from side to side. But he said nothing as we coasted by.

As soon as I got home, I went upstairs to get my trumpet from the top of the desk in my bedroom. Taped to the wall above the desk, I kept a pencil drawing of an old man with a big bandage over his ear, and, as I picked up the trumpet, I gave the picture a glance. My brother Danny had drawn it at the art museum as part of a school project several years ago. I'd dug it out of some old stuff of his and put it there to keep a reminder of Danny, who'd dropped out of school and joined the Marines and no longer shared the room with me.

I took the trumpet downstairs, then outside to the hot muggy afternoon. I steered my bike toward James's house on Fernwood Street. Fernwood had almost no white people. But two streets north, our block on Oakwood Street was all white, except for the Fontenells, who had moved up from New Orleans and lived kitty-corner from us. Only a few years ago, Fernwood had been half white. The whites were slowly moving out as Negroes moved in from the South.

At James's house, I met a sharp incline up the driveway into his yard, which I didn't hit fast enough, and my bicycle began to slow. I stepped on the pedal as hard as I could with my strong right leg, but the bike lost its momentum, and the trumpet pulled me off balance. The bike fell beneath me, and I skinned my elbow on the cinder driveway. At the back of the driveway, a huge brown man lifted his head from under the hood of a car to look in my direction.

"You must be Charlie," the man said in a deep strong voice as he walked down the long driveway and took my arm to help me up. "Are you all right?"

"I'm okay, Mr. Washington," I said, embarrassed by my clumsiness. I tucked the elbow, which had started to bleed, out of sight. He picked up the trumpet case and walked me toward the back yard, with me limping on my shorter left leg.

As we entered the back yard, my eyes came to rest on the most stunning sight I had ever seen, and my lower jaw must have dropped open. Someone had suspended a trapeze from a tree branch, and a girl was hanging by the knees from the bar. A long skirt hung upside down over her head, so she could not see me. My eyes locked onto the sight of two brown legs sticking out from a pair of shiny, white nylon underpants and the legs bent at the knees to support the girl's weight.

The huge brown man saw the look on my face and shouted at the girl.

"Girl! Get out of that tree! Get in the house!"

At the sound of her father's shout, the girl bent up from the waist, grabbed the trapeze, and swung gracefully to the ground, her skirt falling back in place and covering up the delightful vision now fixed in my mind.

As she turned and saw me staring, she lifted her hands to her face in embarrassment. "Go in the house and get James," her father barked.

She darted to the kitchen door. "James!" she shouted. "You got company."

James opened the kitchen door. "Come in, Charlie. I'm all set up." As we stepped into the kitchen, the girl stood at the sink, a hip thrust out as an actress might do in the movies. She was tall for a girl, almost as tall as me, and she flashed an embarrassed grin that made her look very pretty. I noticed a slight hint of perfume as I walked past her, trying to hide my limp. James led me to the living room at the front of the house. A radio by a side window blared an episode from *The Green Hornet*, and James turned it off.

"Who's that?" I asked, nodding my head in the girl's direction.

"That's my twin sister. But don't worry; she won't bother us."

"Twin sister. You never said you had a twin sister."

"What is there to say? She's a pain in the ass."

"How come I've never seen her?"

"I don't know. Maybe she was at the library. She

spends a lot of time at the library."

We sat down to jam, me with the trumpet and James at the drums. After a short while, we quit. "We need a piano," I said. "And a bass or a guitar."

"How about that kid along your route? He plays piano."

"Louis Rubinstein?"

"Yeah."

"He only plays classical stuff. How about an accordion? Bernie Karolak's got one, and sometimes he plays with his dad's polka band."

James made a face. "Polka band? I don't want to play no polkas, Charlie."

"He can probably play other things, too. What do you think?"

"Well, it won't hurt to try."

"I'll talk him into it. We'll come over next week."

As James walked me back through the kitchen to leave the house, I looked for the girl from the trapeze. But she was gone.

CHAPTER 2

J ust after midnight, a car door slammed out front of our house announcing that my parents were back from the end-of-summer party at the VFW Post on Dorr Street. And from the loud voices it sounded like trouble. I put down my Hardy Boys book and looked over at Mollie, asleep at the other end of the sofa, her red hair spread over a pillow. "Wake up!" I said, shaking her shoulder. "Get upstairs. I might need you." I pushed her up the stairs to the bathroom, which had two doors, one opening into the hallway and the other opening out to an outside deck. I stationed Mollie by the door to the deck, then went back to the top of the stairs where I watched my parents walk toward the house. Mollie left her post and tailed along behind me.

"You're an embarrassment!" Mother shouted above the sound of Mr. Byrne's brand new 52 Chevy driving off. "You drank too much again."

"Let a guy have some fun," Da said, slurring his words as he teetered up the sidewalk.

"And you spent an awful lot of time gabbing with those union cronies of yours. You'd better not be planning another strike."

They reached the porch, and Dad tripped on the first step.

"Look at you. You can't even walk straight."

Dad slowed down and forced himself to step cautiously up the stairs. "A guy's got a right to celebrate," he said as he stopped, turned around, bent his tall, skinny frame over, and looked her in the eye, "after all we went through at Normandy."

Mother only came up to his chin, but she pulled herself up to her full height and gave back a hostile stare as her round face started to flush with anger. "Normandy, my ass," she said. "You weren't even there. You were just a Seabee, out in the water someplace."

Da turned back toward the house and, for no apparent reason, started to sing the moment he passed through the door into the living room.

Oh, Danny boy, the pipes, the pipes are calling
From glen to glen, and down the mountain side.

"How dare you!" screamed Mother. "Our own son Danny is on his way to Korea to get shot at. And you're singing about it! I won't have that in my house. Stop it! Shut up! Shut up, I say!"

But Da did not shut up. He loved to sing the old songs, and he always thought everyone else loved them as well. Maybe he thought Mother would join in if he kept wailing long enough. He just kept plodding through the sad song.

"I'll shut you up, you drunk!" She dashed to the kitchen where she lifted a large cast-iron skillet from a bottom cupboard. My stomach knotted as Mother raised the skillet over her head with both hands and chased after Da, threatening to whack him. But Dad moved nimbly for a man who had been drinking all night. He skipped into the dining room where he stood on the balls of his feet behind the polished mahogany table, his fingertips tapping the tabletop for balance. Mother ran after him, and Dad scampered around the table, pulling out a chair to block her way. She ran in the other direction, and Dad skipped to the opposite side. Back and forth they danced, but the heavy cast-iron skillet kept Mother off balance. Her movements got slower, and any minute I expected her to sink into a chair and start laughing at the demon-like grin on his face. She might have, too, if Da hadn't started to mock her just then.

"Ha, ha, ha. You can't catch me," he taunted as he danced back and forth behind the table, faking her into energy-draining lurches with the heavy frying pan. Then he tripped over the chair he had pulled out and went sprawling to the floor. Mother leapt at him like a cat. The heavy skillet swooshed down toward Da's head, but he rolled away at the last instant and, instead of splitting his skull, the frying pan thudded onto the wooden floor, leaving a deep gouge. Da scrambled to his feet, stumbled toward the stairs and headed up, with Mother in pursuit.

"Get set," I barked at Mollie and pushed her toward the outside bathroom door. I pulled the hallway door open, and Mollie did the same with the door that led to the outside deck. Da reached the top of the stairs, darted through my door into the bathroom and out Mollie's door onto the deck. We both slammed our doors shut and locked them by turning the big keys. Mother banged on the door with her fists. "Let me in, you yellow Sea Bee," she shouted, to no avail.

Da paused to catch his breath. He stretched and

pushed his arms out through the sleeves of his unbuttoned khaki uniform jacket. Pinned above the breast pocket was the ribbon for the Silver Star he had won at Normandy. With his arms outstretched and the open coat sagging on his thin frame, Da looked like a scarecrow. Then he lay down on the tarpaper floor of the deck, crawled to the edge, dangled his legs over the side, grasped the down spout with both hands, and slid to the ground. He straightened up, threw his shoulders back, and tramped toward the garage. The light came on in the garage, and I knew Dad would spend the night on the old sofa Mr. Byrne had given to him.

Mother stopped hammering on the bathroom door, and I heard the frying pan drop to the floor with a clunk. With her fury spent and the let up of tension, the knot in my stomach began to ease. I slid to the floor in nervous laughter. My laughter infected Mollie, and the two of us sat there looking at each other, giggling uncontrollably.

Eventually, we stopped chortling, and the house grew quiet. Mother rapped her knuckles on the bathroom door. "Let me in, Charlie," she said in a soft, husky voice. "I've got to pee."

I opened the door and stepped aside. "He's not bad, Charlie," said Mother, apologizing for Da. "He just can't hold his licorice. It's the licorice that makes him do it." Liquor, I said to myself, not licorice. Mother had a tendency to mix up her words, to the great amusement of everyone in the family. This, however, would not be a good time to laugh at her.

Before undressing for bed, I hooked my feet between two wooden bars I had nailed into my closet doorway, and I hung upside down for a moment, putting extra weight on the left leg. This would make the left leg grow longer, I figured, and my limp would go away. The knot in my stomach disappeared, and I felt good as I crawled into bed. Not only did I get my parents apart before anyone got hurt, but I did it without any help from my brother Danny who had left and joined the Marines. What a great story this would be to tell Danny when he came home on leave after boot camp. And we could look forward to a good breakfast in the morning. That was Mother's way to apologize after she got into a ruckus. After breakfast, I would go over to Bernie Karolak's house to recruit him for the band.

Then, just before I fell asleep, the girl from the trapeze wandered into my mind.

CHAPTER 3

Sure enough, the next morning when I got back from serving the early Mass at St. Matthew's Catholic Church, I found Mother stirring pancake batter. She had the radio playing for background noise, and the Mills Brothers chanted one of her favorite songs, "You Always Hurt the One You Love." I sat next to Mollie at the new kitchen table with the modern Formica top. Mother gave us each three pancakes, which we smothered with maple syrup. Dad came in and also sat down for a helping of pancakes. Mother took the last of the pancakes, and we ate in silence, as though the quiet would wipe out what had happened the night before.

I didn't catch up with Bernie Karolak until our Monday night Boy Scout meeting. Boy Scouts was the place where I fit in better than anywhere else. Mr. Jackson, the scoutmaster, wanted to have me for his first Eagle Scout. Getting Eagle Scout would help me out in later life, according to Dad. Mother said I should be especially grateful to Mr. Jackson for his help.

Bernie turned up his nose at the band idea. "A band with you and James? An integrated band?"

"Yeah, we'll make a fortune."

"We're gonna do this at a James's house?" He squinted, skeptically.

"Just to get started. Then we can practice at my house."

Bernie wasn't any more prejudiced than any other kid in the neighborhood, but that in itself would keep most kids out of a Negro's house. So I've got to give him credit for trying. But I worried all night about what he might say when we got to James's house, and the next morning as we trudged down the street, his first words didn't give me much hope.

"Does it stink?"

"Does what stink?"

"James's house. Does it stink?"

"Bernie, it's August. They got the windows open all day. It's full of fresh air, for Christ's sake."

"Well, it could still stink."

Oh God! My shoulders tensed as I grabbed him by the sleeve. "Bernie, we gotta get something straight or this isn't going to work. The house doesn't stink. Everything is clean, and they're going to treat you nice. But you can't say things like that or you're going to kill the band before it even starts. You have to act like you do when you go to anybody else's house."

"I know that. Don't be such a jerk, Charlie. What'ya think I am? A dope?"

"It's just that you got to be careful. We need a drummer for our band, and we don't want to drive James away." I emphasized the "our band" to make it sound as though Bernie were allowing James to audition rather than the reverse.

"Don't worry. Dumb guys like him who drum are a dime a dozen; we can always find another one."

"That's what I mean, Bernie. You've got to stop insulting people. I'd bet you couldn't go through the day without calling somebody a name."

"Not to his face," Bernie protested.

"It doesn't matter. I bet you can't get through the rest of the day without calling somebody an insulting name."

"Don't be such a snob, Parnell. Like you're better than everyone else."

"I'll bet fifty cents you can't go the rest of the day without calling someone a name."

"You're on," Bernie accepted, grinning. "This is going to be the easiest fifty cents I ever made."

And it would be the best fifty cents I ever spent if it kept Bernie from saying some of the things I'd heard him say dozens of times.

"And you think you're so smart!" Bernie gloated as we turned the corner onto Fernwood. "This is gonna ruin your reputation as a sharp bettor."

Our jam session went badly. James and I played loud and fast as though we were already in the high school marching bands we were each aiming for. Bernie played everything to the three-four beat of a polka, and nothing worked. The girl from the trapeze came through the archway into the living room and sat primly erect on a hard-backed chair. My pulse quickened, and I sat up a little straighter. James snarled at his sister. "Get out of here. You're bothering us."

"This is my house, James. I can sit anywhere I want,"

she said in a taunting, sing-songy voice. "Besides, Charlie doesn't mind if I'm here. Do you Charlie?" She turned the corners of her mouth upward in a slight grin and tilted her head to one side, as girls do in the movies.

"Do I mind if you're here?" I stammered. "I don't even know your name."

"Clarice," said the girl from the trapeze. She stood up and walked over to me in short choppy steps, as though she were wearing an extremely tight skirt, even though she wore blue jeans and could take strides as long as she wanted. The older girls walked that way in their tight skirts, and she looked to be imitating them. Still holding that smile on her face, she put out her hand and said, "My name is Clarice. I'm pleased to meet you."

Before our hands could touch, James boomed, "Clarice, get out of here."

She snarled at her brother. "Don't you talk that way to me, James!"

"I'll talk any way I want. Now you get your ass out of here before I kick it out."

"Momma's not going to like it when she finds out you been swearing at me in front of two white boys. She's gonna whop you upside the head."

James thought about this, then retorted. "Well, when she finds out you been embarrassing me in front of my friends, she's not gonna like that either. So sit down and shut up."

Just then James's mother popped her head into the door of the room. "What's all this shouting about?"

She looked sternly at James and Clarice, but neither of them made any effort to enlist her help in the argument. "I want to hear some music out of you, not a bunch of shouting," she said before leaving the room.

Clarice went back to the chair, resumed her prim pose, and put a victorious smile on her face as she shifted her eyes back and forth between the three of us boys. We tried one more song, but with no more success than earlier.

"You know what you guys are doing wrong?" Clarice blurted. "You're doing stuff that's too complicated. You should start with something simple. James, put down those sticks and use your bongos like you do in church." She began humming something I had never heard, but that must be a Protestant hymn. Was it a sin for a Catholic to play a Protestant hymn? And if so, did it need to be confessed? Then I heard her voice chanting the lyrics and forgot all about sins and Catholics and Protestants.

Amazing Grace, How sweet the sound,
That saved a wretch like me.
I once was lost, but now I'm found,
Was blind, but now I see.

I lifted the trumpet to my lips when Clarice paused and quickly picked up the melody. After a stanza, she interrupted.

"Charlie, you're too low for me to sing. What key are you in?"

"C," I said. That was the easiest key to start with when playing something new. It usually minimized the number of flats and sharps.

"You're too low for me. Move up a little. Try starting with an E."

I moved up to the E note and adapted by trial and error to the two sharp notes that would be needed in the new key. Then we got Bernie to add in some chords with his accordion. It took half an hour to belt out a complete version without James and Clarice interrupting each other. When I finally took the trumpet from my lips and rested the bell of the horn on my leg, I had a lightheaded, almost mystical, feeling from blowing the mournful tune, and it echoed in my mind.

We sat around at the end of the session trying to talk, but it was awkward. Finally, Clarice said, "You guys need a piano."

James looked over to me and said, "Are you sure Louis won't do it?"

"Louis?" said Bernie, snapping forward in his seat. "That little kike over on Oakwood? Why would we want him?"

A silence fell over the group, and stayed, until I broke it. "Jew, Bernie. Louis is a Jew, not a kike." But Clarice had an angry pout on her face as she looked at her brother and rolled her eyes. I decided to change the subject. "When should we practice again? How about next Wednesday after supper?"

"I can't," said Clarice. "I always go to the library on Wednesday after supper."

Bernie stared in disbelief. "It's summer. Why do you go to the library in the summer?"

"Momma says I got to get a head start on school so I can make something of myself."

Bernie shook his head, and James said, "It doesn't matter whether you can be here, Clarice. You're not in this band."

My head snapped up. Clarice had me intrigued, and I didn't want James getting rid of her. "James," I said, "we need a singer, and she did a great job on that song.

We need her."

James rolled his eyes but relented. "How about if we meet next Saturday, before we do our papers? In the meantime, feel out Louis."

"Pay up," I said as soon as we got out of hearing distance from James's house.

"Pay up what?" demanded Bernie.

"The bet," I said. "The bet we made that you'd insult somebody."

"I didn't insult anybody."

"You called Louis a kike."

"That don't count. He wasn't there."

"We didn't bet that he had to be there, only that you couldn't go an hour without insulting someone."

"Kike is not an insult. It's what he is. Jews are kikes." Bernie paused, but I did not respond, and he plunged forward, obviously hoping to trip me up. "Everybody's something. It's like being a wop. Tony Morelli's a wop. Old Schmidt's a kraut. And Carl Broda's a bohunk."

"And you're a dumb Ukrainian," I said. "But we don't throw it in your face."

At the phrase dumb Ukrainian, Bernie stopped walking and grabbed my sleeve. His face grew red in anger, and I steeled myself for a punch or at least for an attempt to throw me to the ground. But the heavy accordion strapped over his back made it hard for him to move. He simply shouted,

"And you're—I don't know what you are. Oh, yeah, I know. You're a cripple. That's what you are. A cripple."

My fists clenched. "That's an insult," I said. "You gonna pay up or you gonna fink out on what you owe like everybody says you always do?"

My arms trembled I was so angry, and I clamped my jaw tight as we glared at each other. But I stuffed the urge to lash back and focused instead on making Bernie pay up. "So what's it gonna be? You gonna welch or you gonna do the right thing for a change and pay up?" When Bernie didn't reply, I tried to sweeten the pot. "I'll tell you what. You pay me the bet and I'll split it with you. I'll buy us each a Cherry Coke."

Bernie pulled a fifty-cent coin from his pocket and threw it on the ground. "Up yours, Parnell. Keep your Coke; I'll get some at home."

Tense with anger, I waved the coin in front of Bernie's face as I snarled at him, "Thanks, Bernie." I turned on my heel and headed toward The Norwood Drugstore on Norwood Street where I sat by myself at the soda fountain and drank a glass of Cherry Coke.

But there was no pleasure in it. Bernie had turned our practice session into a disaster. We really needed Clarice as a singer to liven us up, but also needed Bernie's accordion. It was the closest thing we had to a keyboard. But I couldn't see how she and Bernie could fit into the same band. The look on her face made it clear that she did not like him. He, on the other hand, didn't dislike her at all. He simply looked down on her, as he did on all Negroes. I wished I could talk with my brother Danny. He always had good ideas for problems like this. I thought to myself, "There's got to be a way to work this out."

CHAPTER 4

It seemed like forever before Wednesday got here, and after supper I rushed through washing the dishes and piled them up faster than Mollie could dry them. I emptied the sink and went up to my room to exchange my dirty tee shirt for a clean, white polo shirt with a collar. I put on a pair of clean blue jeans, folded up the cuffs, went downstairs, and bolted out the front door.

The Lucretia Mott Branch Public Library on Dorr Street looked like dozens of Carnegie libraries I once saw in a picture book. A dark brick building with stone trim around the doors and windows, it gave me a quiet refuge from the busy street with its noisy traffic. I had to walk up several concrete steps to reach the entrance, because it was built half a level above the street. The top step looked out over the street, and standing there gave me the feel of a judge sitting above and looking down on all the people in his court.

It felt good to step from the muggy summer air into the cool of the building. Mrs. Nordstrom sat behind a counter in front of the door. I spotted Clarice in the section labeled young adults. She sat up straight at a large, wooden reading table, leafing through a magazine. She wore a sleeveless yellow blouse, and I couldn't help but see the white bra straps on the tan color of her shoulders. Trying to hide my limp, I ambled to her table, sat down opposite her, and smiled. She had been watching me from the corner of her eye, and she returned my grin with a wide smile that pushed her cheeks up into little bumps just under her eyes. I marveled at this, then got embarrassed when I realized I was staring at her. I looked down at the magazine. It was *Ebony*.

"That doesn't look like schoolwork."

"Momma doesn't care what I read, just so I read, she says. What are you doing here?"

"I have to pick up a story book for my little sister Mollie," I lied.

"Where is she?"

"She's home finishing the dishes."

"Girls always have to do the dishes. Boys get it easy."

I didn't want to admit that I had to wash dishes as well, so I challenged her. "Well, you don't have to cut the grass or shovel snow or shovel coal into the furnace. Do you know what that's like in January, if the furnace goes out in the middle of the night and you have to go down there in the cold and get it started? Before the sun's even up?"

"Well, you shouldn't let it go out. Then you wouldn't have to go down in the cold."

"Why you arguing with me, Clarice? I stop by to be polite, and you start picking a fight."

I leaned on my elbows, with my hands folded together on the table. She flashed half a smile, then reached her hand out so her fingers touched the back of my hands on the table.

"I'm just teasing you, Charlie. Can't you tell? It's a way of being friends."

"That's a strange way to be friends."

"Doesn't your momma ever tease your daddy?"

I pursed my lips together and thought for a moment. "My mother's not the teasing type."

I paused, then added, "She's more of a hit-you-over-the-head-with-the-skillet type."

"A what?" She drew her hands back and sat up straight.

Oh, God, I thought as I sucked in a breath. Shouldn't have said that. But it was too late to turn back now. "Let me tell you." I described the incident with the frying pan.

"Oh, Charlie," she said. "How often does something like that happen?" She touched the back of my hand again with her fingers, and it felt good. Then, a second later she withdrew them.

"Not very often," I said, trying to make it look okay. "Just once in a while."

"That's awful," she said, then quickly added when she saw me wince, "I'm sorry. I shouldn't have said that."

I moved my fingers up to touch the back of her hands. I asked, "Don't your parents ever fight when your dad drinks?"

"Daddy hardly ever drinks. Momma won't let him."

"How does she stop him?"

"I don't know," Clarice squinted thoughtfully. She sat up a little straighter and pulled back her hands. "I don't know how she does it. Once I heard her talking about Dirty George's father getting drunk all the time, and Momma said her man ever come home like that, she'd kick him out. But I never heard her say that to

Daddy."

We sat quietly for a few moments, and all of a sudden, I felt embarrassed at what I had told her, not knowing what she would think of my family or who she might tell. I stared at the table, glanced at the walls, looked up at the ceiling, anything to keep from making eye contact.

"Clarice?" I finally said.

She looked over as if asking what.

"You won't tell anybody what I said, will you?"

"No, I won't tell anybody. You can trust me."

She reached over and brushed back some hair that had flopped over my forehead. It seemed like a strange thing to do. Maybe she'd seen her mother do it. But it felt good, and I felt a little warm. She looked up at the clock on the wall and said, "I've got to go, Charlie. Did you talk to the piano player yet?"

"I'll see him next week. I gotta do some Boy Scout stuff first."

"You a Boy Scout?"

"Yep. I'm going to be an Eagle Scout. Probably by this time next year."

"Sounds great," she said and smiled, then tried to look stern as she added, "Talk to that piano player, Charlie. We gotta get this band started before everybody loses interest."

She left then, swinging her hips as she walked away. However, you could hardly see the sway, because she had on the same baggy skirt she'd worn when I first saw her hanging upside down from the trapeze, with her legs sticking out of the shiny, white nylon underpants.

I should get a girlfriend, I thought, as I left the library. Directly across the street was the North End Tavern. The doors were wide open because of the hot summer night, and music from the jukebox drifted to the outside. "The Sunny Side of the Street." The upbeat tempo of the song got me skipping as I headed toward home. Yeah, I should get a girlfriend. Maybe I'd fit in better. Maybe Roberta Quinn would go out. I wondered if you can talk with her like you can with Clarice.

CHAPTER 5

Clarice, the band, and the Boy Scouts got put on hold for the next week, because school started. Right after Labor Day I found myself in the eighth-grade classroom of St. Matthew's School waiting for our new teacher to show up, and we were making a lot of noise with everyone talking at once. I tried recruiting Carl Broda to play saxophone in my band.

"That band you tried to rope Bernie Karolak into? The one with James Washington?"

"Yeah, it's an integrated band. James is a great drummer, I'm on the trumpet, and Louis plays the piano. The way you play sax, you'd fit in great."

"An integrated band's never gonna work. I'm not joining a band like that."

Before I could reply, our new teacher walked in, and the moment she stepped through the door we all stopped our jostling. It was Mrs. Hanratty, the only lay teacher at St. Matthew's. An older woman, she wore a long black dress that came down almost to her ankles. She strode across the yellowing wood floorboards to her desk, tapped it with a long blackboard pointer, and announced, "I will not have this noise in my classroom." She swept her gaze across us sitting in the six rows of desks, six desks deep, girls on her left, boys on her right. "You will be polite and be a credit to St. Matthew's School. And you will not cause any trouble."

She read the roster slowly, pausing and staring at each of us as she read our names. She worked her way through the As and Bs, then the Cs and Ds without any problems. Even Billy Byrne, who often got into trouble, escaped unscathed. Then she came to Bernie Karolak, slumped in his seat with his arms folded across his chest.

"You there, slouching like a monkey, are you paying attention?"

"Me?" asked Bernie, a terrified look on his face.

"Of course, you. Who else am I looking at?"

"Yeah."

"Yes what?"

"Yeah, I'm paying attention."

"Are you getting smart with me, young man? Don't get smart with me." She glared at Bernie with her brown eyes. "Haven't your parents taught you any manners? What kind of parents do you have? Sit up straight!" she snapped. "Get those arms off your chest and get that arrogant look off your face. When I ask a question, you answer, 'Yes, Mrs. Hanratty' or 'Yes, ma'am.' You don't say 'Yeah' or 'Naw' like some crude Protestant."

Bernie jolted himself upright into rigid attention in his seat, unfolded his arms from his chest, and put his hands properly on the desktop.

"That's much better," she soothed. A smile almost broke out on her lips. "You must have good posture if you want to grow up to be healthy."

Thirty-five other bodies snapped into good posture as we waited for Mrs. Hanratty to resume. She called, "Charles S. Parnell."

"Here," I said, raising my arm. "I go by Charlie."

"Parnell? That sounds familiar. Did any of your brothers or sisters go here?"

"My brother Danny."

"Yes, I remember." A frown crossed her face as she stared at me for a long moment. It was no wonder she'd remember Danny. When she had sent his class to draw sketches of art pieces at the art museum, Danny looked for something that would shock her, and he found it in the reproduction of the artist with the big bandage on his ear. Danny never tired of telling about the look on Mrs. Hanratty's face when he presented his sketch to the class and he told them about the painter who'd cut off his ear then given it to a prostitute. Words like prostitute were frowned on at St. Matthew's. Especially in Mrs. Hanratty's class.

"What does the 'S' stand for, Mr. Charles S. Parnell?"

"Stewart, ma'am, after my grandpa."

"Named after your grandpa were you? And who was he named after?"

I didn't say anything and Mrs. Hanratty continued. "You are named after a sinner. And not just any sinner, but the second worst sinner in the history of Ireland. And a Protestant to boot. Did you know that?" I didn't know what to say and wanted her to move on to someone else. Why didn't my parents give me a normal name instead of naming me after some dead Irish Protestant? What made him the second worst sinner in Irish history, anyway? And why did anybody care after all these years? Unfortunately, Mrs. Hanratty cared.

"What kind of parents would name their child after

a sinner?" Then she lightened up. "Well, you'd better not follow in his footsteps, Mr. Charles S. Parnell, or your name will be mud with me." She smiled at her little joke, but I didn't smile back. Neither did anybody else.

Turning her eyes back to the roll call, she scowled when she found a name that was out of alphabetical order. "Anthony Morelli."

"Here, ma'am. I go by Tony. My friends call me Tony." Slightly chubby, Tony was the friendliest boy in the class, and never a source of trouble.

"Are you a good Catholic, Anthony?"

"Yes, ma'am," said Tony.

"Didn't I see you last Friday eating a bowl of chili at the North End Café?"

Tony gulped.

"How can you call yourself a good Catholic? Good Catholics don't eat meat on Friday. Maybe Italians don't know how to be good Catholics. Didn't your parents teach you not to eat meat on Friday? What have you got to say for yourself, Mr. Anthony Morelli?"

Never had I heard a nun or priest attack a child's background. To the contrary. They usually preached that we should reject the prejudices that were all over Jeeptown. "We're all God's children," repeated Father Stan, the assistant pastor, over and over. "Even the coloreds."

"Well, behave yourself, Mr. Morelli. I won't have any bad Catholics in my class."

By now Mrs. Hanratty had reached the letter Q, and the Quinn sisters looked petrified as they sat one behind the other. "Stand up, young lady," she barked at Sally Quinn. As Sally came to her feet, her plaid skirt fell barely to her knees.

"Unacceptable," snarled Mrs. Hanratty. "In my class, the skirt must come well below the knee." On the boy's side of the room, we all snuck a glance at Sally's legs.

"And you." She stared at Roberta Quinn. "Is that lipstick on your face? What kind of home do you girls come from? I will not have hussies in my classroom. Both of you go home over the lunch period and change clothes. And don't be late getting back for the afternoon."

Sally and Roberta were so stunned they couldn't move.

"Sit down," barked Mrs. Hanratty.

We all sat in disbelief. Not a shoe scraped along the floor. Not a paper rustled on a desktop. We just sat there without making a noise. Then Mrs. Hanratty abruptly changed tone to one of upbeat cheeriness. "Well, aren't we the sad-faced group of children?" she said with a thin smile on her lips. "Let's get down to business. God wants us to be happy, not glum."

As much as we kids disliked her, Mrs. Hanratty had the best behaved children at St. Matthew's School. Probably in the whole city. Father Doyle, the pastor, repeatedly praised her for keeping all the kids in line. Except for my brother Danny. Especially that one incident about the nine First Fridays, which was the only time I ever saw him come home from school crying. I cringed at the idea of being stuck with her for the whole year.

On our walk home from school that afternoon, Billy Byrne laughed at me. "So you're named after the second worst sinner in the history of Ireland. Who was number one?"

"Damned if I know," I said.

"Oliver Cromwell," said Dad when I raised the question that night at supper.

"Then who was the second worst sinner?"

"Damned if I know," said Dad, furrowing his eyebrows. "Why?"

"Mrs. Hanratty said it was Charles Stewart Parnell."

"Well, sometimes teachers don't know everything there is to know," said Dad. "Charles Stewart Parnell was a great patriot of Ireland. He fought for home rule. He would have gotten it too, if the priests hadn't turned against him."

"So, he must have been a sinner," I said. "Why else would the priests turn against him?"

"He just had a weakness, that's all," said Dad.

"A weakness?"

Dad looked over at Mother before continuing. "He had a girlfriend."

"What's wrong with that?"

"His girlfriend was a Catholic, Katie O'Shea."

"Why did that matter? Lots of Protestants have Catholic girlfriends."

"You were not supposed to do that in those days."

Mother sat across from Dad, annoyed, tapping her fork on the kitchen table. "It was Mrs. Katie O'Shea," said Mother, emphasizing the word Mrs. "She already had a husband when Parnell started playing around with her."

"He just had a weakness," said Dad. "Forget what your teacher said. You have a great name, just like your brother Danny, and you should be proud of it." He strode to the refrigerator to get a bottle of Buckeye Beer. He still bought his beer by the bottle, rather than the new cans that had become so popular. "I'll have to go talk to your teacher." Of course, he never did.

Complaining at home didn't do my friends any good either, I found out. Bernie Karolak said his father slapped him and reaffirmed that he must indeed sit up straight, keep his shoulders back, and his chin up. Especially so because everybody was watching to see how Ukrainians behaved. "I didn't spend three years fighting that goddamned war so you could give us a black eye. Act like you're proud to be Ukrainian," Bernie reported his father saying.

Tony Morelli said he got bawled out by his mother when she found out about the Friday chili. Italians, too, were being watched. "It was bad enough before the war with everybody thinking we weren't good Americans. Even Roosevelt. The last thing we need is you convincing them we're not good Catholics."

The only parent to object about Mrs. Hanratty was Mr. Quinn, who owned a construction business and did a lot of work for the churches in the diocese. I pried the information out of Sally Quinn.

"What did your Da say to Father Doyle?" I asked her.

"I believe in discipline, and I want my children educated. But I will not have them humiliated," she said. She pushed her shoulders back and her chin out, like she was proud of him. I could believe he had said that. He was a tough cookie. Once at a VFW picnic he and Dad got into a ferocious argument about the union. They stood toe to toe shouting, almost to the point of pushing each other, when the union president came and led Dad away by the arm.

"What else did he say? He must have said more than that."

"I can't tell you," she said. "My da told me to keep it a secret."

"Is it true your dad paid for that big stained glass

window above the church entrance?"

"Charlie, I said I can't tell you. You'll just have to wait and see."

"Wait and see what?"

She snapped her arms down and refused to say anything more.

Whatever her father had said to the priest, it had a big impact. When we showed up for school the next Monday, Mrs. Hanratty was gone.

CHAPTER 6

A young, short nun with a square dark face stood waiting for us as we filed into class that morning. A white ruffle in the shape of an upside-down U framed her face, as it did for all the Sisters of Notre Dame. In the entire history of schools, no teacher had ever faced a class happier to see her rather than the person who'd been there the week before. "I am Sister Mary FAH tee mah," she said. "It is spelled like this." She wrote F a t i m a on the chalkboard. "But you pronounce it FAH tee mah. Now say it after me, 'Sister FAH tee mah.'"

We all called out in amusement, "Sister FAH tee mah."

"Wonderful," she said, a big smile lighting up her face. "Many people cannot say my name properly. But now I have taught you how to say it the right way, and that is how I want you to say it." She had a slightly odd accent. During the roll call, she pronounced my name like "Sharles" instead of "Charles" as though she had trouble making the sound "ch." And when she said the word "spelled," it had sounded like "spell ed" as though it had two syllables. From the squints in the other kids' eyes, they too had noticed something different. No one said anything, however, until Billy Byrne raised his hand in the middle of religion class.

"Yes, William?" said Sister FAH tee mah after checking the seating chart she had made.

"Billy, Sister. I go by Billy."

"What is your question, Billy?"

"Sister, where are you from?"

"When a girl enters the convent, she leaves her old life behind and marries herself to Jesus. What matters is not where a sister comes from but whether she can help you live a holier life."

Billy did not reply. He just sat with his mouth drooping and looking puzzled.

"I am not supposed to dwell on my old life before becoming a sister. But I can see you are curious about it, so I will tell you." I could hear some rustling on the girls' side of the room, as they leaned forward to hear what this small nun had to tell us about her background.

"I'm from Massachusetts."

She had a slight smile in the turned-up corners of her mouth and her eyes twinkled. She seemed to be teasing Billy as she stood in front of us waiting for him to say something. Billy wasn't the quickest kid at St. Matthew's, but finally, he said,

"But Sister, you don't look like someone from Massachusetts."

"What do you mean?" she asked.

"Well, you don't look like Ted Williams, for example."

Butch Bower piped in, "He's a baseball player, Sister." I nodded in agreement. It was good to clarify that point, since a nun could hardly be expected to know anything about a baseball player, even if he had been the greatest batter of modern times.

She paused to look down at her seat chart. "I know who Ted Williams is. You can't be from Massachusetts and not know about Ted Williams, Baldwin."

Sally Quinn snickered. Butch Bower did not like to be called by his proper name, and Sally frequently called him 'Baldwin' to get his goat. And now Sister FAH tee mah had unwittingly done the same thing. Butch sneered at Sally, then replied.

"Butch, Sister. I go by Butch."

She wrote 'Butch' on her seating diagram. "I know who Ted Williams is, Butch." She stood silently for a moment, then directed her attention back to Billy Byrne who had asked where she came from. "I came to Massachusetts from Cape Verde when I was a young girl. Do you know where Cape Verde is, Billy?"

He shook his head no.

"Billy, we do not just shake our heads. We say, 'Yes, Sister' or 'No, Sister.'"

"No, Sister," said Billy.

"How about you, Butch?"

"No, Sister," said Butch.

Even Brenda Delaney, the best student in the class, did not know where to find Cape Verde. Sister said, "Let us take a short geography lesson. Butch, go to the map and find the Cape Verde islands."

Butch had never shown interest in any geography beyond the Old North End, much less Cape Verde. Nevertheless, he rose from his seat and swaggered to the mission map on the wall. This map portrayed the Christian world as bathed in sunlight and everywhere else as covered with darkness. Each year we donated money to a special mission collection to spread the light of Christianity to the heathen world, and the map had little patches of light where the largest Catholic missions existed in the darkened parts of the world.

"Can anybody help Butch?" Sister asked as Butch stared blankly at the map.

"I can help Baldwin," piped up Sally, grinning as she walked over to the map and stood next to Butch. He waited until Sister's eyes were diverted elsewhere then poked his elbow into Sally's ribs. She jabbed him back with her knuckles.

Sister turned her attention back to the two map explorers and said, "Look for a group of islands in the Atlantic Ocean, between Africa and the Caribbean."

Butch slouched back from the map and kept his hands in his pockets as Sally used her index finger to trace a line eastward across the Atlantic from Cuba. "Here they are," she said, pointing to a spot that lay right on the border between the lighted up Christian side of the world and the darkened heathen world.

Butch moved up a step to peer at the map. He pointed his finger at the islands and asked, "What's this 'Port' that's written under the name?"

"Let's see if we can figure that out," said Sister. "Look at Puerto Rico and you will see the letters 'USA' are written there. What does that mean?"

Brenda Delaney waved her hand back and forth in the air. At Sister's nod, she said, "That means Puerto Rico is owned by the USA."

"Exactly," said Sister. "So if 'Port' is written by Cape Verde, who owns Cape Verde?"

We looked quizzically back and forth. How the hell were we supposed to know that? Sister frowned with irritation at our lack of knowledge. Then she walked over to Butch Bower, grabbed his wrist, and pointed his hand at Europe. "What is this?"

He looked carefully at the map. "Spain," he said.

"No, not Spain. What is next to Spain?"

Butch peeked again at the map. "France."

"Not France. What is on the other side of Spain?" She dragged his hand westward until it fell into the Atlantic Ocean. Half the class suppressed giggles.

"Portugal," said Butch. "I get it. Portugal owns Cape Verde." He beamed a big grin as he swaggered back to his seat.

"Yes, Portugal," said Sister. "My father was a poor sailor from Cape Verde. He wanted to go to Massachusetts where his brother had settled, but his ships never sailed in that direction."

She pronounced sailed as two syllables, 'sail ed,' but no one snickered.

"His ships only took him back and forth to Portugal. One time, he visited the shrine at FAH tee mah, or Fatima, as we pronounce it in English. He made a promise to Our Blessed Mother that, if she would get his family to America, he would give his oldest child to the service of Jesus." She pointed her fingers at her chest. "That was me."

Roberta Quinn gasped and brought the palms of her hands up to her cheeks in horror. "You mean he forced you to be a nun?"

"On, no, my child," said Sister. "By the time I became a nun, we were already in America. You can't force people to do that in America. But even in Massachusetts, the Cape Verdeans were very poor. Until my father learned English and got a good job as a taxi driver, he suffered many insults and indignities. But Our Lady of FAH tee mah got us to America and got us through those times. We owed a great debt to our

Blessed Mother. So after high school, I entered the convent."

Every girl in the room stared at her with fascination. Even we boys paid attention. "My mother wanted me to enter the Franciscans so I could stay in Massachusetts and work with the poor there. But I wanted to be a teaching nun, so I joined the Sisters of Notre Dame and took the name, Sister Mary FAH tee mah." She smiled proudly and added, "Maybe one of you will decide someday to give your life to the service of Jesus, either as a sister or as a priest." She slowly scanned the room.

"I must tell you one more thing," she said. "It is why I do not look like Ted Williams. And it is a thing of great pride to Cape Verdeans. Hundreds of years ago, North Africans conquered Portugal and intermarried with the Portuguese there and in Cape Verde. Then during the years of the slave trade, many Africans ended up in the Cape Verde islands. So Cape Verdeans are partly European and partly African." She beamed proudly as she spread this astonishing message.

I could hardly wait to deliver this news to my parents and see the looks on their faces when they heard my teacher was part Negro. And proud of it. I wondered what Clarice would think.

Sister squinted her eyes for a second as though something had just occurred to her. "But maybe I'm getting ahead of myself. Maybe you don't know about FAH tee mah. Can anyone tell us why it's important?"

Brenda Delaney waved her hand again. "Our Holy Mother appeared there before some children and thousands of people." Brenda beamed in delight. She could never contain her desire to show off how smart she was. "The sun grew so bright it seemed to spin in the sky. And many people were cured of crippling illnesses."

As Sister nodded her head yes, Butch Bower broke in, "Maybe she can cure Charlie. He's a cripple." A burst of laughter erupted from the class.

I looked down at my desk so I wouldn't have to make eye contact with anyone, but from the corner of my eye I could see the smiling face of Sister FAH tee mah turn to a grimace. She had seen me limp into the classroom at the start of the day, so she obviously knew who that son-of-a-bitch Butch had in mind. "Baldwin, you go to the coat room and wait for me," she snapped.

As Butch walked into the coatroom, she turned her attention to the class. "We must get back to our lessons, but first I must send a note to Father Stan." Father Stanislaus Drybczyk was the assistant pastor. But nobody except Bernie Karolak could pronounce a name that had no vowels. So Sister FAH tee mah, like the rest of us, just called him Father Stan. She scribbled something on a piece of paper, folded it, and sealed it with Scotch tape. "I need someone take this to the rectory for me?"

We boys all raised our hands at the chance to escape the classroom for a few moments. She picked me and told me to wait for a reply from Father Stan. The big wooden door swung shut behind me, but her voice drifted out over the transom, and I couldn't help listening.

"I will not tolerate cruelty in my classroom. When you laughed at that boy, you were cruel. We all have a cross to bear in life. I have mine. Each of you has yours. I never again want to see any of you being cruel to one another." She paused, and I imagined her eyes sweeping slowly across the class, attempting to make eye contact, as she had done earlier. But I doubted that anybody looked at her.

"When you laughed, you mocked Our Lady of FAH tee mah. Do you doubt that Our Lady of FAH tee mah could cure that boy's limp? Do you doubt that she can help you with your burdens? I already told you what she did for my family, and yet you still doubt her powers. You must not mock the Blessed Mother."

Another long pause followed.

"For your punishment, you will each write out a hundred times, 'I must not be cruel,' and you will turn it in tomorrow morning. With perfect penmanship." I could hear a general rustling of displeasure, as the girls shifted in their seats and the boys scraped their shoes along the floor.

"Furthermore, you must not breathe one word of this to that boy. If he finds out I gave you this punishment, you will each have to write it again."

Then Brenda Delaney asked, "Sister, what about those of us who didn't laugh? Do we have to write it out, too?"

Sister FAH tee mah paused. "True, you did not laugh," she said. "But if you knew it was wrong and you failed to object, that is even worse. You must write it two hundred times."

I was stunned, standing outside the door, and before I could move, there came the sound of her shoes stepping someplace, apparently to the coatroom where Butch waited. By now her voice was muffled as it floated through the transom, and I could no longer make out her words. I did hear Butch's voice, followed by the sound of three sharp slaps.

I don't know what the note said, or if my face was betraying the shame I felt, but Father Stan gave me an odd look. After writing a response on the note and telling me to return it to Sister FAH tee mah, he asked me to come back after school to help him with some task he needed to do.

When classes ended at three fifteen, I slogged over to the rectory to keep my appointment with Father Stan. We bent over some boxes to unpack a shipment of missals that had just arrived. Our heads came very close together as we pulled the books from the boxes, and he smelled of cologne. Why would a priest bother to wear cologne? And why would he be so close to me? As I started to back away, Sister FAH tee mah knocked on the door. Father Stan dismissed me, and I quietly shut the door to his study behind me. Standing outside the door, I paused to eavesdrop on them. I shouldn't have done that, but I still felt humiliated from what had happened that morning and wanted to know what she had to say about it.

"I did not know what else to do, Father," she said, and it sounded a little like she was crying. "I lost my temper when he said 'Everybody calls Charlie a cripple. He doesn't mind.' Of course he minds! Everyone cares when they are humiliated. I remembered what it felt like to be called a 'dago' or a 'spick.' And I lost control of myself. I know I should not have slapped that boy. But I cannot let the children be cruel to one another. I hate myself for being cruel, but I lost control. I am sorry, Father. Please give me absolution so God will forgive me."

"I understand your anger, Sister. Under the same circumstances, I might have slapped the boy myself. We are only human. But you must not hit the children over small transgressions. Let us make the Act of Contrition so God will forgive you." The long brown rosary hanging from her waist clinked on the floor as she knelt down to pray and receive the words of absolution.

I walked out of the rectory and was barely out of sight around the corner of the building when she came down the stairs. She walked over to the church and knelt in the front pew, fingering the brown beads of the huge rosary.

I felt very bad for her, and that made my own shame easier to bear. Sister FAH tee mah never slapped anyone again and rarely had to make anybody write anything a hundred 100 times. I grew to admire the ability of this small smiling nun to command our obedience and loyalty. In fact, until May, the eighth grade was my most rewarding year in school.

CHAPTER 7

W here is everybody?" Billy Byrne complained as he walked into our Boy Scout meeting in the gymnasium of Lincoln Junior High School. Only eight of us had shown up. We expected low attendance at our summer meetings, but this was our kick-off meeting for the new school year, and we'd been hoping for a bumper crop of new scouts.

"Where's Tony Morelli? He used to come all the time."

"He quit," said Bernie Karolak.

"Quit? Why?"

"I don't know. He went to the camp-out last spring, then just quit. He never said why."

"We gotta work harder to find more kids," I said. "I could get my friend James."

"James?" exclaimed Billy Byrne as he took off his jacket. "That colored kid you hang out with over on Fernwood?"

I scowled. "James is a great guy, and he'd make a good scout."

Billy paid no attention. "Let him join some other troop," he said, hanging his jacket on a hook and turning away from me.

"Boys! Boys! Hold it down," said Mr. Jackson, the scoutmaster. "Let's get started. We have to make plans for our fall camp-out." He was a bachelor in his thirties and had sharp, well-pressed creases in his khaki Boy Scout shorts. He lined us up at attention to start the meeting, then set his camera on a tripod. "I want to get a picture of us all lined up," he said.

Mr. Jackson always had his camera in reach, a classy looking thirty-five-millimeter Kodak in a brown leather case. "It has a 3.5 f-stop," he bragged. He was so proud of his photography he always carried pictures around with him. On a long table he spread out the photos he had taken at the camp-out last spring. He developed the pictures himself in the photo lab where he worked.

"Wow! Remember this!" said Billy Byrne. He picked up a picture I had snapped of Mr. Jackson lying in his undershorts on his cot, holding a cigarette lighter in his hand, getting ready to light the hairs on his chest to show how tough he was. "I don't know how you did that without burning yourself," said Billy. "And God, that hair sure stunk when it started to burn."

I picked up a picture of Tony Morelli standing naked, except for his jockey shorts, and Mr. Jackson snatched it from me right away. "That shouldn't have been there. I planned to give it to Tony, but he isn't here tonight."

After the meeting ended, I helped straighten up the room. That was one of the jobs of being patrol leader, and I figured it would help me move up toward my Eagle Scout. As we left the building, Mr. Jackson said, "Hop into my car, Charlie. I'll give you a ride home."

I liked sitting in the front seat of the shiny, red Ford convertible with the top down and the warm summer

air blowing through my hair. He pulled the car to a stop
in front of my house on Oakwood Street.

"I can't wait to get to our fall overnight," I said.

"You're going to love it," He smiled and reached over
with his right hand to pat my shoulder.

CHAPTER 8

James bugged me once again to line up Louis for our band. "We really need that piano, Charlie. You gotta talk to him."

"I'll see him next week. It's too hot to do anything hard today."

The thermometer only said eighty degrees, but the air was so humid the sweat from our skin pasted our tee shirts to our backs. It was Saturday afternoon, and we were sitting on our heels in the alley, on the shady side of the paper station, holding green Coke bottles we had bought from the mom-and-pop grocery store around the corner. The paper station was a ramshackle garage near the corner of Dorr Street and Collingwood Boulevard. Collingwood had once been a magnificent avenue with big fancy houses. But where the paper station sat, it was now little more than a rundown lane on the edge of Jeeptown's Negro neighborhood. The paper station's doors sagged on rusted hinges, and they were swung wide open in a vain attempt to let out the hot stale air.

Inside the garage, Old Schmidt sat behind a big counter waiting for the newspapers to arrive. He scratched out a living as a neighborhood distributor for the *Jeeptown Gazette*. None of us boys knew his first name. We called him Old Schmidt. His skinny frame and wrinkled face made him look ancient, while his constant frown made him seem tough. That and his accent. Words like street or storm came out as shtreet or shtorm. "They" became "zey" and "with" came out as "viss." He sounded like a Nazi soldier in a movie.

Eventually, a pickup truck stopped in the alley to drop off the bundles of newspapers. We carried them in to the long wooden bench, where Old Schmidt lined them up. He called out the route numbers, starting with number one. The boy with route number one came up to the counter, Old Schmidt looked at his large notebook to see how many papers were destined for that route, counted out that many for the boy, and then shouted, "Number three." He skipped over Number two, because that carrier was behind on his payments. As punishment, Old Schmidt sent him to the end of the line where he would be the last one to get his papers. I had route number four, with 55 customers. I took my bundle and went to a bench facing the side wall, where I could fold the papers and put them into the newspaper sack. Picking up a paper, I held the folded edge up and pressed the bottom half of page one against my stomach. With my right hand, I folded the paper over twice, then tucked the folded portion into the opening on the left hand edge of the paper. I placed these folded papers into the newspaper sack. The more papers I folded, the more the black newspaper ink stained my white tee shirt. The combination of sweat and newsprint slowly turned my white tee shirt to an ugly, dirty gray-black.

When I reached the last paper, I stopped and waited

for James, who had route number fifteen and did not get his papers until I was halfway finished with my folding. But we always left the station together, because our routes ran in the same direction. Waiting for James to finish folding his papers, I skimmed through the news about Korea.

"Lookin' to see if there's gonna be any communists left for your brother to shoot when he gets there?" chided James with a smile as he tucked the last paper into his sack.

"Nothing there," I said, and we headed outside to lift the paper sacks onto our bicycles.

I often made a game of doing my paper route, and today I brought the great Boston Red Sox slugger Ted Williams back from the Korean War, where he currently served as a jet fighter pilot. I devised a game that gave him one more shot at batting .400 again. While rolling down the sidewalk, pulling papers from the paper sack with my right hand and throwing them towards my customers' porches, I increased Ted's batting average by one point for each paper that landed on a porch. Since I started him with a .345 average and I only had fifty-five customers, every single paper had to reach its porch for Ted to be the only modern era player to hit .400 twice.

I had already hit forty-nine porches when the Rubenstein house came into view. The sound of a piano drifted out the open front door as I pulled a paper from the sack and made ready to bring Ted's average up to .395. This one was tricky, however, because a tall rose bush blocked the widest part of the Rubenstein porch. I had to loft the paper high enough to clear the bush, but not so high that the paper would crash through the plate glass picture window again. The paper sailed from my hand, clipped one of the petals, and fell behind the bush.

"Damn," I said as I stopped the bike, got off, and set it upright on its kick stand. "Now I'm going to get stuck with thorns." As I limped across the grass to pull the newspaper from under the rose bush, I decided to go ahead and do what James had been urging. I walked up to the porch and rang the bell.

"A dance band?" asked Louis.

"I'm the trumpet. You know James, over on Fernwood? He's the drummer, and his sister might be our singer."

"I hear you practicing sometimes when I walk by your house. You're not so bad. But what about James and his sister? Are they any good?"

"They're great," I said, speeding up my voice a little, delighted to see Louis's indication of interest. "What we really need, though, is a piano. Why don't you join us once and see what it's like?"

"I can't right now. I have a recital next week, and I can't do anything until that's over."

"What are you playing?" I asked just to be polite. I didn't really expect to know it.

"A medley from *Porgy and Bess*."

I had no idea what it was, but I nodded agreeably, even though his recital wouldn't draw a single kid from the neighborhood. And suddenly fearing he might ask me to show up for it, I said, "Let's get together after that's finished." Then I turned and got off the porch as quickly as I could.

I knew Louis would join the band, because he did not get out much, and joining the dance band would give a boost to his social life. This made me feel that I had done a good deed, and somewhat made up for the sleazy feeling I had about getting away from him before he trapped me into going to his recital. I rode off humming the tunes I had heard every afternoon for the previous two weeks as I had tossed papers onto the Rubenstein porch.

It was too muggy to stay out in the hot sun. I headed for the coolest place I could think of, the art museum, a big, cool stone building barely a mile away. With its marble walls, it was the grandest building in the Old North End, maybe in all of Jeeptown. I turned right toward a gallery marked Impressionists-Post Impressionists, and the sweat under my tee shirt started to cool. I walked past the picture of the old man with the bandage on his ear that my brother Danny had sketched. He always laughed when he talked about the shocked look on Mrs. Hanratty's face when he told the class the painter had cut off his ear and given it to a prostitute. I sat on a wooden bench to gaze at a picture I liked much better than the weird one that had appealed so much to Danny. The one I liked showed a street scene in Paris painted by a famous artist named Renoir. I marveled at the fuzzy green-yellow colors that mingled together. The young women with ankle-length dresses and small children in tow. The buildings and trees that formed imaginary lines that faded into a point in the back of the picture.

God! How I envied the people in Renoir's painting! Everyone looked so peaceful. No brothers going to war or parents bickering over the union or kids who made fun of you because you had a limp. No sweaty tee shirts covered with dirty newsprint. As I sat in the cool gallery, my mind slowly drifted to the dance band we were trying to start. And this pretty girl Clarice who was fun to be around.

CHAPTER 9

Because Billy Byrne couldn't come, I was the only older boy to go to the Fall camp-out, and that's probably why things fell apart. Billy had gotten a job setting pins at the bowling alley on Monroe Street and couldn't get the weekend off.

That left me as the one Mr. Jackson put in charge of the younger kids. But they rebelled at taking my directions. "I ain't taking orders from no cripple," one said when Mr. Jackson stepped outside the cabin. I grabbed the boy's lapels and jammed him against the cabin wall so hard his head snapped forward from my push, then thudded backward into the wall. The shock brought tears to the boy's eyes, and I hissed in his face, "Watch your mouth you little twerp, or I'll break your goddamned neck." No sooner did I let go of him, however, than I realized I was behaving like Butch Bower when he bullied the little kids in the playground.

Despite feeling bad, I couldn't help but notice I had brought a quick end to the rebellion of the younger scouts. Within a short time, we brought in the water cans from the station wagon Mr. Jackson had borrowed as well as our food supplies we piled on the big wooden table in the cabin. And we dumped our sleeping bags in a corner. A fire roared in the big stone fireplace, and we had stacked up enough firewood to last the entire night. The boys stood chattering loudly in front of the fire, repeatedly turning around so they could warm their faces, then their backs, from its glow. The guilt I felt from bullying the smaller boy softened when I overheard him talking to a friend.

"He didn't have to do that. Feel this bump on my head."

"Served you right. You shouldn't have called him a cripple."

After chores, Mr. Jackson let the boys run around outside. I felt awkward and out of place without Billy or anyone else my age around, so I lingered at the table where Mr. Jackson had just lit a cigarette. I sat with my fingers clasped around a cup of hot chocolate. With no older boys around, I had a new status with Mr. Jackson.

"Do you want to play a game of gin?" I asked.

"Sure."

"Penny a point?"

"I can't gamble with you, Charlie. What would it look like if your scoutmaster took your money? Let's just play for points."

I chuckled at the idea that he thought he could beat me. But I dealt the cards, and in short order won the game.

"Another game?"

"Maybe you better go outside and get some fresh air while it's still light."

He had a funny look on his face. He must not have expected to get beaten so easily. I rinsed out my mug and went outside, putting on a jacket first, because the temperature had dropped to near freezing.

I loved Camp Miakonda, the land of the crescent moon, according to the legend of the Ottawa Indians who originally owned the site. In the fall, it was one of those quiet places that made you feel peaceful. I headed out one of the trails to get away from the noise of the other kids milling around the cabin, and I gazed at the rugged trading post building that teemed with kids during the summer camp. But it was dark and quiet now on the last Saturday in September. I looked up at the tall flagpole that had once served as the mast of a Great Lakes freighter and had been donated to the Boy Scout Camp. I strolled along various trails, searching for any signs of rabbits, racoons, foxes, or other animals. The leaves on the giant white oaks were starting to turn color, which left traces of red and orange in the big canopy of green over my head. It wasn't quite dark, but the sky was overcast, and when the rain drops started to fall, I headed back to the cabin.

Late that evening, Mr. Jackson announced it was time for lights out. Because the temperatures were expected to dip down into the forties, he said the boys could double up in their sleeping bags if they wanted to. None of the boys wanted to share a bag with me, and Mr. Jackson said, "When that fire dies down, it's going to get cold, Charlie. Maybe you should double up with me."

As I changed into my pajamas and slipped into Mr. Jackson's sleeping bag, it seemed like the thickest, warmest, most luxurious sleeping bag I had ever felt. The lights were out. Mr. Jackson stood by the picnic table, taking one last drag from his cigarette. With his forefinger he flicked the cigarette into the logs, and for an instant it flickered brightly from the heat. He disrobed down to his shorts and tee shirt and crawled into the sleeping bag.

The cabin was perfectly peaceful. The only sounds were an occasional snore and the crackle of the burning wood. As I grew drowsy, Mr. Jackson shifted position, and suddenly his big, hard prick pressed against my butt, jabbing me right in the crack. I tried to move away, but that luxurious sleeping bag was cramped, and he edged closer.

"There isn't much room in here," he said softly. "I have to put this thing someplace."

I didn't say anything. A hand slid inside my pajama pants and gently closed around my penis.

"Don't," I said quietly, not wanting to draw the attention of the other boys. The hand released its grip, then softly stroked my penis.

"No," I said, pushing the hand away, then shifting position to get away from the hand. But I was now lying on my back, which made it even easier for the hand to reach me. And Mr. Jackson's face was now only inches from my own. I could feel the breath and smell the stale odor of cigarettes.

"Do you like to do it, Charlie?" he whispered.

"No!"

"It's not bad, you know. Just two people making themselves feel better."

Feeling trapped, I did not say anything.

"I'd like to do it with you."

The hand came back, resisted my weak attempt to move it away, and stroked my penis until it became hard.

"Oh, that feels good," said the stale cigarette breath voice. "Now you touch me." He moved my hand onto his own hard penis, but I recoiled.

"No!" I said, trying to sound emphatic.

The hand went back to my penis, and all resistance faded as my legs stiffened and I came into the pajama pants. The hand wiped the wet semen on my pant leg.

"Now you do me," whispered the voice with the stale cigarette breath.

"I have to piss," I said. I pushed myself up in the sleeping bag, slipped into the hiking boots sitting beneath the cot, picked my jacket off the hook on the wall, and stepped into the cold night where I pissed onto the dark ground. Coming back inside, I threw two more logs onto the fire, picked up my own sleeping bag from the corner of the big room, and dragged it over to the fireplace. I threw one more log onto the fire, unrolled the sleeping bag, and slipped in. I twisted in the sack, trying to rearrange the pajama pants to avoid the wet spot that had grown cold. I lay there on the floor next to the fireplace and dully watched the logs flare in the heat. After a moment, someone stepped onto the floor and walked toward me.

"Are you all right, Charlie?"

I continued staring silently at the fire. Mr. Jackson bent over very close to me, and I could smell the cigarette breath again.

"Please come back to bed, Charlie. You're going to freeze out here."

I did not say anything. There was a pause, and then the cigarette voice went on.

"When somebody does something nice for you, you should do the same thing in return."

"That wasn't nice!" I blurted. I hadn't meant to say anything, but I was too upset to stop myself. I glared at him for a second before turning my gaze back to the fire.

"Oh, you liked it, Charlie. I could tell. You were so hard, and you came so fast. You could come a couple more times. Don't you want to do that?"

I said nothing.

"There's nothing wrong with this, Charlie. It's a perfectly natural thing to do. You know you like it, and I'd like to do it with you."

I still didn't say anything. After a long wait, the man gave up and returned to his luxurious sleeping bag. His cot squeaked for several minutes as he moved in it. Then everything went quiet. I clenched my fists with shame and anger, and I had to blink hard to keep from crying. I stared blankly at the logs crackling in the fire until I finally fell asleep.

The station wagon pulled to a stop to let me out in front of my house on Oakwood Street, and the scoutmaster leaned over to remind me of a special event coming up in two weeks, a program to help kids prepare to be Eagle Scouts. "I hope you'll go. I could pick you up at six-thirty that night." When he spoke, what I noticed more than anything else was the smell of the cigarette breath.

But he looked so sincere and sorry for what had happened that I nodded and said, "Okay." I turned away from the stale smell of the cigarette breath and limped up the walkway to my front porch. From that day on, I could not stand the close presence of people with cigarette breath.

CHAPTER 10

I usually had no trouble banning unpleasant thoughts, but for the next several days I felt consumed with rage and shame. The memory of Mr. Jackson's prick pushing against me and the photo of Tony in his jockey shorts kept popping into my mind. Was I a pervert? And what would Clarice think of me if she learned what had happened? Fortunately, she would never find out.

"So, you talked to Louis," she said as she glided into a chair across from me at the library table.

"How'd you know?"

"James told me. Do you think he'll do it?"

"Sure. Why wouldn't he?"

"Maybe he's like your bigot friend Bernie and won't play in an integrated band."

"He's not like Bernie," I said. "He'll play. And if he doesn't, we've still got Bernie's accordion for a keyboard. We'll get Bernie to shape up what he says."

She put a sullen pout on her face and stared me in the eyes for a second before responding. "Charlie, it's deeper than what he says. It's the way he thinks. If he says insulting things about Louis, what does he think of James and me?"

There really wasn't anything to say, so I kept quiet. And she kept watching me with that sullen look, until she said, "You better tell him to watch what he says. Someday he's gonna pay a price for that mouth of his."

Her saying that reminded me of winning the fifty cents from Bernie, and I must have started grinning about it, because she said, "Charlie, what are you laughing at? This isn't funny." Her eyes narrowed.

"Just something about Bernie. He's already paid a price."

"What?"

"Can't tell you."

"Tell me!" She started to lose her sullen look now, and her usual lively mood was popping up. "Tell me!" she repeated, raising her voice. Mrs. Nordstrom looked over at us and put her finger to her lips.

"I can't tell you now. I'll tell you some day."

At least she had stopped pouting, which made it easy to change the subject.

"My new teacher's part Negro."

"How can she be part Negro?"

"I don't know, but that's what she said."

"What's she like?"

"Well, she's got a funny accent. She pronounces my name Sharlie instead of Charlie."

"Sharlie?" she repeated and started to laugh.

Whatever was bothering Clarice, she was at least starting to laugh. The laugh was infectious, and in a moment I began laughing, too. We stopped when Mrs. Nordstrom looked over.

"She sounds kind of cool, for a nun."

"Well, you can see for yourself. She said she's gonna come to watch us play football Saturday at the fields on

Monroe Street."

"You play football? You never told me you play football." She tilted her head down to one side and gave me that smile that pushed up the bumps under her eyes.

"Well, I spend most of the game on the sidelines. But I am on the team," I bragged.

"Maybe I'll just come and watch you," she said as she began picking up her books to go home. Suddenly, I felt anxious. Maybe it hadn't been such a good idea to tell her about the football team. I was a terrible football player. I only joined the team so I could fit in better with the other eighth-graders. If she came to the game, she'd see me make a fool of myself.

We walked out of the library, crossed Dorr Street, passed by the North End Tavern, and headed toward our homes. It felt good when our shoulders occasionally bumped together.

"Why are you walking so slow?" she said. "Move a little faster."

"What's your big hurry? You won't be late. Let's just enjoy the walk." I looked across at her and smiled.

"Okay," she said and smiled back.

Of course, I walked slow with her because I wanted to hide my limp. It didn't show up as much when I walked slow. But I wasn't going to tell that to Clarice.

On Saturday, Sister FAH tee mah showed up at the football field, along with another nun. So did Clarice with two girls I didn't recognize. They were the only Negroes out of all the people gathered around the various football fields in the huge open area. Clarice and her friends edged over to the two nuns and giggled when Sister FAH tee mah joined in with the kids cheering for our team. "Charge team! Charge!" Judging from Clarice's giggle, Sister must have said "Sharge" instead of "Charge." Sister FAH tee mah started talking with Clarice and her two friends, but I had no idea what they said to each other.

Late in the fourth quarter, I got into the game. We had built such a big lead the other team had no chance of beating us. Coach Ned Delaney put me in for a punt return. I drifted over to my right and raised my hands to catch the ball as it spiraled downward. But it slipped through my fingers, bounced off my shoulder pads, and skidded to the ground. I dove after it, but so did four opposing linemen. They thudded down on top of me and recovered the ball. My replacement jogged onto the field, forcing me to take off my helmet and walk to the sidelines. Nobody said anything. You'd think somebody could have at least said, "Nice try" or "You'll get the next one." Coach Delaney, with his horn rimmed glasses, didn't even look in my direction, and I felt too dejected to look down the field at Clarice.

Nobody noticed when I skipped practice the following Monday. Or Tuesday. Or Wednesday. I felt like an invisible person. Being on the team wasn't helping me fit in at all. I had learned enough about gambling from Danny to know that at some point a guy has to cut his losses. Maybe fitting in with the football team wasn't that important, and I felt relief as I came to that decision. Playing football was a lot less fun than starting a band with James and Clarice. Once we brought in Louis, our band might actually get off the ground.

CHAPTER 11

Mr. Jackson still weighed on my mind when Danny came home on leave from Boot Camp. He arrived at two-thirty on Monday afternoon while Dad was still at work. I got off school early so I could show up for his arrival. Grandpa and Grandma Parnell picked up Mother, Mollic, and me in grandpa's red Pontiac, and drove us to the train station. Danny tossed his khaki duffel bag into the trunk, then hopped into the front seat next to grandpa.

"We're proud of you, Danny," said Grandpa Parnell. "We're so proud I'm going to let you keep my car for your entire leave. Just check in with your grandma each morning and drive her anyplace she needs to go."

When I heard about that, I figured grandpa just wanted some relief from driving Grandma around. For Danny, though, driving Grandma around was a small inconvenience for having a car at his disposal for two weeks. He changed out of his uniform as soon as we got home from the train station. Then he disappeared with the car. He didn't even show up for supper.

"Get your trumpet, Charlie, and we'll give Danny a reception when he gets home," Dad instructed me. At nine-thirty that night, we heard the tires roll to a stop on the cinders in the alley behind the house, and we all ran to the kitchen door. I put the trumpet to my lips, depressed the first and third keys to give the trumpet the pitch of a bugle, and played reveille. Dad put one of his old, fragile 78 rpm records on the phonograph, turned the volume up high and began waving his arms up and down like a conductor as the record played an old Irving Berlin song.

Someday I'm going to murder the bugler,
Someday you're going to find him dead.
And then I'll get that other pup,
the one that wakes the bugler up,
and spend the rest of my life in bed.

"You guys are too gung-ho," said Danny. But he flashed a big smile at our reception. Mother was crying, and she threw her arms around Danny.

"Where did you go?" she asked.

"I went to watch football practice at Albertus Magnus. But the coach kicked me out, so I just drove around."

"Why'd the coach kick you out?" asked Mollie.

"He said I was disrupting the practice for their big game against DeVilbiss. But he was pissed because he doesn't have me there at fullback. And I could see why he's pissed. That guy in my place is terrible. Well, screw them!"

"You don't talk that way in my house, young man," said Mother. "Is that the way they teach you to talk in the Marines?"

"Yep," said Danny, laughing. "Besides, we're not in the house. We're in the yard." Before Mother could reply, he picked her up by the waist and began carrying her toward the kitchen door.

"Stop that!" she ordered. "Put me down before you drop me." But she laughed the whole time.

Uncle Jim stopped by to say hello. Unknown to Danny, Mother had gone to her brother Jim right after Danny enlisted and asked him to get Danny out of the Marines. Uncle Jim stood six feet two and had huge fatty jowls that hung down from his chin. He was not only big, but his positions as precinct captain and a superintendent in the city's public works department gave him the biggest connections of anyone in the family.

He talked to the mayor and the mayor called the congressman and the congressman sent an aide along with Big Jim to speak to the Marine recruiters. Afterwards, Big Jim came back to tell Mother the bad news. Nothing could be done, the recruiter told Big Jim while they drank coffee in the recruitment office. Even the aide from the congressman's office couldn't change the recruiter's answer. Seventeen-year-olds did not need their parents' permission to enlist, and Danny's enlistment was an official legal act. I remember the pinched lips on Mother's face when she got the news. But she felt grateful to Big Jim for trying. She also felt grateful to the congressman and the mayor for trying. So did everyone else in the family.

"We're proud of you, Danny," said Big Jim. "You're not like those weenies at the university who went there to get a draft deferment. Win a medal for us!" The jowls under his chin bobbled as he told Danny of the great times he had had in the Army during the war. He turned his steely gaze in Dad's direction, but Dad just stared blankly. Unlike Dad, Uncle Jim never won a Silver Star. Nevertheless, I could see Danny lift his chin a little higher. Strange, I thought. Uncle Jim, who had spent the war as a quartermaster handing out supplies wanted Danny to become a hero. But Dad, who had won a Silver Star and really was a hero, said nothing of the sort. He didn't even offer Uncle Jim a bottle of Buckeye Beer.

On Friday night, Danny took me to the football game. It was a close game until the very end. Late in the fourth quarter, Albertus Magnus got the ball on the DeVilbiss five-yard line, and the high school kids were on their feet screaming. Danny leaned over and punched me in the ribs with his elbow.

"Look at that," he exclaimed, bouncing up and down on the bench in the grandstand. "That hole on the left side of the line has been there all night, but the fullback keeps going to the right side where he gets creamed. I'd get two or three yards every time just going over the left side, maybe more if the linebackers closed up too slow. We'd have a touchdown for sure." And I didn't doubt it. Danny had been an explosive runner who could blast through the smallest opening. But Albertus Magnus ran out of downs without scoring and lost the game by four points.

"I gotta take you home now, Charlie. I'm going to a party," said Danny. "See that cheerleader down there. She's the one who's putting it on. If I'm lucky, maybe she'll put out."

It shocked me to hear Danny say such a thing, but I had to recognize that the idea of it titillated me as well.

I looked closely at the cheerleader and I recognized her immediately. She was Roberta Quinn's older sister. She wore the gray sweater with the big red letters "A M" across her chest and a thick red skirt that came down almost to her knees. As a church school, Albertus Magnus made its cheerleaders wear modest, thick, long skirts. Nevertheless, when she jumped and kicked her legs apart or did a cartwheel, she showed off plenty of thigh.

"The party's gonna be at the Quinn house?"

"You know her?"

"Oh, yeah. I been trying to put the make on her sister Roberta all summer. This would be perfect. Going as part of a football party. Let me come, Danny."

He looked down and gave me his cocky grin. "All right," he said. "Maybe that's not a bad idea. I'll give you some pointers."

Danny stopped at a liquor store to pick up a six pack of 3.2-percent beer. He had turned eighteen during boot camp and could now buy 3.2-beer, the watered down beer with less alcohol than the regular full strength beer. Nothing like a six pack of beer to get you into a party, he said. He took a can opener from his pocket and punched two holes in one of the cans. "Tastes like piss," he said and made a face after he took a huge gulp.

"It's against the law to drink and drive," I warned him.

"So what are they gonna do?" He laughed. "Send me to Korea?" He looked over at me to see my reaction, which made me nervous because we were traveling quite speedily down Monroe Street in the direction of the Quinn house.

"Watch the road, Danny. Christ, there's a car coming

at us!"

He swerved to avoid the car. "When did you turn into such a nervous Nellie?" he chided me as he handed the can over to me. "Take a slug. It'll relax you."

I pretended to take a sip. Danny would be in plenty of trouble with an open beer can if a cop stopped us. No point in me getting into trouble as well.

Roberta's house was fantastic! So fantastic it looked like it belonged in the movies. It was a two-story brick house north of Monroe Street, where all the houses were nice. Instead of the dark interior of my house, the woodwork was a bright, glossy white. A breakfast nook sat between the dining room and the kitchen. The living room ran the entire depth of the house, and a screened-in porch at the rear provided a cozy place where several teens sat joking with each other. A fireplace in the side wall of the living room crackled, and wall-to-wall shag carpet covered the floor. "Someday, I'm gonna have a house like this," I said to Danny. But he wandered off to talk with the football players and left me standing by myself. Then Sally Quinn saw me, gave me a big welcoming smile, and pulled me down to the carpet in front of the fireplace where we sat and watched the older kids.

"What do you think of our new teacher?" she asked. She sat cross-legged, pulling at tufts of the shag carpet.

"She's all right," I said. Sally was not as pretty as her sisters, but she was the most likable girl at St. Matthew's. "I almost fell over laughing when you and Butch were at the map poking each other every time Sister looked away. And Butch is so dumb he couldn't even find Portugal." Sally giggled. But nice as she was, I felt awkward. We were both annoyed at her sister Roberta, me because Roberta flirted with the football players and gave me no attention and Sally because of all the attention Roberta got from the football players.

Danny also didn't look to be having such a great time, but I couldn't figure out why. You'd think he'd be having a ball talking with all those guys who had been his teammates the previous year. But he didn't really seem to care about them anymore. Most of the guys he talked about were the members of his squad in boot camp at Parris Island.

Danny perked up when Roberta's sister, still wearing her scarlet-and-gray cheerleader uniform, came over, smiled up at him, and gave him a big compliment. "You should have been in there at fullback, Danny. We'd have gotten that touchdown for sure." Looking at her up close, she was even prettier than Roberta. She had the same long, blonde hair pulled back in one of those ponytails that had become so popular. It seemed as though half the girls in the room had a ponytail. But Roberta's sister stood up straighter than the other girls and seemed more sure of herself.

"Thank you," said Danny. "But the way you cheered them on, they should have won anyway." It had been a long time since Danny had felt the admiring attention of a girl. He gave her his cocky grin in which he twisted up the corners of his mouth the way tough guys do in the movies. It was then that the team captain interrupted.

"What are you doing here, Parnell? You don't go to school here anymore."

"I was invited," Danny lied, throwing out his chest. He was wearing his own letter jacket that contained the big A M he had earned from his three years of football at Albertus Magnus.

"First you run out on us. Then you come back trying to be some big shot Marine making time with our girls." He reached his arm around the waist of Roberta's sister, but she twisted away.

"You're pissed because you can't find a fullback as good as me."

"Why don't you go back to the Marines where you belong?"

"Up your ass, dickhead," said Danny, pushing his jaw into the team captain's face.

All of a sudden, my stomach knotted. Danny was a terror if you got him mad. But the cheerleader wedged herself between the two of them. "Come on you guys. Let's not ruin a good party." She gave a funny look at the team captain and nodded for him to back away. "Let me talk to Danny for a minute." She put her hand on Danny's arm and led him toward the kitchen so easily it looked as though she had spent her entire life breaking up fights between angry boys, and defusing this conflict was a piece of cake. I got up from the floor where I was sitting with Sally and followed my brother to the kitchen. Roberta's sister guided Danny to the kitchen table where she sat him down, then put her foot up on one of the kitchen chairs, making her skirt ride up her thigh. The shiny tights of the uniform made her legs gleam, and I could see almost to the top of them. From Danny's angle, he could see even more. His eyes bugged out at the sight.

"He's just mad about losing the game, Danny. It's not you," she said with sympathy. She wrote down her phone number. "Call me and maybe we can do something."

"I've got a car," said Danny. "Maybe we could go to a drive-in."

"Maybe." She smiled. Then she ushered Danny and me out the back door before we even realized we were being kicked out of the party. As we walked toward grandpa's car, we heard the loud talk and laughter that was still going on inside the house.

But the cheerleader didn't answer when Danny called the next morning. After the third try he gave up and dragged me to a side street to throw a football back and forth. My friends Dirty George and Billy Byrne came by and challenged us to a game of touch football. George held a cigarette between his fingers, and his white tee shirt was stained with dirt. His greasy hair was long, uncontrolled, and matted on the top of his head, and his fingernails covered up a layer of dirt. He had a long chin and nose that gave him an animal look. Although I didn't really want to play football, I also didn't want to offend him, so I flipped him the ball and told him to kick off to Danny and me. He took one last drag from the cigarette before flicking it into the gutter and setting himself up to kick the ball.

In truth, I felt sorry for George. Not only did he smell bad and look dirty, but he lived in a dingy duplex on Norwood. His father got drunk almost every weekend, and on top of it, you never knew what to expect from George. He could be pleasant one day or just plain insulting the next. He was pathetic, and that was the real reason why I tossed him the ball. It was like Father Stan who kept telling the story of Jesus. "Whatever you do for these, the least of my brethren, you do for me."

But two minutes later, Dirty George started to taunt me after catching a pass and dodging past me for a touchdown. He held the ball up in the air and smirked as he waved the ball back and forth in front of my face.

"You're a pig, George."

"Don't be such a sore loser, Parnell. It's not my fault you're a cripple and can't run fast."

I lowered my head and charged him, knocking him over with my impact. But as he got to his feet and threatened to pound me to the ground, Danny got between us.

"C'mon you guys. Cool off. Man, it's just a game."

But I was too angry to play anymore. I headed home, muttering to myself. That stupid dirt bag! I'll never feel sorry for him again. It doesn't pay to feel sorry for people. I entered my back yard where I took a seat in the swing I had built for Mollie. It wasn't much of a swing, just a notched board, resting in long brown ropes that hung from a limb of the silver maple back of the house. Soon Danny wandered into the yard.

"Jesus, Charlie. You shouldn't go messing around with guys like that."

"I'm not afraid of him," I boasted. "He didn't have to say what he said. It makes me mad that I'm no good at sports. God, I'll never win a letter like you did."

"Letters don't mean much once you're out of school, Charlie. That letter wasn't worth squat at Parris Island."

"I want one anyway, and I'm gonna get even with him some day."

"Well, if you do, don't go picking a fist fight. That guy's a moose. Only a fool plays into the other guy's strength. Look at me when I'm playing fullback." Danny paused for a second and looked over at me until I calmed down. "If there's some great big lard-ass lineman on the right side, do you ever see me charge right into him?"

Before I could say, "No," Danny kept on talking. He grinned broadly and flung his arms around as the words came out of his mouth. "No way! I look for the weak spot on the other side of the line so I can smash into it like a battering ram. And that's what you gotta do. Look for the weak spot. Then smash into it like a battering ram." He actually waved his hand to the left, just as though his brain saw that hole in the line he had pointed out to me at the game the other night.

Danny was right. Look for the weak spot. And I wondered, "How could I find Mr. Jackson's weak spot?"

CHAPTER 12

To complete our recruitment of Louis, James, Clarice and I treated him to a Sunday movie at the World Theater on Dorr Street. A red velvet curtain covered the movie screen and would not be pulled open until the newsreels started. To give Louis a sense of fitting in, we sat him between James and me, and I maneuvered Clarice into sitting on my other side. We munched popcorn as we talked and waited for the theater to go dark.

"This movie is about a band like ours," I said.

Finally, the red curtain parted, and we sat through five minutes of news reels before the movie came on, *Young Man with a Horn.* It featured Hoagie Carmichael as a great piano player and Kirk Douglas as a great trumpet player who drank too much and fell in love with a tragic Lauren Bacall, when he should have stayed sober and fallen for the perky Doris Day. In the end, Lauren Bacall disappeared, Kirk Douglas sobered up, and Doris Day got her man. She sang some wonderful songs, and the movie ended happily. Much more happily than the life of the jazzman Bix Beiderbeck, on whom the newspaper said the movie was based. Bix died from drink before the age of thirty.

After the movie, we stopped at the North End Café to put the final touch on recruiting Louis. He annoyed me by squeezing into Clarice's side of the booth, forcing me to sit on the other side with James. We ordered ice cream sodas, except for Clarice who settled for a small glass of Coca-Cola.

"You know what they should have put in that movie," I said. "Doris Day should have sung 'My Melancholy Baby.' She'd have been good at that song." Then I looked at Clarice. "You have a good voice for ballads, Clarice. That would be a good song for you, too."

"I don't want to be no Doris Day, Charlie." She riffled through the juke box selector at the window end of the booth until she found the rhythm-and-blues section. "Ah, I'll show you who I want to sound like," she said. "James, give me a nickel."

"I don't have a nickel. Use your own."

"You just did your newspaper collections. You must have a nickel."

"Well, you just got paid for babysitting. Use your own money."

"I'm saving that for college. That's what Momma wants me to do. So, give me a nickel or I'll tell her you been hanging around again with your hoodlum friend Rafer Jones."

"You do that and I'll tell her you been stealing her perfume again."

To end their bickering, Louis pushed a nickel across the Formica counter to Clarice. It slid through a puddle of spilled Coke and ice cream soda, and as she picked it up, she said, "At least there's one gentleman at this table." She turned her smile toward Louis, looking slightly downward, since she was half a head taller than he was. Then she daintily wiped off the coin on a paper napkin before dropping it into the slot and pushing a button. "Now, listen to this."

It was Dinah Washington singing, "Blue Skies," and I realized immediately that she was the one Clarice had been trying to mimic when she had sung "Amazing Grace" some weeks earlier. When the song finished, Clarice folded her hands together on the tabletop and looked triumphantly across at James and me. "Now that's the way I want to sing."

"You don't like Doris Day?" asked Louis.

"Doris Day's good. I liked her in that movie." Clarice browsed through the jukebox selections once again. "But if you want a white singer with a real cool sound, listen to this one. Give me another nickel, somebody."

I slid another nickel across the table before Louis had a chance, and James shook his head from side to side as he made an ugly face at Louis and me. She put the nickel in the slot, and Peggy Lee began singing the song "Golden Earrings." Clarice sat straight up on the bench and shifted her gaze between the three of us boys. "Now here's the part I like," she said as the husky voice of Peggy Lee wailed about a gypsy lover wearing golden earrings.

"But Clarice," said Louis, "guys don't wear earrings."

"That's what makes it so great," she said as she bounced excitedly up and down next to Louis on the bench in the booth. "In real life, all you guys walk around trying to be he-men. And here's this guy in the song being just a little bit different." She smiled triumphantly again.

"Clarice, you're weird," said James.

We went on to argue about the R&B tones of Dinah

Washington, the perkiness of Doris Day, and the husky sound of Peggy Lee. This was by far my most fascinating conversation in ages. Other than my trumpet teacher, Mr. Kneusel, I didn't know a single person who could talk about music for more than a minute. Now I had three such people. Right here in the booth of the Old North End Café, with the windowpanes steaming up from our breath on the inside, the rainy October air on the outside, and Clarice smelling faintly of her mother's perfume.

As we pulled on our jackets to leave, James said, "Do you know what you two guys ought to do?" he said, glancing back and forth from Louis to me. "You should come to our church when the teen choir sings. Louis, you need to hear what a gospel piano sounds like. And Charlie, you ought to hear Clarice when she's got a choir behind her."

Louis said, "But James, I play classical piano. I don't play gospel. What would it look like for a Jew to play gospel?"

"You don't have to play it. Just listen to it. What about you, Charlie?"

"James, I'm Catholic. I'm not even supposed to go into a Protestant church."

Clarice laughed. We looked at her. "You two guys are a riot," she said. "Here I thought you'd be afraid to come because it's a colored church. But Charlie's afraid because it's not Catholic and Louis is afraid because it's not Jewish."

Normally, I liked Clarice's bluntness, but this was an insult. The words must have stung Louis, too, because neither of us said anything. After a moment of silence, Clarice saw she had offended us. "I'm sorry," she said. "I shouldn't have said that. You guys got to do what you believe. But Louis, lots of Jewish musicians have played Christian music. If they can do that, why can't you listen to a gospel choir?"

"I never thought of it that way," said Louis, "and it would be nice to hear that gospel piano James talked about. Count me in."

Clarice then turned her eyes to me. "Charlie, suppose it was just a concert and not a church service. You could go to that, couldn't you?"

"Well, a Catholic isn't supposed to go into a Protestant church at all."

"What if the church was on your paper route? You'd be allowed to go inside to collect your money from the pastor."

"That's different. That's my job. I'd just be doing my job." But she had planted a seed in my mind. "Maybe playing in our band is my other job. Then going to your concert would be sort of like doing my job. I don't know." I put my palms on the table, pursed my lips, and looked up at the ceiling. I'd have to make sure Mother didn't find out. She'd blow a gasket if I went to a Negro Protestant church.

"Let's do it," I said.

CHAPTER 13

The scoutmaster continued to float in and out of my mind, especially when I failed to keep busy. I would relax and picture Clarice breaking into the smile that pushed up little bumps under her eyes, when suddenly I'd remember Mr. Jackson's prick pushing against me in the luxurious sleeping bag. Or I'd remember that picture of Tony Morelli in his jockey shorts. These thoughts made me afraid I was becoming queer, and I'd try to drive them from my mind by focusing on Mr. Jackson's disgusting cigarette breath. I dreaded the day when I would have to tell this in confession. In truth, my resentments of Mr. Jackson kept growing as all kinds of thoughts like this invaded my mind.

He phoned one Friday afternoon as I moped on the sofa. Mother picked up the phone, and I bolted out the front door the instant I heard her say, "Oh, hello, Mr. Jackson. It's good to hear your voice."

I hopped on my bike and rode around the block so she couldn't call me in to take the phone. She meant well, I knew, and she really wanted me to get my Eagle Scout. I, on the other hand, wanted to smash him in the face. But he was much too powerful for me to attack him that way. He had to have a weak spot, as Danny had said to me. How could I find his weak spot?

When I got back from riding around the block, I went into the kitchen, and she said, "Call Mr. Jackson. He wants you to come to the Boy Scout meeting next week, but right now I need you to do this for me."

She handed me a spoon and added, "Stir this pot for me while I make a salad for supper."

The pot contained her god-awful macaroni and cheese. I should have known; after all, it was Friday, and we couldn't eat meat.

"Why is it always macaroni and cheese?" I moaned. "Why can't we have tuna fish once in a while?"

Mother, however, handed me the spoon and said, "Stop complaining, Charlie. Just stir this for me and don't forget to call Mr. Jackson after supper."

Instead of calling him after supper, however, I went out to do my paper route collections. Many paper carriers hated doing their collections and frequently fell behind on their payments to Old Schmidt. I loved going door to door getting people to give me money. When I got back home, everyone was gathered around the kitchen table.

Mollie called to me. "C'mon over, Charlie. Danny's gonna teach us Hearts."

"It's best with four people," said Danny. "We got me, Charlie and Da. We need one more." He looked over at Mother, who was rearranging the dishes in the kitchen cupboards. Once she started a task she did not like to be taken away from it, but she hadn't yet refused a single request of Danny's since he'd been home on leave.

"Me! Me!" yelled little Mollie.

So, Mollie sat on Mother's lap, across from me. "Everybody gets thirteen cards," Danny explained. "The highest card in the suit led takes each trick."

"What's a trick?" asked Mollie.

"I'll show you when it happens," Mother told her. "What's trump?"

"There is no trump," said Danny, laughing. "You're thinking of pinochle. Whoever gets the least points wins. Each heart counts one point, and the queen of spades is thirteen points. However, if you get all the hearts and the queen of spades, that's called shooting the moon. And everybody else gets twenty-six points, while you get nothing. We play to a hundred." Danny rattled so fast no one could follow his directions. Once the game started, however, we picked it up easily. As I figured out how to keep track of cards outstanding in the key suits, I began to dominate the game.

"You lucky creep," he snarled from the corner of his mouth when I shot the moon.

"Don't call your brother names," said Mother.

Dad plucked two bottles of Buckeye Beer from the refrigerator and gave one to Danny. Mother frowned, but she didn't say anything.

"Can I have one?" I asked.

"When you're eighteen," said Dad.

Danny smirked at me as he lifted the bottle of cold beer to his lips. But I got even on the next hand. I held onto the queen of spades until the last minute and stuck Danny with it.

"Damn!" he said as he slapped his cards down.

The doorbell rang, and Mother went to answer it. "Oh, come in," she said, in a fast, anxious tone of voice. "He's in the kitchen. Charlie, there's someone here for you."

Oh God, I thought. Mr. Jackson has come to my house to pester me. I looked over my shoulder and, with great relief, saw Clarice walking over to me, looking a little awkward. "You left your music book at our house. James told me to bring it over to you. He said you might need it tomorrow." She handed me the book.

Why I might need it tomorrow, I could not imagine. Or why James had not brought it over himself. Or why she did this for James tonight when she never did anything else he wanted. As long as she was here, however, I should try to keep her for a while.

"Let me introduce you," I said, leading her to the kitchen table. "This is James's sister, Clarice. She's gonna be the singer in our band. This is my mother and dad, my sister Mollie, and my brother Danny, who's home from the Marines." Clarice nodded at Danny with a slight smile. "Do you want to play Hearts with us," I asked. "Danny, can five people play this game?"

"Oh, no," she said. "I don't want to disrupt your evening." Her head jerked slightly when she spotted the collection of beer bottles on the table, and I wished to God I had never told her last summer about Mother chasing Dad around with the cast iron skillet.

"No, you won't disrupt it," said Mother. "Take my place and help Mollie out with her hand. I'll make us some hot chocolate and popcorn. I can't keep up with Charlie anyway. He's always mooning the shoot."

Clarice frowned in puzzlement. She had never heard Mother's word mixups before.

Everybody else laughed. "She meant shooting the moon," explained Danny.

As she moved Mollie off her lap, Mother motioned for Clarice to sit down. Mollie jumped onto Clarice's lap, saying, "I never sat on a colored girl's lap before."

We all froze except for Clarice, who smiled at Mollie and said, "And I've never had a little white girl on my lap before, either. I think we'll get along just fine."

"I'm not a little white girl," said Mollie. "I'm a big white girl."

Danny brought Clarice up to date on the rules of the game, and we started over. Every time it was Clarice's turn to play, she carried on a discussion with Mollie. "Should we play this one?" she would say, lifting the card up a little from Mollie's hand, "Or this one, or this one?"

"This one," said Mollie, pointing at the first card.

"Let's save that one for later." When she led the jack of spades, I was sure she did not have the queen, so on the next move I played the ace of spades only to have her stick me with the queen. That annoyed me.

"Why did you lead that jack when you had the queen in your hand. Nobody plays the game that way."

She bent over toward Mollie. "We can play it any way we want. Can't we Mollie?"

Mollie shook her head up and down. She didn't understand the game anyway, and she was grateful for the attention Clarice lavished on her. I rolled my eyes, while Dad and Danny laughed.

Mother poured popcorn into a big pot. Holding the lid on with her left hand, she used her right hand to shake it back and forth over the flame. As the kernels popped, their aroma drifted over to us at the kitchen table. Mother set a bowl of popcorn on each corner of the table and then brought cups of hot chocolate for Clarice, Mollie, and me, while Dad sent Danny to the refrigerator for more beers. Finally, at nine-thirty, Clarice said she had to go home. She had made a big impression on my family, and it had been a fun evening.

"It's pretty dark. Do you want me to walk you home?" I asked.

She nodded and we walked out the front door.

When I got back, Danny chided me. "Charlie couldn't find a white girlfriend, so he got himself a colored one!"

"She's not a girlfriend. She's just a friend. She's gonna be the singer in our band."

"She's seems like a very nice girl," said Mother. "But you shouldn't go out with colored girls, Charlie. All they want is a white boy to give them a baby. And once you do that, you're trapped."

My mouth dropped open. "That was a mean thing to say," I objected. "She's not like that."

Mother scowled. "Well, I don't care if it sounded nice or not. You're too young to know what life is like, and I'm telling you about the real world. The real world's not going to accept a white boy and a colored girl."

She folded her arms across her chest and shifted her eyes from Danny to Dad, looking for someone to agree with her. But Danny didn't say anything. When he had chided me about having a colored girlfriend, there had been a hint of envy in his voice. His leave had almost ended, and he still hadn't found any girl to give him attention. He'd probably be grateful to have a colored girl as lively as Clarice. Or any girl at all, for that matter. Dad silently picked a bottle of Buckeye Beer from the refrigerator and wandered into the living room to turn on the radio.

On Tuesday the whole family walked two blocks up Oakwood to Aunt Bridget's house so we could watch a comedy, "The Milton Berle Show."

"Da when we gonna get a TV?" I asked as we trudged up the street to Aunt Bridget's house. "Everybody's got one but us. Even the Fontenells have one."

"If everybody jumped in the lake," said Mother, "would you jump in after them?" That was her way to end a conversation when she didn't want to talk about something. She liked the excuse to spend Tuesday evenings at her sister's house. If she had her own TV, there would be less reason to go out on Tuesday nights.

"When the union gets us a raise, then maybe we can think about a TV set," said Dad.

"Hmph!" said Mother.

"How about a car," asked Mollie. She dawdled as she walked, and I had to pull her by the hand to speed her up so we wouldn't be late for Milton Berle's opening skit. "If we had a car, we wouldn't have to walk everywhere."

When we reached Aunt Bridget's house, Grandma and Grandpa O'Rourke had already arrived and sat waiting for the big cabinet model Zenith TV with the round screen to warm up. Dad gave grandpa a big grin and walked over to shake hands. Strangely, Dad got along better with Grandpa O'Rourke than he did with his own father, who scorned Dad's union activities. Grandpa O'Rourke, however, always had many questions for Dad about the union. He always warned Mother to stop badmouthing the union.

The only problem with Grandpa O'Rourke was his reluctance to wear his hearing aids. They made him feel self-conscious, and he often refused to wear them. When Mother told him she was going to get a new pink dress, he thought she said pig dress and asked her what a pig dress was. In June, he'd gotten into an argument at the North End Tavern with an old union member who planned to vote for Eisenhower. Then he noticed other people saying nice things about Eisenhower, so he used that as an excuse to take off the hearing aid in protest. "There's nothing worth listening to anymore," he said. However, he always read the *Jeeptown Gazette* I dropped on his front porch every day. Why hearing about Eisenhower was more painful than reading about him made no sense to me.

The previous August, Grandma convinced him to reinsert the hearing aids so he could hear the news about the Democratic National Convention. "You'll be needing to keep up with what's going on," she said. She kept the radio playing all day long so grandpa could hear the news. But one day he came into the living room and the radio was playing a song, "Aba Dabba Honeymoon," which featured a monkey and a chimpanzee chattering about their wonderful life together. This he might have tolerated, but it was followed by the immensely popular Arthur Godfrey singing "The Too Fat Polka." With an overweight wife, grandpa hated that song. When it came over the airwaves that day, he used it as an excuse to pull off the hearing aids.

"That music isn't worth listening to," he sneered. "In my day we had good music. Even the coloreds had good music. Did you ever hear Count Basie?"

Grandma kept nagging him and finally convinced him to give the world one last chance, especially while visiting with his own daughter and his own grandchildren. So, grandpa wore the hearing aids as we sat in Aunt Bridget's living room that Tuesday night, waiting for the television set to warm up. But it was too much for grandpa O'Rourke when Milton Berle opened the show with a skit in which he dressed as a woman. "That's disgraceful!" shouted grandpa as he took off the hearing aids. "First, we got union men voting for Ike, then 'The Too Fat Polka,' and now men walking around in dresses. There isn't anything worth hearing anymore."

"But Grandpa," I asked, "if you don't want to see Milton Berle in a dress, shouldn't you take off your glasses instead of your hearing aid?"

"Don't get smart with your grandpa," Mother warned. But Grandpa had already disconnected his hearing aids by this time. He didn't even hear my question.

CHAPTER 14

As his leave drew to a close, Danny kept more and more to himself, and he didn't swagger so much. He spent a lot of time driving around in Grandpa Parnell's big red Pontiac. One day we hopped into the car, and he drove out to the amusement park on the South Side that overlooked the river. We wandered the length of the game arcade while we stuffed nickels into machines, tossed baseballs at milk bottles, and threw basketballs at undersized hoops.

"Let's ride the tilt-a-whirl," I said.

"That's for babies," said Danny. "All these rides are for babies. They don't even have a roller coaster."

We wandered through the picnic area to the edge of the hill above the river. Down below was a boat club that was closed for the season. Dozens of canoes and rowboats were turned upside down and chained together. A big muddy plank floated slowly down the river, gathering weeds and debris as it drifted. We picked up stones and flung them at the plank, but our stones just splashed into the water around the plank. When our arms grew tired, we sat down on the bench of a picnic table, leaning back with our arms draped across the table. We looked out at the trees on the other side of the river that glowed in their spectacular fall colors of reds and oranges and greens and yellows. Danny didn't say very much.

"Did you know?" I said, "That the Great Lakes are the biggest body of fresh water in the world."

Danny looked at me, pointed at the muddy plank out in the water. "Whoever called it fresh water never saw all the crap flowing into it from this river."

I couldn't help smiling, but Danny's face held no hint of humor as he said it. We headed back to the car and as soon as we got home, he phoned Roberta's sister, the cheerleader, one more time. She couldn't come to the phone, however, and Danny got moody.

"Those high school kids don't know shit," he told me. "Maybe heading out to California won't be so bad. At least I can get a real beer at the Enlisted Men's Club. None of this three-two piss." He held up a can of the three-two beer he had picked up at the liquor store on the way home. "And when I get to Korea, there might even be a whorehouse near camp." That really rocked me back on my heels. I worried for Danny.

When we got back from watching television at Aunt Bridget's the next Tuesday night, Dad sat in the kitchen with Danny and tried to get him to talk. Danny had his big, khaki duffel bag sitting on the floor and was packing it from the piles of clean clothes Mother had laid out on the kitchen table. I sat at the dining room table, finishing off my homework.

"I wish you had talked to me before you signed up."

"It wouldn't matter, Da. It's something I have to do."

"Why?"

"I want to get a medal like you did."

"Oh, Danny. After you get those medals, they don't mean anything. Believe me, they're not worth it."

This intrigued me. I got up from my homework on the dining room table and moved to the kitchen. If medals didn't mean anything, why did Dad wear the ribbon of his Silver Star on his Seabees jacket when they went to parties at the VFW?

"Uncle Jim doesn't think it's nothing," I said. "The other night he looked like he was jealous of your Silver Star."

Dad involuntarily grinned at that but quickly suppressed it. Mother swatted me on the head. "Don't badmouth your Uncle Jim. The war couldn't have been won without him."

"How'd you get that medal?" I asked.

"At the Normandy landing," he said. But I don't want to talk about it."

"Normandy, Hmph!"said Mother. "You were just a Seabee driving a bulldozer." Dad's medal reminded her of the VFW party and the fight they'd had afterwards. A red flag to Mother.

I was squirming on my chair I was so eager to hear more of this. "How'd you win a medal driving a bulldozer?"

"I said I didn't want to talk about it." To end the conversation, he got up and pulled a bottle of Buckeye Beer from the refrigerator.

Mother changed the subject. "Well, the war wasn't exactly a piece of cake for me, either," she said, "And I didn't get any medals to wear on my chest." She put another batch of Danny's khaki colored underwear on the pile. "At first, things were good," she smiled as she looked around at us. "Everyone had jobs, because we had become the 'arsenic of democracy.' That's what President Roosevelt said."

"Arsenal," laughed Dad as he turned to the kitchen table. "The arsenal of democracy."

"Whatever," said Mother, undeterred from her story. "Your dad got a job in construction and got lots of overtime, as all those factories expanded." From his pay envelopes she gave them each a weekly allowance of spending money, paid all the household bills and secretly put some aside in a savings account. When the war ended, that savings account plus the GI Bill enabled them to take out a mortgage on our two-story house on Oakwood Street. "For the first time in our lives," Mother beamed, "we were homeowners. If the bankers had managed their money as well as I managed ours, that Depression would have ended a lot sooner."

"But during the war, I had to raise two boys all by myself." She smiled at Danny and me, then went on telling us how the monthly allotment from Dad's military pay did not go very far and she took a job sorting generator parts at the Jeep Factory. She even won a "Certificate of Proficiency as a Vehicle Technician," signed by a Jeep Company vice president. She framed it, and it still hung on the dining room wall. "I was like Rosie the Riveter," Mother beamed. For a while, she even picked up extra money by taking in laundry. One of my earliest memories was of Mother down in the basement feeding the wet clothes from the round, green washing tub through the wringer that squeezed out the excess water. I worried that her long black hair might get caught in the wringer. So I would sit on the basement steps watching just in case I'd be needed to pull out the electric plug to stop the wringer if such a disaster should occur.

Mother gave everyone a job. Danny became my babysitter, and I was taught to pick up toys. Mother took pride in her efficiency and said, "If General Marshall had organized the war effort as well as I organized my house, that war would have ended a lot sooner. But we got through it, and your dad came home."

I still remember the Sunday afternoon when he returned. Mother and Dad hugged each other and gave Danny money to take me to the World Theater on Dorr Street where we could celebrate Dad's return by watching a movie. When we got back home, they seemed warm and happy.

However, Mother always felt that Dad could have done better than work at the Spark Plug Factory. And as we sat at the kitchen table the night before Danny's departure, Mother tried one more time. "You were so good with a bulldozer. Why don't you get out of that dirty factory and go back to construction, where you'd make more money?"

"No future in driving a bulldozer," replied Dad as he went to get some Buckeye Beer for himself and Danny.

"There certainly is," replied mother. "Just go out to the suburbs and take a look. It's one bulldozer after another flattening out the land for all those ranch houses being built. I want one of those ranch houses," she told him. "Get a job in construction so we can afford it."

"Construction sounds good," said Dad. "But you get laid off in the winter. I want a job that's steady."

"Steady?" Mother's voice grew louder. "You've had two strikes since the war. What's steady about that?" Mother scowled. "What's steady about losing several weeks pay? I save and save and save to build up a little safety cushion, and then it all goes down the drain when that damned union of yours calls a strike." She swatted a pile of clothes with the palm of her hand. "You better not go on strike this time," she warned Dad as we all sat in the kitchen. "The coloreds are moving in, and I want to get out of here. It's not safe. I want a ranch house in the suburbs." It seemed like a bad argument to have on Danny's last night home. But we had all heard the same argument many times, so it couldn't have surprised him. I glanced in his direction to see his reaction, but he kept looking down and packing the clothes into his duffel bag.

The next morning, while Mollie attended kindergarten, Grandpa Parnell walked to our house to take back his big red Pontiac. Dad took off work, and they let me take the morning off school so we could all drive to the train station together. When it was over, I wished I hadn't come.

Danny had tickets for the New York Central Twentieth Century Limited to the LaSalle Street Station in Chicago where he would have to find his way across something called the Loop to the Union Station to get the train to Camp Pendleton in California before shipping out to Korea. Dad pressed a five-dollar bill into his pocket. As he put his arm around Danny's shoulder, Dad began to choke up. "Don't be a hero, Danny. Just do your job and keep your head down. Before you know it, you'll be coming back home again." Dad's eyes were dull, while Mother and Grandma Parnell had tears on their cheeks.

As he stepped onto the train, it came to me that

Danny had brought us together in some strange way. With him home and the family complete, we all seemed to fit together better. Then he disappeared into the carriage. We couldn't see him through the windows, but we stood on the platform to watch as the train gathered speed and headed West.

When we got back in the car, Grandpa turned on the radio. Tommy Dorsey was playing an old World War II song. "I'll be seeing you in all the old familiar places."

"Turn that off!" snapped Mother.

CHAPTER 15

S o Danny's off to Korea?"

"Yep," I said, leaning back in my chair at the library table. "He left this morning."

"What's his middle name?"

"Why?"

"I'm curious," Clarice grinned. "Middle names can be interesting."

I couldn't argue with that after the way that Mrs. Hanratty had humiliated me for my middle name. However, I didn't want to get into that with Clarice, so I said, "Give me an example."

"Jackie Robinson," she said, "the baseball player. Jackie Roosevelt Robinson, after Teddy Roosevelt."

"I didn't know that."

"So now you know. What's Danny's middle name?"

"O'Connell," I said. "Daniel O'Connell, a great Irish patriot. My mother and dad named Danny after him."

"See," she smiled. "Middle names are interesting. Who were you named after?"

"You first," I said. "What's your middle name?"

"Nope. I started it. So you have to tell me first."

"Stewart. Charles Stewart Parnell."

"Another Irish patriot?"

"Yep. But he was a Protestant," I added, thinking that might be impress her.

"What about your sister? Who did they name her after?"

"Nobody," I said. "Da could only think of one woman patriot. Somebody called Countess Markievicz or something. He said someone even wrote a poem about her. But Mother said she refused to saddle any daughter of hers with a name like that." I smiled at the memory of Mother's look when she told Mollie how lucky she had been not to be stuck with the name Dad wanted.

"So they named her after a song."

"A song?" She looked quizzical.

"Molly Malone."

"Never heard it. What does it sound like?"

"We can't sing it here in the library."

"Of course you can. Just lean over and sing it low so Mrs. Nordstrom doesn't hear."

We leaned our heads together over the polished wooden library table until our foreheads were almost touching. I had never been this close to a girl's face before, and I caught a whiff of her perfume. It smelled good. James must have been joking about Clarice stealing it from her mother. A middle-aged woman couldn't possibly smell this good. I softly sang the song's lyrics.

In Dublin's fair city, where the girls are so pretty,
there first I laid eyes on sweet Molly Malone,
as she wheeled her wheel barrow
through the streets broad and narrow,
crying "cockels and mossels,

a live a live oh."

Suddenly, Mrs. Nordstrom strode over to our table and crossed her arms over her chest as she glared down at us. We jolted back into proper sitting positions. "We do not sing in the library!" she snapped, waited a moment, and then headed back to her circulation desk by the front door.

Clarice and I each suppressed a giggle, but she didn't say anything. Maybe she found the song dumb.

"Mollie likes it," I explained. "She asks me to play it on my trumpet."

Soon we left the library and ambled slowly up the street, letting our shoulders bump together as we walked. Just as we passed The North End Tavern, I saw a police car move slowly past us. It was the cop with the fat face again. He stopped by the curb, and though he didn't say anything to us, he watched us walk by. When we reached Fernwood, Clarice peeled off to the right and headed home. The cop car moved off, and I headed up toward my house on Oakwood Street. Only then did I realize I had never learned her middle name. I hoped she was not insulted that I had forgotten to find out this little piece of information.

Just as I entered the house, Mother said, "Your scoutmaster called. He wanted to remind you of the special meeting for Eagle Scouts on Monday. He said he'd pick you up at 6:30."

"Okay," I said, without any zest. I definitely did not want to go to that meeting. Unfortunately, it would be hard to get out of it now that Mother knew about it.

"Write it down on the calendar so you don't forget

it," she said.

"I won't forget," I said. As if that were possible.

"Let's write it down anyway." She penciled it in on the calendar that hung in the kitchen. Then she came back to the living room and did something she seldom did. She put her arm around my shoulders and said, "Charlie, I'm so proud of you. This is going to be so good for you. Just think of all the great men who started out as Eagle Scouts."

Before my meeting with the scoutmaster, I had to go downtown for my Monday afternoon trumpet lesson with Mr. Kneusel, who rented a studio room in the Fine Arts Building, an old brick structure next to the Greek diner. The Fine Arts Building wasn't classy, like the Art Museum was, but I always felt and warm and comfortable in the dirty old structure. Today it seemed like a cocoon, because I didn't really want to leave it and go out with the scoutmaster. Before going up to the studio, I stopped at the Greek diner to get a cherry Coke. I sat in a booth watching Mr. Papadoka fling his dark and hairy arms around as he wiped off countertops and used his spatula to scrape off the grill. The old Greek flirted with a young secretary who stopped in to buy a pack of gum on her way to the bus stop. I dropped my nickel next to the big brass cash register that popped open with a clang when Mr. Papadoka punched the keys. Then I walked past the counter and out the side door of the diner which opened into the lobby of the old studio building.

A bank of elevators stood across the faded marble floor of the lobby. Going into the one with an open door, I said, "Eighth floor" to the operator. He wore a white shirt and old blue pants. He always had something to say to his passengers, and he asked me, "Did you practice hard this week?" He turned the crank handle, which sent us soaring upward. He didn't bother to close the accordion style metal gate in the shape of large X's that kept the passengers from falling against the outside wall as the elevator sped upward. At each floor, he looked through a glass window in the door for anybody to be picked up. On the third floor, he stopped and waited for a pretty girl who ambled slowly down the hall and didn't even step faster when she saw the elevator waiting for her. On the fifth floor, however, he shot right past a dumpy looking artist standing right in front of the door.

"Hey, you skipped Leonardo," said the pretty girl.

"He can wait. I'll get him on the way back down," said the operator. When the girl looked in the other direction, the operator stared at her ass, which must be why he overshot the landing on the eighth floor. He stopped the elevator with a jerk and had to back down where he undershot the floor and finally brought the cage to a bumpy halt on his third try. Even with these adjustments, I had to step down several inches to reach the floor.

Immediately to my right, the owner of the Violin Repair Store was locking up his shop for the end of the business day. On the hall to the left stood the door to a large rehearsal room with a floor made of wood strips about three inches wide that had been worn smooth by many years of use. Inside someone practiced arpeggios on a grand piano. The autumn afternoon sunshine poured through the large windows, and I wished James and I could rehearse our band here. Inside the room was a brand new tape recorder we would be able to use to hear how we sounded. Perpendicular to the elevators, another corridor led to an open door where Mr. Kneusel bent over a table organizing some 45 rpm records. He used them to play selections from the Ohio State Marching Band and point out subtleties of the trumpet section to me.

After the trumpet lesson, I couldn't bear the idea of going home and meeting up with Mr. Jackson, so I went back down to the diner and ordered a Greek sandwich with all the roasted meat, tomatoes, onions and mayonnaise. But even after taking my time eating the sandwich and watching Mr. Papadoka go through his routine of closing up for the night, I still didn't want to go home. Mr. Jackson might still be there. I wandered through the downtown department stores until closing time, and then dallied by the downtown movie theater, reading all the posters. By the time I caught the bus home, it was 8:00 o'clock. The scoutmaster had come and gone, and Mother fumed.

"In this family, we keep our commitments. We don't tell someone to pick us up at 6:30 and then not show up."

"I forgot," I lied.

"That's no excuse," she snapped. "You've got to learn responsibility."

I couldn't blame Mother for being mad, and I could understand that she wanted to keep me from ending up as irresponsible as Dad was sometimes. But the incident made me afraid to tell her I wanted to quit the scouts. She and Dad both wanted me to make Eagle Scout. "You're so close," Dad kept saying. "And it'll really help you get ahead later in life." I knew he was right, but I also knew that never again did I want to see Mr. Jackson. I just didn't know what to do.

CHAPTER 16

Our troubles started about this time. The day after skipping out on Mr. Jackson, I met James at The Norwood Drugstore so we could each get a cherry Coke like we always did after doing our papers. Just as we pulled open the door to enter, we suddenly heard the sound of shouting. Standing in front of the Norwood Avenue Grocery Store, across the street, Mr. Levy, the owner, screamed. "Stop, thief!" A large Negro teenager was running away from the store. Mr. Levy chased after him, but he couldn't match the boy's speed, and he came to a gasping stop.

"Oh Jesus," said James. "Rafer Jones has got himself in trouble again."

I started moving toward the scene, but James grabbed me by the arm. "What're you doing?" he demanded.

"I wanna see what happened."

"No, you don't," he said. He pushed me through the door into the drugstore. "Just sit down and get a Coke, just like you always do. And be quiet for a change."

It didn't take long for Mr. Levy to show up, and a cop trailed behind him, the cop with the fat face and the mean eyes.

Mr. Levy pointed at James and me. "Those boys saw the whole thing."

"Would you boys please come outside for a moment?" asked the cop in a very polite voice that didn't match the mean look in his eye. The four of us went through the door, and the other customers looked at us like we were guilty of something.

"What do you two know about the robbery at the grocery store?" he asked.

"What robbery?" I said.

"Don't get smart with me," he said as he pushed the palm of his hand against my chest and jammed me back against the building. "You kids saw what happened. And I want to know what you saw."

"I saw some colored kid running down the street," said James. "Mr. Levy shouted, and I saw him chasing after the kid."

"What's his name?"

"I don't know," said James.

The cop looked at me. "I never saw him before," I said.

"Something tells me you kids know a lot more about this than you're letting on," he said. He wrote down our names and addresses and warned us not to leave town, as if we were about to get on a plane to New York or some place. He spit on the sidewalk. "Decent man like Mr. Levy here sells you groceries day in and day out. Gives you credit when you need it. Then some hoodlum robs his cash register, and you won't even tell us who he was."

Neither James nor I said anything. My stomach churned with a twinge of guilt, because I agreed with the nice things the cop had said about Mr. Levy. But if

I snitched, I also knew the cop would be nowhere in sight when Rafer Jones came looking for me. Maybe my guilty feeling showed in my face or something, because the cop pushed me back against the building again.

"How come I always see you in suspicious circumstances?" he said, his mean eyes glaring at me. "The other night I saw you and some girl walking past that beer joint on Dorr Street. What are you two doing next to a beer joint? Now I see you covering up for some hoodlum robbing this decent businessman here. You're cruising for trouble, kid. You better learn to stick to your own kind."

If he had slapped me in the face, it wouldn't have stung any more than his words. I couldn't bear to look at James. We parted without saying anything to each other, and I just prayed to God he didn't tell Clarice what the cop had said about her and me.

CHAPTER 17

On Friday night, things got worse. I came home after doing the collections from my paper route, and Mother sent me outside to keep an eye on Mollie. "Play with her or get her doing something, Charlie. She's been under my feet all afternoon and she's driving me crazy."

"Why don't we get a TV? That will keep her busy."

"Don't be starting up on that again. TVs cost money, and if your dad goes on strike we'll need that money more than a TV."

I slouched out to the front porch. Mollie was riding a scooter I had built with an orange crate I had picked up one night from the trash behind the Norwood Avenue Grocery. Watching Mollie glide back and forth made me proud of my handiwork. The crate was nailed upright on a two-by-four board. I had split an old roller skate in two and mounted the two sets of wheels on the ends of the two-by-four. On top of the orange crate, I had nailed an old broom handle to serve as handlebars. Then I'd painted the scooter bright red, almost scarlet, and put the word mollie in gray letters across the front. Scarlet and gray were the school colors for Albertus

Magnus High School where Danny had gone and where I planned to join the marching band the next year.

As she rode the scooter up and down the sidewalk, the roller skate wheels made a ratchety sound on the pavement. The front wheels got stuck in a crack, and Mollie looked up at me swaying back and forth on the porch swing. She dropped the scooter in the middle of the sidewalk and ran up to the porch. "Let's play tiddlywinks," she said.

We pulled the game of tiddlywinks from the cabinet at the end of the porch. For a table, we used the old giant cable spool that lay on its side on the porch. Dad had grabbed it one night when the telephone company left it behind after doing some work in the neighborhood. We sat by the makeshift table and snapped tiddleywink chips toward the cup that rested on the small piece of plywood I nailed over the hole in the center of the spool.

"You know what's nice, Charlie," she said as she curled up her nose and focused on snapping a tiddlywink toward the cup.

"What?"

"Da hasn't done anything really crazy in a long time."

"What's he doing now?" I asked.

"He said he's gonna clean his shotgun."

"Wow, this I gotta see." I got up so fast I knocked the tiddlywink game onto the floor. Mollie followed me inside. We sat down at the dining room table next to Dad, who'd spread a newspaper over the tabletop to protect it from the oils and cleaning solvents he needed to clean the gun. A scrap of paper fell from the table and landed on the gouge Mother had put in the floor with the frying pan last August. Draining his bottle of

Buckeye Beer, Dad sent me to get him a new one from the refrigerator. Mother looked over skeptically from where she was polishing the top of her walnut china cabinet. "Why are you doing that?" she asked.

"I might go hunting this fall. We were talking about that at the union meeting last night."

Mother shot a sharp glance at Dad. She suspected that the union was plotting another strike, which she didn't want, and the mere mention of the union could set her off. But she did not react. She simply asked, "Why do you want to go hunting?"

"I need a hobby. It's not good to sit around too much with no outside interests."

"I don't like guns," Mother said. "But this neighborhood's going downhill, and maybe we need something to protect ourselves." She rambled as she kept polishing the cabinet top. "We should buy one of those ranch houses out in the suburbs. Then we wouldn't need a gun."

"Maybe we can think about that after we get our raises," said Dad.

It felt good to sit by my dad in the small dining room. He took another swig of Buckeye Beer before picking up the big 12-gauge shotgun to check the gun sights. He aimed at a spot of peeling paint on the wall just above Mother's head and just to the left of the "Certificate of Proficiency" that Mother had earned from the Jeep Factory during the war. He peered across the two sights on the gun barrel to see if they lined up properly.

"Don't point that gun at me," said Mother.

"I'm not pointing it at you. I'm sighting it on that spot on the wall."

"Well, sight it someplace else. It might go off." She

bent down to spread some polish on the legs of the cabinet.

"It can't go off. It's not loaded. I'll show you." Just as Mother ducked down to polish the cabinet legs, Dad squeezed the trigger and the gun exploded with the loudest bang I'd ever heard. Unprepared for the recoil, he got kicked back and almost fell off his chair. Mother peered up, her chin barely above the tabletop, her face fixed in horror.

"You tried to kill me!" she shouted.

Dad looked stunned by what he had just done. "No, I didn't. I was aiming above your head." He pointed with a shaking finger at the spot where a patch of plaster the size of a bushel basket had just been shredded by the blast of the shotgun, a blast that would have taken off Mother's head if she hadn't ducked down at that moment to polish the cabinet legs. "It wasn't even close to you," said Dad, as his shaking finger pointed toward the big hole he had just blasted in the wall next to Mother's Certificate of Proficiency that was now tilted at an odd angle.

"You almost killed me," she shouted. "Get out of my house!"

Dad just stood there shaking, as Mother screamed at him. "Get out of my house!"

Dad grabbed two handfuls of beer bottles and sheepishly moved toward the kitchen door. His fingers were coiled around the necks of the bottles, four of them in each hand. Before disappearing from sight he turned and said, "I'm sorry. I didn't mean to do that."

"Get out!" Mother screamed. "Get out of my house!" She collapsed on the floor and began to sob. I had never seen her like this. Without saying anything to Mollie or me, she stumbled to her feet, her shoulders shaking as she moved toward the stairs, and climbed up to her bedroom. Mollie began to whimper. I put a hand on her shoulder, but she shrank from me and ran upstairs after Mother.

With everyone gone, the silence in the dining room was deafening, and the sour smell of the gunpowder was everywhere. My whole body shook as I stared at the big hole in the wall directly above where Mother's head had been.

I went to the kitchen for a half dozen brown paper lunch bags and spread them out on the dining room table. After checking to make sure the gun held no more shells, I slowly began to take it apart. This took some time, because I had never seen the gun broken down before and had to figure out from scratch how to do it. But slowly the pieces came apart. I placed the trigger on top of one paper bag, the trigger guard on top of another, the firing pin on another and so on until all the small pieces of the gun were scattered out on the paper bags. I put each collection of pieces in its own sack and crumpled the sacks so they looked as though they contained nothing more suspicious than an old apple core or maybe a half-eaten sandwich.

Leaving the blue metal gun barrel and the paper sacks on the table, I took the wooden gunstock down to the basement, where I pushed it against a pile of coal in the coal bin and used the coal shovel to cover it. Thank God Dad had not yet converted from a coal furnace to a gas furnace like the neighbors had done. I could just wait until the cold weather arrived and toss the wood stock into the blazing coal fire in the furnace. I stuck the gun barrel down my left pant leg, and grabbed all of the paper sacks, clutching the tops of three of them in each hand. I went outside, going out the front door so Dad couldn't see me from where he was in the garage. I headed toward the alley between Oakwood and Norwood, but the gun barrel dropped out of my pant leg and began dragging on the sidewalk. Bending over, I stuck the end of the gun barrel into my sock, and that held it in place. I slowly moved through the alley, dropping a paper sack in every third or fourth of the metal trash cans that stood by each garage, carefully choosing only trash cans that already had something in them, so that each crumpled paper sack could be stuffed under some other piece of trash. No point in making it easy for some snoopy neighbor to find any of this evidence of Dad's irresponsibility and call the police. Finally, I reached the end of the alley, crossed the street toward the Norwood Avenue Grocery Store and pulled the gun barrel from my pant leg, wiping it clean with my handkerchief. I had learned enough from crime movies to know that one should never leave any fingerprints to be found by the police or the FBI. Then I tossed the gun barrel into the dumpster and walked deliberately down the street toward my house, clenching my fists in an effort to control my trembling hands.

Nobody ever asked me what had happened to the gun. Mother did not care what had happened as long as she couldn't see it in the house. Dad was curious, I knew, because he looked around for the gun when he came into the house the next morning. But he didn't ask Mother about it, and he never suspected that I could have gotten rid of it the way I had. As part of a deal with Mother to let him stay in the house, he vowed to turn over a new leaf. He agreed to become an usher at the church, join the Knights of Columbus and stop drinking at the VFW, although he drew the line at quitting his union steward position. This satisfied Mother. Now that Dad went to mass each Sunday with the family and stayed in the good graces of the church, maybe she could put up with the hardship of another strike.

I felt proud at Sunday mass when Dad put the usher's sash over his shoulder and moved up the center aisle in his freshly polished shoes, passing the collection baskets back and forth. Billy Byrne's father had never had the honor of performing this important duty; nor had Bernie Karolak's. I bragged about this to Clarice. One Sunday, while serving the 10:00 o'clock high mass, I made a special effort to stand as straight as possible as Dad watched from the congregation. I slowly toted the heavy missal from the right side of the altar to the left side so Father Doyle could read the gospel. It seemed so natural for the priest to stand with his back to the congregation reading the gospel words in Latin. The Latin gave the words a mysterious quality that was missing from the English translation in my personal missal.

Events at the Knights of Columbus, however, did not proceed as smoothly. The Jeeptown Knights were undergoing their biggest conflict in memory. The bishop of the diocese was pressing them to integrate and had even picked a Negro doctor as a candidate for admission. The Knights objected and delayed action so often that the bishop finally lost patience. He refused to allow the Knights to use any church facility in the diocese until they integrated.

"The bishop's right!" Dad announced, when he came home one night with a grin on his face. He told us about the bitter arguments in which he had stood practically alone shouting at the majority of the Knights who adamantly rejected integration. "You sound like a bunch of bigots," Dad said he shouted. Then he grinned as he added, "They almost kicked me out. They would have, too, if Big Jim hadn't intervened."

Never before had Dad stood up for integration, and the family debated why a man who felt the way he did about Negroes would go out of his way to antagonize the majority in an organization he had just joined. "He just likes to argue," Mother told her brother, Uncle Jim. But Big Jim's fat jowls shifted from side to side as he shook his head. "That husband of yours is a troublemaker. No sooner did I save him from being expelled than he up and quit. Tell him next time around he's going to have to find someone else to cover his ass. Brother-in-law or not!"

To me it seemed that Dad just didn't like the Knights of Columbus and was looking for an excuse to quit. But his decision couldn't have been better for me. My family would look good in Clarice's eyes if Dad could be portrayed as a champion of integration. I debated in my mind the best way to tell her this wonderful news.

At any rate, family life became more peaceful. With Dad going to mass and serving as usher, Mother seemed more relaxed. One Sunday afternoon when I brought Mollie home from the movies at the World Theater, the door to their bedroom was closed. They had fallen asleep. They were cheerful and mellow when they woke up, and Dad even peeled the potatoes for Mother as she prepared supper.

Dad patched the hole in the wall, but he could not

get the plaster evened out perfectly. No matter how many times he repainted, there was always a small bump left on the wall that stayed as a silent reminder of that hideous moment none of us ever mentioned again.

But old habits are hard to break. Mother eventually became stern and unhappy again. And Dad slowly started drinking. He had few non-drinking friends to hang out with, and the North End Tavern was so close to the bus stop on the way home from work. What really did him in was Halloween.

CHAPTER 18

On Wednesday, I reached the library before Clarice. By the time she showed up, I had The *Wall Street Journal* spread out on the table along with some other stuff Mrs. Nordstrom had found for me. I was so engrossed in these materials I didn't notice Clarice arrive until she slid into the chair across the table from me and pulled her arms out of her jacket sleeves.

"What's all this?" she asked. I looked up a little anxiously, worrying whether James had told her what the cop had said about her and me. However, when she gave me that big smile that pushed up the bumps above her cheeks, I knew James hadn't told her a word about it.

"Mrs. Nordstrom found all this for me. I'm helping out the union. My da asked me to look up some stuff on the Spark Plug Company while I was over here at the library."

"Why?"

"He wants to find out how much money the company makes."

"What did you find out?"

"I haven't got that far yet. This stuff is complicated. But look what I did find." I twisted the newspaper so she could see my finger point at the stock listings. "Dad's gonna shit when I show him this."

"Don't talk that way, Charlie. Jesus don't want that," she scolded.

"I'm sorry. I forgot that you don't like that." Of course, I really wasn't sorry, and I really hadn't forgotten. Sometimes I just liked to provoke a reaction from her. "Here's the price of a share at the start of the year." I pointed my finger for her to see. As she reached over to put her finger on the share listings, her hand brushed coolly against mine.

"What's a share?"

"That was hard to figure out. It's like owning part of a company. Sort of like my paper route. I have fifty-five customers, and if James wanted to buy my route, he'd have to pay me five dollars for each customer."

"That's a lot of money."

"But he makes almost nine cents a week per customer, so he'd have it all paid for in about a year, and after that everything would be a profit."

"I see."

"Now, I only have fifty-five customers, but the company has millions of shares. So it's worth a fortune. Now look at this." I bobbed up and down in my chair with eagerness, now that I had an audience. "Here's what a share cost at the start of the year, twenty dollars. And now it's worth twenty-six." I looked over at her expectantly, but she had no reaction. "That's more than thirty percent."

"How did you figure that out so fast?"

"Six divided by twenty is point three. Thirty percent."

She grinned at me in frank admiration. "Wow, you're good at this math, Charlie."

"Clarice, you're missing the point, and you're getting me sidetracked."

"What's the point?"

"Don't you see? That's why Dad's going to flip when he sees this, and the union's going to flip when he tells them. The company is thirty percent richer than it was in January, but it still doesn't want to give anyone a raise."

"But Charlie, if it's in the paper, doesn't the union already know that?"

I sank back in my chair, deflated. "Why you throwing cold water at me, Clarice? I'm trying to help out the union, and you're just trying to get even with me for cussing."

She stiffened in her chair. "You want to cuss, Charlie, you can go sit by yourself."

"Let's drop it," I said and jumped back to what had really excited me so much. "I wonder how you get in on these shares."

"Why?"

"Can't you see? Look at the money they made. Thirty percent. That's a lot better than selling newspapers. Or babysitting. Or working every day at the factory like my dad does. The guys that have these shares make all that money and they don't even have to work."

"I don't know," she said. "You know more about getting in on it than I do. You're the wizard with numbers. I'm just a little old gospel singer." Those bumps showed up under her eyes as she flashed a big smile. "When you gonna come and hear me sing?"

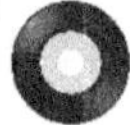

Mother was on the phone when I strolled through the door, still feeling good from spending time with Clarice, recalling the smell of her perfume and the touch of her hand when it brushed against mine.

"I'll make sure he's here, and thank you so very much for calling. You are very kind, Mr. Jackson."

"Mr. Jackson?" I stiffened.

"Yes." Mother smiled. "He is giving you another chance to attend that Eagle Scout meeting you skipped out on. He'll pick you up at 6:00 a week from Tuesday."

I looked down and the floor and stammered. "Oh, Mother. I really don't want to do that."

She grabbed my hand, obviously not understanding what I meant. "Charlie, I know it'll be awkward for you to see him after you forgot the last meeting, but he's forgiven you."

I paused for a moment, then raised my eyes from the floor.

"It's not that," I said. "I just don't want to go to the meeting."

"Charlie, we can't leave things half-done. We have to finish what we start. And you are so close to finishing your Eagle Scout."

"I don't need that meeting to get my Eagle Scout," I said. "All I've got to do is get enough merit badges, and that's what I intend to do."

"The road to hell is paved with good intentions," she replied. "You need to take action when you have the chance."

She walked over to the big calendar in the kitchen and wrote in Mr. Jackson's name for 6:00 a week from Tuesday. Then she gave me a big warm smile.

"Even if you feel awkward, Charlie, do it for me. Afterward, you'll feel better."

CHAPTER 19

L ouis and I made our way to the huge, dark brick Pentecostal Evangelical Church of Jesus at the corner of Pinewood and Lawrence, just around the corner from Clarice's house. For Louis it was not hard to get out of the house on Sunday morning, because his Sabbath was on Saturday, and his parents had no objection to his visiting a church from a different religion. It would broaden his horizons, they told him. I, however, had to create an excuse to avoid going to the 10:00 o'clock mass with Mother and Mollie. I made a swap with Billy Byrne, offering to take his place serving the Sunday 8:00 o'clock mass in exchange for him taking my place at a Saturday mass. Going to the 8:00 o'clock mass meant I could skip the 10:00 o'clock service with Mother and Mollie.

"No deal," said Billy. "You have to go to mass on Sunday anyway, but I don't have to go on Saturday. That makes it a better deal for you."

He held out for my taking his place on two separate Saturdays, and I hated letting him get the best of me on the deal. However, I had no other way to go to Clarice's church without Mother finding out about it.

The sidewalk in front of Clarice's church was crowded with brown, black, and even cream colored people wearing their Sunday clothes. The men wore neatly pressed slacks, white starched shirts, neckties, and some even wore full-blown dark-blue or charcoal gray suits. The women had bright looking dresses, high heeled shoes, and carefully done hair. I had never seen so many Negroes all dressed up. Much more dressed up than the people I had just seen an hour earlier at St. Matthew's. I felt a little awkward, since I was just wearing slacks and a sweater under my jacket. Standing on the steps of the church before going in, the people waved their arms, talked, laughed, and made much more noise than I was used to from people about to enter a church. Louis and I fidgeted self-consciously as we looked for James, who had agreed to meet us on the church steps. Finally, James showed up, dressed in navy blue slacks, a stiffly starched white shirt, and a necktie. I had never seen him wear a necktie before.

"You're in for a treat," he said, beaming a broad smile at Louis and me. "We've got a faith healer today. Man, that's always special. I get to help with the drums, and Clarice is going to sing a solo. She's all dressed up. She's something else, today, Charlie."

Hearing James brag about his twin sister made me do a double take, since he usually regarded her as a nuisance. He led us into the still-empty church. We headed toward a pew in the back, but James said, "No. You guys got to sit up front so Louis can see the piano." He walked us up the center aisle, and, not wanting to stand out, I did my best to hide my limp. As though Louis and I wouldn't stand out in a room where we had the only white faces. James ushered us into the fourth pew. I had to remind myself not to genuflect. We moved into the center of the pew and waited for the church to fill up.

"I've never been inside a Christian church before," said Louis, looking around in wonderment. "Do they all look like this?"

"It doesn't look much like mine," I said as I followed his gaze around the church. There was no crucifix above the altar. No statues to the Sacred Heart of Jesus or the Blessed Virgin Mary. No stations of the cross up one side and down the other. No confessional booths along the sides and at the rear. Not only were there things missing, but there also things in sight that didn't seem to me to belong in a church. An upright piano. A set of drums. Two rows of metal folding chairs on each side of the altar. In my church, the altar was the most sacred of all the sacred places. Only the priest and servers were allowed on the altar during mass.

I glanced at my watch. The service was slated for 10:00 o'clock, but it was already 10:00 and the church was only now beginning to fill up. Louis and I huddled closer as people filed into our pew. I looked over to see if he was as nervous as I was. A tall, black-skinned woman in her fifties gave us a friendly smile as she entered the pew and sat down next to us.

The adult choir took its position on one of the sets of folding chairs. The choir members wore long white robes with vertical and horizontal gold stripes forming a huge cross that ran from the neck to hem and from sleeve to sleeve. The teen choir filed in next, the boys in blue pants and white shirts, the girls in white blouses and dark blue skirts that came down well below their knees. James sat behind a set of bongo drums. Next came the pastor, a tall man with steel-rimmed glasses. Behind the pastor came a short, fat woman in a bright blue paisley colored dress and a head wrapping that looked like a turban.

When the choir broke into its first hymn, Louis and I sat dumbfounded. Never had I felt such a beat and movement. The choir swayed from side to side and everybody clapped their hands in rhythm with the music. Louis and I joined in the swaying. The drummer slapped the bongo drums setting up a beat for the choir. Louis stared, with his mouth half open as he watched the man at the piano. The pianist not only played melody and chords to back up the choir, but his fingers beat out a rhythm that seemed to guide the swaying of the choir members. "I never heard a piano played that way before," Louis whispered.

The pastor took the pulpit, introduced the order of the day's service, then asked the congregation, "Do we have any guests to welcome today?" A few people stood up to introduce relatives or friends visiting from other places, and the congregation applauded at each introduction. James stood up at the back of the altar and called, "Reverend?"

The pastor turned and gave his attention to James who said, "Reverend, I want to introduce my friends Charlie and Louis, who are sitting in the fourth pew."

"Oh no!" whispered Louis, as he slid down a few inches in the bench. The pastor smiled and said, "Stand up, Charlie and Louis so the church can welcome you."

I felt awkward as we stood up. But everyone was kind. "Brothers and sisters," said the pastor, "Let us welcome our young visitors." The entire congregation clapped loudly in response. From the altar, Clarice joined in the clapping and gave me a broad grin. Then the attention shifted away from us, as the pastor stepped up to the pulpit to introduce the Reverend

Sister Sheila Mae Jackson, the short, fat woman with the turban and the paisley blue dress.

She held the congregation spellbound from the moment she opened her mouth. Unlike Father Doyle, whose sermons were a droning sequence of points that left everyone bored in their pews, the Reverend Sister Sheila Mae had no sequence of points. She had just one message. "Trust in Jesus, my brothers and sisters. Put your faith in Jesus, and Jesus will heal the pain in your heart. Jesus made the lame to walk, the deaf to hear, and he raised Lazarus from the dead. Jesus will heal you, my friends, either in this world or in the one to come. We must trust in Jesus."

The same message kept pouring out in a dozen different ways, a dozen different modes. Jesus had saved Sister Sheila Mae at each crisis point in her life: when her father had abused her, when she had found herself homeless in the streets, when her first husband deserted her and left her two children to raise by herself.

"But I called to Jesus, and Jesus saved me," she cried in a loud voice.

"Amen!" came a chorus of voices from the congregation.

"Then I got married again, and we had two happy years together. But my new groom is now low sick and has a tumor the size of an orange. So many times I have walked through the Valley of Despair. And here I am again. How many times, Sweet Jesus, must I walk through that Valley of Despair?" Tears streamed down the face of Reverend Sister Sheila Mae Jackson, as she told her story. "I asked Jesus," she repeated, emphasizing the word Jesus. "How much do I have to do, Jesus? After all my pain, why do you give me this burden?"

To my right, tears were streaming down the face of the tall, elegant woman sitting beside me. Even her husband, two seats over, had tears welling in his eyes at the misery afflicting the Reverend Sheila Mae. The passion of the moment spilled over to everyone, and I had to swallow hard to keep the tears from looming in my own eyes. Louis seemed to be doing the same thing. Then Sister Sheila raised her arms toward the ceiling and called out.

"But I trust in Jesus."

"I trust in Jesus," came a chorus of replies from the congregation.

"I trust in Jesus," shouted Sister Sheila Mae.

"I trust in Jesus," came back the congregation.

"I trust in Jesus!" shouted Sister Sheila Mae a third time in a voice too thunderous and loud for such a small body.

"I trust in Jesus," replied the entire congregation, except for Louis and me, who sat transfixed with our jaws dropping.

Then dead silence for an entire minute, which seemed like an hour, until Sister Sheila whispered in a throaty voice that barely carried into the congregation.

"I trust in Jesus."

The bongo drums began a soft rhythm right at that moment. James stood standing next to the drummer and held a little musician's triangle. The teen choir rose to its feet. Clarice stepped out to begin her solo, the same song she had rehearsed with James, Bernie, and me two months earlier, "Amazing Grace." The bongo drum died out, and James tapped the triangle lightly with a drumstick to set up a tempo for the slow hymn. The teen choir and the adult choir began to hum in the background as Clarice sang her solo. She sang strongly, hitting the high notes without even a crack in her voice and producing a lusty, throaty sound on the low notes. The humming of the choir in the background, the ting of the drumstick keeping time on the triangle, and Clarice's solo lay a quiet, mysterious trance over the entire congregation.

The Reverend Sister Sheila Mae Jackson once again stepped forward and announced in a strong, confident voice.

"Martha and Mary used the holy oils to anoint the body of Jesus. And Jesus rose from the dead." She lifted a brass container for us to see. "We too will use the holy oils to anoint the sick and infirm, to heal their wounds, and heal their souls. My brothers and sisters, if you have a pain in your heart, come and be anointed with the holy oils. Let Jesus into your soul to soothe your aches and pains. Trust in Jesus my brothers and sisters."

Slowly, people left their pews, walking uncertainly to the front of the church where Sister Sheila Mae stood with her holy oils. The women came first. Then came the children. Then a few men began edging toward the aisle, and in only a few moments there a long line of people formed in front of Sister Sheila Mae, to be anointed and healed. She asked for two strong men to stand behind the people being anointed and catch them if they should be overcome by the holy spirit and start to fall backwards.

In fact, that happened. A very tall, thin, light skinned man, who barely looked Negro, started to faint. Someone caught him by the armpits and eased him to the floor where he lay for several minutes before he rose to his feet and went back to his pew.

The congregation sat perfectly still as Sister Sheila Mae Jackson applied the holy oils to the forehead of a short, bent-over woman who had struggled up the aisle on crutches. She moved very, very slowly, pushing the left crutch in front of her with great care, then dragging her left leg forward with painstaking slowness and then repeated the process with her right leg, "Oh, thank you, Jesus!" the woman shouted after being anointed. "Thank you, Jesus!" She dropped her crutches to the floor, stepped forward and gave a grateful hug to Sister Sheila. Then she turned and walked unaided back to her pew, with a slight limp no worse than my own. "Thank you, Jesus!" murmured a dozen voices in the congregation.

If I hadn't seen it, I would not have believed it. Louis and I just sat in our pew, our jaws drooping downward.

CHAPTER 20

Mother took to heart Father Doyle's preaching that "The family that prays together stays together." She extended it beyond the family and organized a block rosary for Thursday evenings during the school year. We all went except Dad, who went bowling on Thursday. Each family took turns hosting the rosary. Four or five mothers and twice as many children got down on their knees in the living room of the host and prayed their way through the rosary. Fifty-three Hail Marys, seven Our Fathers, and seven Glory Bs. One prayer for each bead of the rosary, and, of course, the Apostle's Creed for the crucifix. I knew the numbers exactly, because I counted them off one boring bead after another as we worked our way down one side of the beads and back up the other. Finally, each person finished, kissed the crucifix, put the rosary away for the week, and retreated to the dining room for cookies and coffee or milk. The block rosary was the most boring thing I did all week, but it was important to Mother who offered it up for the safety of Danny in the Marines in Korea. A new family joined the block rosary this year, the Fontenells who had moved up from New Orleans. They were the only Negro Catholic family on the block.

"Mother," I asked later that night, "if you don't like Negroes, why did you invite the Fontenells to the block rosary?"

"Don't get smart with me," Mother snapped. "The Fontenells are different."

"They got white blood," said Dad. That was how he explained any Negro who made good in life. Dad's list of Negroes with white blood grew each time the subject came up. It had started with Joe Louis, the boxer. It now included Jackie Robinson, Ralph Bunch, Nat King Cole, Sammy Davis Jr., the Mills Brothers, Lena Horne, and its most recent addition, the entire Fontenell family. But he continued looking down on Negroes in general. I had no idea where Clarice fit into this picture, since he had never said anything the night that Mother had accused Clarice of wanting a white boy to give her a baby.

Toward the end of my paper route the following Tuesday, I came across Dirty George sitting on the sidewalk in front of his house playing solitaire with a tattered deck of cards. Stopping and straddling the cross bar on my bike, I asked, "What'ya doing?"

Dirty George looked up and sneered, "What's it look like I'm doing, Chump? I'm playing solitaire." I guessed he was still mad at me for time I knocked him down and called him a pig.

I continued to watch. "Did you ever play gin?" I asked.

"What's that?"

I took the deck, dealt out the cards, and showed

Dirty George how to play gin, just as Danny had taught me before he went off to join the Marines. I deliberately let George win the first several hands.

"D'ywanna play for money?" asked George after he started feeling good about the game.

"I don't know," I said. "I didn't bring any money."

"I'll stake you a quarter. Then, after I beat you, you can pay me back tomorrow." He fumbled in his pocket and pulled out 5 nickels.

"Nickels are too much. Let's play for pennies."

George rearranged the coins, still lending me twenty-five cents, but making it three nickels and ten pennies. I started badly, and in short time had lost all ten pennies to George.

"Well, you're out of pennies," George gloated. "It looks like you're going to have to play for nickels after all."

In fact, I had several pennies in my pocket, but I did not let on. "You could sell the pennies back to me for these nickels," I said, extending my palm with two of the five-cent coins.

"No dice," he said. "I'm not going to sit around all day playing for chicken feed."

We continued at a deadlock, sitting in the shade of the giant elm tree in front of George's house. Finally, I agreed to play for nickels. It took nearly twenty minutes to win all of his money, which amounted to a whole dollar.

Getting back on my bicycle and heading toward the drugstore for a cherry Coke, I felt a little guilty about taking George's money. I tried to ease my guilt by reminding myself that he's the one who had called me a chump and earlier a cripple. And he was the one who challenged me to play for money, not the other way around. A guy shoots his mouth off like that, he has to expect some payback. Too bad I couldn't think of a payback for Mr. Jackson. And thinking of that reminded me that I had no way to get out of the Eagle Scout meeting that night. I shivered at the thought of being near him.

When I opened the front door at 6:00 to let him in, he strode directly to Mother in the middle of the rug in the living room. He flashed a warm smile, shook her hand, and said how pleased he was to see her again. Handing her a photograph he had taken of me in my Scout uniform saluting the flag, he told her what a great mother she was to be raising such a fine boy and how I should be so grateful to her. She blushed and walked him back toward me. As we headed out the front door, he rested his hand on my shoulder. I flinched.

Instead of heading downtown toward the Boy Scout headquarters, he turned onto Fernwood and headed in the opposite direction. When he came to a stop sign, I unlatched the door so I could push it open and jump out the moment the car came to a stop. But he reached over with his right hand and grabbed my left arm. His grip was so powerful it felt like a vise squeezing me. After waiting for the cross traffic to pass, he drove through the stop sign and parked down the block in front of a duplex.

"I left something in my apartment, Charlie. Come up with me while I get it."

"I'll wait here," I said.

"No, come up," he said. "I'll get you a glass of Coke. You look thirsty."

"Let me alone," I said, "or I'm going to report you for

what you did."

He smiled confidently. "Who will believe you?"

As he opened his door to get out of the car, I saw my chance. I pushed my door open, jumped out of the car, and started running up the street. With my limp, however, I was no match for him, and he caught me before I'd even gone half a block. He clamped his hand tight on my arm again and had a strange smile on his face as he pulled me to a stop.

"Whoa, Charlie. Slow down. Everything's okay. We just need to get something from my apartment."

"Let me go," I shouted, and an older couple walking on the other side of the street looked over at us. He kept his hand clamped over my arm.

"Let me go or I'm going to scream for help."

He relaxed his grip slightly but didn't let go of my arm.

"If you don't have what it takes to become an Eagle Scout, Charlie, I can't force you into it. Nevertheless, we could still have a place for you in the troop," he said softly.

Then he tightened his grip on my arm and sneered, "But so far as reporting what you did, forget it. Remember, you did what you did of your own free will. If you ever tell anybody what happened, everyone will know what kind of person you are. And the first chance I get, I will break your ugly little neck."

He gave an agonizing squeeze that made my arm feel like it was going to break off. The older couple on the other side of the street stopped walking, stared over at us, and took a step toward the curb as though they might cross the street to intervene.

When he saw that, Mr. Jackson let go of my arm. I began running off, and I kept running until I reached the Lucretia Mott Branch Public Library where I went inside and leafed through magazines until I could safely go home without Mother asking why I'd come home so early.

CHAPTER 21

I badly needed to ask something of Sister FAH tee mah. But to get her alone, I had to wait until after our end-of-the day cleanup. At 3:15, she passed out a hand brush to the students at the back of each row, girls on the left side of the classroom, boys on the right. We each swept the dirt from under our seat toward the seat in front and passed the brush forward to the next kid who did the same until we had swept the dirt into piles in front of each row. Two girls used push brooms to sweep down each aisle and pile all the dirt in one spot where they brushed it into a dustpan and dumped it into the waste basket. Two boys started at the left of the chalkboard and began erasing the chalk. Behind them trailed two girls who wiped the black chalkboard with damp rags until it gleamed. Carl Broda and I went outside to clap the erasers against each other to get rid of the excess chalk, holding them far enough from our bodies to keep from getting the chalk dust on our clothes. Sister FAH tee mah warned us not to clap the erasers against the side of the building and leave chalk dust all over it. She kept an eye on the others as they got their jackets from the coatroom and filed out of the building. Some younger girls were playing Red Rover in the schoolyard, and Sister stood in the building doorway watching them for a moment, before going back inside. After returning the erasers to the blackboard, I lingered until Carl Broda left, and I was finally alone with the nun. I went up to her desk, where she sat copying numbers into a large, black grade book.

"Sister?"

She looked up and smiled, her square face framed by the u-shaped white cloth ruffle on the headdress of her habit. "Yes, Sharlie?" she said. Even after six weeks at St. Matthew's, my name still sounded like "Sharlie" when she said it.

"Sister, can people be cured by faith?"

"Yes, we know that. God performs miracles every day at FAH tee mah."

"But Fatima is very far away. Does God perform miracles in other places, too?"

"Oh, yes," she said. "There is Lourdes, as you know, and Guadalupe in Mexico. God has performed miracles in many places where our Blessed Mother has interceded."

"But Mexico is far away, too. Could God perform miracles here?"

"God can perform miracles any place he wants. You know that. If a person's faith is strong and the Blessed Mother intercedes, it doesn't matter where the place is."

"Would it have to be the Blessed Mother who interceded? Could somebody else intercede instead of the Blessed Mother?"

"Well, Jesus is more disposed to grant a wish made by his mother than by somebody else, just as you are more disposed to do favors for your mother than for a stranger. So the Blessed Mother is the best intercessor. But, I suppose, somebody else could also be an intercessor."

"Would the intercessor have to be a Catholic?"

Sister FAH tee mah pursed her lips tightly together and paused as she thought about this. The longer she paused, the more I wondered whether it had been such a great idea to start this conversation.

"Nobody can know that for sure. After all, God loves everyone. We do know that it is always a person of great faith to whom the Blessed Mother appears. At Lourdes, it was just a young girl, Bernadette. The Blessed Mother can appear to whomever she wants, and God can choose to cure whomever he wants. Why are you asking these things, Sharlie?"

I pondered how to ask my question without embarrassing myself. "What if somebody had a problem—a big problem—and he couldn't afford to go to Fatima? Could he ask someone else to intercede for his problem?"

"Somebody with a limp?"

At first, I clenched my teeth as the anger rose up that always comes when someone makes an issue of my limp. But I quickly realized she had meant no insult in what she said.

"Just any kind of a problem. It could be anything."

She stood up, her long black robe swirling as she did so, and the huge brown rosary drooping from her waist clicked against the desk as she stepped around it. She guided me to sit at one of the student desks and sat down opposite me. "Sharlie, I know you sometimes get teased because of your limp. But as you grow older, your limp will matter less and less, until someday it will not matter at all. Asking God to cure us is a very important favor to ask. We must not ask it lightly. We all have a cross to bear, just like Jesus bore his cross on the road to Calvary. Some people have terrible crosses like cancer, a deformity, starvation—all kinds of bad things. You and I just don't know what each other person's cross is."

With all the horrible things happening to other people in the world, I began to regret I had raised the subject in the first place. But I was a little like Charles Lindbergh when he got halfway across the Atlantic Ocean and he could no longer turn back. He had to go forward, and so did I.

"Well, is it a sin to ask God for a cure?"

"It is never a sin to ask God for a cure. But it is better to ask him for the strength to bear our crosses until he sees fit to lift them off our shoulders. I know it is a big cross to have a limp when you are fifteen. But ten years from now, it will not be so big. And twenty years from now it will be even smaller. By then you will be married to a nice Catholic girl, and to her your limp will not matter. She might even be proud of the way your bore your cross."

"But I can't wait twenty years. Would it be a sin to ask a non-Catholic to intercede?"

Sister FAH tee mah looked puzzled. "I do not know who that would be. Tell me a little more." So I told her about Sister Sheila Mae Jackson, the people lined up in front of her, the women in tears as she anointed them with oil, the tall, light skinned man who fainted, and the lady who walked all the way back to her pew without her crutches. As each word tumbled out of my mouth, Sister FAH tee mah's shoulders sagged deeper. And very, very, very slowly she finally asked,

"You went—to—a—Protestant church?"

"Sister, I only went to keep Louis company as we watched our friends perform. He wanted to see the piano player, and I wanted to see Clarice sing. She's the colored girl you met at the football game a couple of weeks ago. I didn't know a healer would be there."

"As nice as that girl seemed, you must stay away from her if she's going to lure you into Protestant churches. You cannot go to Protestant churches! And you should talk this over with your confessor!"

I noted that she had stopped short of telling me I had committed a sin that needed to be confessed. Getting moral guidance from one's confessor is far different from having to confess a sin, and I started to feel bolder. "But would it be sinful to ask the lady to pray for me?"

"Sharlie, faith healing is not like going to Lourdes where God performs miracles. This woman you saw might be very sincere, maybe even holy. But there are many charlatans posing as faith healers. The lady with the crutches might have been a fake."

I did not believe that. Nobody could fake the pain of that lady tottering down the aisle on her crutches. She had walked back to her seat without so much as a cane. What difference did it make whether she had been given that gift at Fatima or at the Pentecostal Evangelical Church of Jesus? However, I kept this thought to myself. Sister FAH tee mah's own father had made a petition at Fatima, and she would not like anybody comparing that shrine to a Protestant church.

"I won't go to the church services, Sister. But would it be a sin to ask the lady to say a prayer for me?"

Sister FAH tee mah looked thoughtfully at me for a moment before responding. "You have to stay away from that church. But it is never a sin to ask someone to pray for you."

Mr. Jackson never called back after the night I ran away from him. But I resented the fact I had to drop out of the Boy Scout troop and miss out on my Eagle Scout. Rather than quitting the scouts, I should have driven him out so we could get a new scoutmaster. But I had no idea how to do that. If I told anyone about what he did with the boys, they would know he did it with me as well. And the mere thought of people knowing that made me cringe. At best, I could look around to find his weak spot.

So before meeting Clarice at the library on Wednesday, I stopped by the drugstore first. I wore the scarlet-and-gray letter jacket from Albertus Magnus High School Danny had left behind when he joined the Marines. Wearing his jacket gave me the nerve to take the first step in what I was planning. I slipped into the phone booth, closed the door behind me, and dialed Mr. Jackson's number.

"Hello?" came his deep voice.

I didn't say anything, and he said "Hello?" again.

I blew a heavy breath into the mouthpiece, then just let the phone dangle from its cord. As I stepped out of the booth I chuckled to myself. Danny was right. You have to look for the weak spot.

"Will you do me a favor?" I asked Clarice.

"What?"

"It doesn't matter what. Will you do it?"

"It always matters what. What if it's something bad?

Jesus don't want that."

"Why do you think I'm going to ask you to do something bad? That's not a nice thing to think about me."

"Well, you're a boy. So it's only natural you'd want me to do something bad."

"It's not bad. I just want to see that healer lady who was at your church Sunday.

"Why?"

"It doesn't matter why. I can't tell you why."

"You're always not telling me something. First, you can't tell me what was so funny about your bigot friend, Bernie. Now you can't tell me why you want to see Sister Sheila Mae Jackson."

I did not respond, and stayed there in awkward silence leaning toward her over the library table. Eventually, she said, "Okay, I can take you there."

"I need to go by myself."

"There are some tough kids on her street. Rafer Jones lives on that block. He's mean, Charlie. It'd be better if James or I went with you."

"I don't want James to know about this."

"I'll call her up and find out when we can come over."

CHAPTER 22

Clarice was right about the faith healer living on a rough block, and it made me anxious. Several houses badly needed paint and at least two places had old cars parked on the grass, one with no wheels and the other with the windshield knocked out.

Having Clarice along only increased my anxiety. She'd said Rafer Jones lived on this street. Suppose he challenged me for walking along his street with a colored girl? We passed two girls skipping rope. One end of the rope was tied to a rusted chain link fence, and one girl jumped while the other girl twirled the rope. I felt sure they stared at me as I walked by. We passed a dilapidated garage with an iron hoop on an outside wall. Four teen-age boys played basketball in the dirt yard where the grass had been worn away, and the basketball bounced at odd angles because of the uneven ground. They each shot me a glance that felt hostile.

When we reached Sister Sheila's house, she welcomed us with a big smile. "Honey Child," she said to Clarice, "I have a big glass of sweet tea for you, and you can sit right here on the swing and sip it while I talk to your friend inside."

She followed the woman's direction so promptly and quietly it didn't seem like her. I followed the woman into her living room. Instead of the bright blue, paisley colored outfit she wore at the church, she wore an old pair of slacks and a gray sweatshirt. She looked more like a cleaning lady than the preacher who had dazzled 300 people the previous week.

She gave me a glass of sweet tea as well, put a coaster for it on the end table, and said with a friendly smile. "Yes. You were at church Sunday with the other white boy."

"That was Louis," I said. "We weren't supposed to be there, because he's Jewish and I'm Catholic, but Louis plays the piano in our band and James wanted him to hear the church's piano player and I wanted to hear Clarice sing." The words tumbled out of my mouth as they always do when I'm nervous.

"You and James and your friend have a band?" She looked puzzled, trying to figure out the connection between the band and my visit.

"That's why we came to the church. But I never saw a healer before." I stopped.

"Jesus is the healer, Charlie." She smiled and lifted her hands as she shrugged. "All I do is ask for his aid and get the person to have faith in him. Do you have faith?"

"Oh, yes," I said.

"There's something troubling you, child, but I can't see what it is. Maybe things aren't right at home or maybe you don't know if you should be here. Or maybe it's just that slight limp you have. I can see many things that might trouble you, Charlie. But you've got to tell me more."

Her face had the same pained look she'd had when she told the congregation about her father abusing her as a girl. The look made me feel so comfortable I was tempted to tell her about Mr. Jackson and my troubled remembrances of the photo of Tony Morelli in his jockey shorts. However, I came to my senses and resolved to put first things first. "It's my limp. Can you cure my limp?"

"I don't cure anything, Charlie. I've already explained. It's Jesus who does that. I help you heal."

"Can you heal my limp?"

"I do that at the church. Why didn't you come to me at the church?"

"I couldn't. I'm Catholic, and it would be a sin for me to see you in the church."

"I can see you are very serious about your faith. That is good. But why isn't it a sin to see me here if it would be a sin to see me at church?"

"It's not a sin to see you," I explained. "It's never a sin to ask someone to pray for you. That's what Sister FAH tee mah said."

"Who is Sister FAH tee mah?"

"She's my teacher. She's a nun."

"She sounds like a very wise lady," smiled Sister Sheila. "Indeed, it is not a sin to ask someone to pray for you. But what do you want me to pray for?"

"To cure my limp."

She frowned for a moment as if she had been expecting me to say something more.

"Only Jesus can cure your limp. He can do it, like he multiplied the loaves and fishes, like he healed the leper, and like he raised Lazarus from the dead. But he does these things in his own time. He might heal you now or in twenty years or maybe even in the next world.

But if you have faith, Jesus will heal you. We must pray not just that Jesus will cure your limp but that he will heal the pains in your soul and give you the strength to bear all your burdens. That your soul shall not lose its faith. That your mind stays open. And that your heart continues to show love. That is what we must pray for."

"That's sort of what Sister FAH tee mah said," I responded.

"She is indeed a wise lady," said Sister Sheila, her eyes beaming and her lips parting in a broad grin. "I know Catholics kneel down to pray, so, to make you comfortable, let's get down on our knees, Charlie." She reached out to the end table to steady herself as she sank stiffly to her knees on the big area rug in the middle of her living room. From a pocket in her blouse, she pulled a little cannister of holy oils and dipped her thumb into it. The oil felt cool on my forehead and I felt the palms of her hands come to rest on the top of my head.

"Oh, Jesus, have mercy on this young boy. This is a good boy, who tries to do right in a very sinful world. He is true to his church, Jesus, and he comes to you in hope. He has faith in you, Jesus. Do you have faith, Charlie?"

"Yes," I mumbled.

"Say, 'I have faith in you, Jesus,'" she instructed.

"I have faith in you, Jesus," I said.

"I trust in Jesus," she said and nodded for me to repeat after her.

"I trust in Jesus," I repeated.

"I trust in Jesus," said the healer.

"I trust in Jesus," I said.

"I trust in Jesus," she said a third time.

"I trust in Jesus," I repeated a third time.

"Oh, Jesus," prayed Sister Sheila, "This boy comes to you with faith in his heart. He comes to you with trust in his heart. He comes to you with a burden in his heart. The other boys can run and jump freely. But Charlie here has a limp that slows him down and limits his jump. And the boys mock him, Jesus, just as the soldiers mocked you on Golgotha. Help this boy, sweet Jesus. This is a good boy. He has an open mind and a big heart. Help him never to lose that open mind and big heart. Help him carry his burden, Jesus, just as you help us all carry our burdens."

I lost track of the many prayers uttered by Sister Sheila Mae. She seemed to have a huge stock of Bible sayings that she invoked in a sing songy voice that lulled me into a semi-trance. Eventually I noticed that the room had become quiet. Not even the sound of birds chirping came through the closed windows to stir the quiet stillness of the room. It was like coming out of a dream as I slowly began to notice the ordinary objects around us: a television set in the corner and a sofa along the sidewall. Outside the front window, Clarice's soft black hair shifted as she swayed back and forth on the porch swing.

Sister Sheila Mae put a hand on the end table and stiffly pushed herself to her feet. I took her free hand to help her. "All we can do is pray," she said, "and have faith in Jesus. Trust in Jesus to make your burdens a little lighter."

I didn't know what to do next. Did I owe her money? I pulled a dollar bill from my pocket to offer her, but she refused. "This is not like making a contribution to church, Charlie. Here's what I want you to do with that dollar." She pointed through the window at Clarice on the swing. "You owe a debt to that pretty little girl out there who brought you here. Now you take her to the nearest soda fountain and buy yourselves a treat. Whatever's left over from your dollar, you drop that in the collection plate at your church on Sunday."

I felt peaceful as Sister Sheila ushered me out of the warm house into the crisp October air. I said to Clarice, "Let's go to the drugstore, and I'll buy you a soda."

"Charlie, my daddy's not gonna let me go on a date with no white boy."

"It's not a date. It's what Sister Sheila Mae told me to do." I looked over at the faith healer still standing in the doorway. She beamed her smile at Clarice and nodded her head up and down, signifying yes.

"Oh, that's different," said Clarice.

We headed down the street toward The Norwood Drugstore. We passed some small boys playing hide and seek. One of them hid underneath a parked car and Clarice snapped at him, "Get out of there! It's not safe." He ignored her. We walked closer together than normal, and when our arms brushed together, I took her hand. I'd never held hands with a girl before, and I'd never felt so good walking down the street. After a couple blocks, a police car coasted into view. It was the cop with the fat face and the mean eyes, the one who had pushed me in the chest two weeks ago. He stared at me, but I didn't stop holding hands.

CHAPTER 23

The leaves fell steadily off the trees now, and when I returned home from the drugstore, Mother sent me outside to rake the yard. "We've got a card party tonight, and I don't want the yard looking like a pigpen," she said.

After raking the leaves into a big pile by the curb, I sat on the porch steps and watched Mollie jump around in the big leaf pile. The littlest Byrne girl came over from across the street and joined her. Then the two Fontenell sisters came over, and the Byrne girl stepped back as though she were going to go home. This got me curious. Would she think it beneath her to play with the Negro girls. That's the way most white kids in the neighborhood felt. However, the Fontenell girls and Mollie looked to be having a great time as they laughed and jumped in the mound of leaves. They pulled the leaf pile apart, spreading the leaves around in little squares, pretending that they were rooms of a house. The little Byrne girl finally rejoined the other girls to play house in the leaves.

It was warm for October, so Mother left the front door open, and the sound of her arguing with Dad drifted outside.

"Well, why won't you do it?" Mother said.

"Because I don't drive bulldozers anymore."

The city had started a big construction project by the Sports Arena on the East Side and needed to complete the ground preparation before the winter snows came. The city needed heavy equipment operators to work on weekends. Uncle Jim had told Mother about it. As a precinct captain and a supervisor in the Public Works Department, he knew about the opening even before it was posted. A mere word from Big Jim would land the job for Dad.

"But you only have to do it on weekends. And only till the snow comes. If you go on strike, Lord knows we will need the money. You could start tomorrow."

Dad didn't say anything. Mother looked at him and added, "Just do it tomorrow and if you don't like it you don't have to go back."

Dad finally gave in. "All right. I'll drive the goddamned bulldozer." While Mother picked up the phone to give Big Jim the good news, Dad marched out of the house and slammed the front door behind himself. He did not even pass through the kitchen to pick up a bottle of Buckeye Beer. He looked at the girls playing in the leaves.

"Look at that goddamned mess they're making," he growled at me. "Let's get those leaves raked down to the curb so we can burn them."

After we raked them to the curb, Dad flicked on his cigarette lighter, and soon the sweet smell of burning leaves drifted through the air. We went back to the porch steps where we watched the blaze of fire and relished the sweet aroma of the burning leaves.

"Da, did you notice how quiet Danny got just before

the end of his leave?"

"He knows now that he made a mistake joining the Marines to get a medal. But he can't admit it," said Dad. "And he's scared, but he can't admit that, either."

"Why is he scared? You weren't scared when you won your medal."

Dad turned his eyes away from the burning leaves and looked over at me. The stubble of unshaved whiskers gave his face a bony look. He frowned, like he was trying to decide whether to tell me something. "Charlie, I can't say this in front of your mother, because if she knew had bad it was at Normandy, her nightmares about Danny in Korea would be even worse than they are now."

He paused, then added. "I was scared shitless. We were all scared shitless. I was with the 111th Construction Battalion and we actually landed on the beach before the combat troops did. We had to clear paths through the minefields so the troops had areas where they could move up from the beach. We had to use our bulldozers and tanks to clear out all the obstacles the Germans had installed to block our vehicles from moving forward. If we hadn't gotten those out of the way no vehicles could have gotten off the beach. No tanks. No trucks. No jeeps. No artillery pieces. No nothing."

He clenched his jaw and bobbed his head toward me for emphasis. This was all new information that stunned me. In the movies and the newsreels, all you saw was the infantry troops and the military vehicles. You never saw construction workers.

Dad swallowed and went on talking. "And all the while we're doing this, the Germans are pouring artillery shells down on us. One shell destroyed the dozer on my left and another shell the three machines over on my right. It was random who got hit and who made it through. We were all paralyzed with fear. But the worst thing we could do was to stand still so some gunner could get a bead on you. The only way to survive was to keep going forward. It took the entire first day to clear 10 gaps through those land mines so troops and vehicles could pass through. And another couple of days to clear all the obstacles off the beach."

"So that's how you won your Silver Star."

"No. There were hundreds of us doing that." He chuckled. "They didn't have enough Silver Stars in their stockpile to give one to each of us."

"Then how'd you get it?"

"As the beach got secured, the troops and the vehicles began moving inland. On the second or third day, I got assigned to a convoy that needed a bulldozer to clear a path. It sounded easy enough. All I had to do was use my bulldozer to fill in any bomb craters or push aside any obstructions the Germans had put up to block our progress. We had barely gotten a mile inland when we ran into a German demolition team wiring a bridge so they could blow it up and slow down our advance. To protect them while they did this, they'd placed a machine gun in a foxhole right behind a small hill. Our whole convoy was brought to a halt by the machine guns blasting away at us. Every time somebody raised his head, they'd shoot a round of machine gun bullets at us. They had us pinned down in. But if we didn't go forward, we couldn't capture the bridge before the Germans blew it up. And if that happened, who knows how long it would have taken to get our army across that river."

"So what'd you do?" This story excited me so much I

couldn't sit still on the porch steps. I got up and began walking back and forth in front of him. He grabbed my arm and pulled me back down to a sitting position.

"We got lucky. The bullets were killing anyone who poked up his head, but they bounced off the plow of my bulldozer."

Discovering this, said Dad, he headed the bulldozer toward the hill in front of the foxhole. He had to raise the plow high enough to keep from getting his head ripped off by the bullets whizzing past him while at the same time keeping it low enough to protect the Cat's radiator from being shot. An empty radiator would stop the bulldozer dead in its tracks in the middle of a no-man's land between the American riflemen and the German machine gunners.

"Those bullets just kept flying by my head. Did you ever see how big a 50-caliber bullet is?" He spread his thumb and forefinger apart to show me. "And the noise from that machine gun was deafening. This was worse than being on the beach. At least on the beach it was random who got hit by an artillery shell. But here they were aiming their fire directly at me. I was never so scared in my life. But once I started moving, I had no choice. I had to keep going."

Dad paused. His Adam's apple bobbled as he swallowed hard, and little beads of sweat formed on his forehead. He looked almost as though he was afraid all over again. I wondered how that could be. After all, this had happened eight years ago. But I didn't say anything for fear that he might not go on with the story.

"When I reached the bottom of the hill in front of the foxhole, there was a moment when the machine gunners could see me. So I lowered the plow, dug into the hill and buried them under a huge load of dirt."

I had never felt so proud of Dad. And I must have had a stupid grin on my face, because he looked annoyed at me.

"I killed them, Charlie. Don't you understand. I buried them alive and smothered them under a pile of dirt."

"But Da, they were trying to kill you."

He looked at me again as we sat on the porch steps watching the leaves burn. For the first time, I noticed some gray in the stubble of hair on his chin.

"Of course they were. That's what war is. You kill or get killed. But that doesn't mean you feel good about what you have to do," he snarled.

"At least I'd shut down that damned machine gun, and our infantrymen were able to attack the demolition team before they could blow up the bridge. But there were bullets flying everywhere. I turned the dozer engine down to an idle, leaned over the side, and puked in the dirt. And I spotted a GI lying on the ground and groaning. A young guy, just a kid Danny's age. I jumped off the tractor to help him, and one of the rifle shots hit my helmet and knocked it off my head. It felt like getting hit with a baseball bat, and my head felt like it was exploding. Some Army nurse told me later on that I had a concussion. But this kid was still lying on the ground, with a fountain of blood coming out of his leg. He was holding his leg and crying for his mother. Our medic was busy with someone else, so I made a tourniquet as best I could from some slices of cloth that I cut from his pant leg. And all the time I'm doing this, I'm hearing him cry, 'Mother help me! Mother, help me!' until I finally passed out from the concussion I'd gotten. But I'll never forget that kid weeping like that."

"Did he live?"

"Apparently. If he'd died, there wouldn't have been much reason to give me the Silver Star."

"So, if you were wounded, how come you didn't get a Purple Heart?"

"Who knows? Maybe a concussion's not enough. Maybe you've got to shed some blood or something."

He stopped talking abruptly for a moment, stared at me, and barked, "Charlie, pay attention. You're missing the point. It's not whether I won a Purple Heart or a Silver Star or any medal at all. The point is that it's not worth it."

Then his voice softened.

"It know it's confusing, Charlie. I'm proud of what we did at Normandy. If we'd failed, your world would be a helluva lot less nice than it is. But I'm telling you this for a reason. Don't get some crazy ideas in your head like Danny about joining the Marines to get a medal."

"Why is it crazy to fight for your country?"

"It's not crazy to fight for your country like we did in the War. But it's not the same in Korea. They lost thousands of men on that march into North Korea they shouldn't have done. And for what? They had to retreat, and they're right back where they started. Thousands of men dead, and they're right back where they started. The people running this war can't be trusted. And what's crazy is voluntarily placing yourself under the trust of people who are untrustworthy."

Dad had never talked this way before, and I couldn't think of anything to say. However, he was so wound up he didn't need any prodding.

"If Danny keeps his head down and doesn't try to be a hero, I think he'll be okay. But some night he's gonna be out on some godforsaken hill under attack. Some of his buddies will get shot and be crying for their mothers just like that kid in Normandy. Danny and the others will be so scared they'll be shitting in their pants and shooting at every noise they hear. And for what? To hold some goddamned hill they'll probably give back again as soon as we get a truce. I think he'll be okay, Charlie. But it's going to change him. Spending a night sitting in his own shit praying for his life."

So that's what happened. No wonder Dad didn't want to drive bulldozers anymore. Who would? Not after you'd crapped your pants because of it all. We sat there quiet until Dad stood up to go back in the house. He looked down at me.

"Medals aren't worth it, Charlie," he said. "Don't get any crazy ideas in your head like Danny has about winning a medal."

Mother was still busy getting ready for the family card party. She sent me across the street to borrow a card table from the Byrnes. Then she gave me a batch of steak knives to take down the street to the man who earned money on the side as a knife sharpener. As he held the knife blades against the sharpening wheel on his machine, sparks flew off the cutting edges of the knives. Dad put out a supply of mixes and soft drinks, pretzels and peanuts. Mother made up a platter of crackers and cheese slices. By 7:30, we had the kitchen loaded with crackers, celery sticks, dips, potato chips, whiskey, gin and mixes. Dad also set out a laundry tub filled with Buckeye Beer bottles and bags of ice. Mother went upstairs to change into a good dress, then came down and asked Dad to fasten some buttons in the back.

"Mother," I asked. "Why do you wear dresses with buttons where you can't reach them?"

"Don't get smart with me," she replied. "Just go out in the kitchen and make sure Mollie doesn't eat all the potato chips."

Dad laughed.

Relatives and friends began to stream in and gather around the tables to play cards, and I got to hang around the fringes, eavesdropping on the conversations and peering over the shoulders into the card hands held by our favorite aunts and uncles.

"Get some horses durves," said Mother to each person who came through the door. Dad chuckled to himself but didn't say anything. Her brother, Uncle Jim, however, couldn't stand her word mixups. After the third time she did it, he corrected her. "Hors d'oeuvres!" he said. "Not horses durves. Hors d'oeuvres!"

"Well, pardon me, Mister big shot know-it-all," Mother replied.

They talked a lot while they played, and this year they were split over the election. Most of the family stuck with their party and pledged themselves to vote for Stevenson. But Mother announced, "I'm voting for Ike."

That did not sit well with Big Jim who had used his influence as precinct captain for several years to hire her as a paid election judge. Those few extra dollars every election day were a welcome addition to Mother's personal funds.

"What's it gonna look like if my own sister, a Democratic election judge, votes Republican?" Uncle Jim challenged.

"I'm not voting Republican. I'm just voting for Ike.

Everyone else will be a Democrat."

"What kind of Democrat votes for Ike?" he persisted.

"One that doesn't want her son killed. That's what," Mother glared at him. "Ike says he'll go to Korea. Somebody's got to stop that war before any more of our boys get killed."

"Danny's not gonna get killed," snapped Big Jim. "He's just got to do his duty like we did in the War."

Dad looked over at Big Jim with the meanest look I had ever seen him show. "It's not the same, Jim. Danny's gonna be out on some cold hill getting shot at. You were safely back in a warm quartermaster's tent handing out clothes."

All of a sudden everyone stopped talking. Dad and Big Jim sat there glaring at each other.

"This is the thanks I get!" snorted Big Jim, his voice growing loud and angry as he bolted upright and leaned down on the table with his fingers clenched around the table edge. "I get my sister a job on Election Day and I get work for you at the Sports Arena. And this is the thanks I get! Just think for a minute what it would have been like sitting on that bulldozer of yours in France if you hadn't had a quartermaster to give you clothes and equipment. Think of that before you shoot off your mouth about me."

Dad also jumped up and glared back at Big Jim. I thought for sure one of them would slug the other or that Big Jim would walk out of the house in a huff. But just at that moment, Uncle Benny, the jovial fireman, fell backwards out of his chair in a comical way, and lay sprawling on the floor, sort of like the fat comedian Lou Costello, whom he resembled. I went over to help him up, and he put an arm around my waist. "Charlie, could you go to the kitchen and make a sandwich for your old

Uncle Benny?"

"Sure," I said. "What kind of sandwich?"

He paused. Having caught everyone's attention, he tilted his head to one side, puckered his lips and stared at the ceiling. "Peanut butter and mustard," he said. Everybody burst out laughing at the idea of such an atrocious sandwich. Uncle Jim sat back down, shaking his head as he did so, and the players went back to their cards.

Eventually, the card players lost their zip. "I must be getting old," said Aunt Bridget as the clock pushed toward midnight. "I just don't have the energy I once had."

In the end, the card players seemed to have enjoyed a great evening. But some of them looked like they were not going to be feeling too good the next morning.

Mollie and I sat on the stair steps, basking in the glow of the evening, in which we got to stand around with our favorite aunts and uncles. I wished Mother would host the card game every week.

CHAPTER 24

As Halloween approached, Mollie and I pestered Dad to tell us his plans. He always made a spectacle out of trick-or-treats, and each year he tried to outdo what he'd done the year before. Two years earlier, he had built a coffin, which he set next to the door on the front porch. Then he dressed himself in a shroud with a dark hood that covered his entire head and cast a shadow on his face. Against the wall next to the coffin, he leaned an old broomstick, on the end of which he had taped a curved blade cut out of stiff cardboard and painted jet black. I watched the first group of kids approach the house. He slouched down in the coffin and waited until they walked up the steps. Just as they reached the porch, he lifted himself up, groaned as though he was rising from the dead, and swung his homemade scythe through the air.

This sent the bigger kids stepping back and the littler ones running down the porch steps to the safety of the sidewalk. At this point, Dad pulled the hood off his head and give a loud chortling laugh. Then, to show his actual harmless, good hearted nature, he dropped Snickers Bars and Mars Bars into their sacks. After the kids walked off the porch, he grabbed a bottle of Buckeye Beer from the foot of the coffin, sat back down and waited for the next unsuspecting batch of kids he could scare.

Last year he outdid the coffin caper, as he started calling it, when he got his hands on an actual human skeleton. He dreamed up the scheme while drinking at the VFW Post with another Normandy veteran, Greg Mendel, who now taught science at DeVilbis High School. He persuaded Mr. Mendel to let him wrap the skeleton in his old Navy peacoat, sneak it out of the Science Lab on a Saturday morning, and stick it in the trunk of Mr. Mendel's car. They hid the skeleton in the garage until Halloween day when they tied it to a kitchen chair Dad had dragged onto the front porch. They propped it into a sitting position, draped the torso with a black cape, wrapped the neck with a bright orange scarf, and adorned the head with a big top hat they had borrowed from the school's Theater Department. Inside the chest bones, they mounted a light bulb that shone up and gave an eerie glow to the yellow jaw and the empty eye sockets.

Before getting any candy, each trick-or-treater had to kiss the skeleton on the lips. Well, the jawbone, actually, the lips having long since gone. The two men giggled and roared with laughter at the looks on the faces of the kids as they approached the skeleton. If a kid hesitated to kiss the skeleton, Dad or Mr. Mendel showed how easy it was by bending over and giving the dead bones a big slobbering smooch, wet with spit and beer. Also roaring with laughter at the sight of this were Danny and me. Danny had stolen a bottle of Buckeye Beer when Dad wasn't looking, and he shared some with me. Lumbering over from across the street to get in on the laughter and the Buckeye Beer came Mr. Byrne. The hilarity ended when Mother came out to investigate the noise.

"What are you drunks doing?" she yelled. "You can't make the children kiss a skeleton."

She did not think it was funny at all. Of course, she had not shared a case of Buckeye Beer with an old buddy from Normandy and the various neighbors who, like Mr. Byrne, came over to join in the fun. For the rest of the night, Mother took charge of handing out the treats.

The next day she confronted Dad. "Get that creepy skeleton out of my house."

By the time Dad asked him to take back the skeleton, however, Mr. Mendel had sobered up, and he worried about what trouble he'd be in if he were seen dragging the missing skeleton back to his Science Lab. He said it had all been Dad's idea to begin with, so Dad was stuck with the skeleton. If anyone asked him about it, Mr. Mendel said he would deny he had ever brought the skeleton over to our house in the first place.

"That wimp!" Dad complained. "Just like a teacher to come up with his brightest idea when he's all liquored up, but then not have the guts to take responsibility for his actions."

"Well," demanded Mother, "if he won't live up to his responsibility, then you take it back!"

"Are you crazy? They'd arrest me on the spot the minute they saw a bone sticking out from whatever I wrapped it in. I'll just wait till winter and throw it into the furnace."

Mother looked horrified, her eyes opening wide and her mouth drooping. "You can't do that. It's a mortal sin to cremate a human body."

"This isn't a human body. It's just a bunch of bones."

"I don't care. You can't cremate it. Get rid of it."

From that day on, the science students at DiVilbis no longer had a skeleton from which to learn the bones of the body. However, our basement did have one wrapped in Dad's old Navy peacoat tucked under some old rags by Mother's washing machine where it was out of sight.

One day in January the skeleton disappeared. Mother apparently didn't want to know how Dad had gotten rid of it, because she didn't ask. But later in the week, as I raked ashes out of the furnace, I pulled out some long pieces of something that hadn't burned completely and looked nothing at all like coal ashes.

This year, Dad said he had a gag to top all the previous ones. That didn't seem possible, since I didn't see how anything could top the skeleton gag. We were sitting at the supper table, and Mother looked skeptical. Mollie bounced up and down on her chair. "What is it? What is it?"

"You'll just have to wait and see," said Dad with his grin. "I can only say one thing. It's a variation on the coffin caper."

On Halloween night, I rushed Mollie through her trick-or-treating. I wore a thick sweater over a flannel shirt and a Lone Ranger mask that covered my eyes. Mother dressed Mollie in a cowgirl's outfit to go with my Lone Ranger getup. We stopped at barely a dozen houses before I brought Mollie back home. "That's not fair, Charlie," she complained. "This is too soon. I don't even have half a bag." She held up a mostly-empty pillow case.

"You can get all you want at home," I said, tugging her along. "Besides, we need to get home so you can see what Dad is up to."

As we neared the house, Dad came into view, and I had to admit that this, indeed, was a clever prank. He wore a striped prisoner's suit and stood precariously on a barrel set up next to the front porch steps. A hangman's noose around his neck dangled down from the porch roof overhang where he had fastened it. When he spied some children coming up the walk, he tilted his head to the side and bent his knees slightly to take up the slack in the noose so he looked like an executed convict hanging in the air. Just as the children reached the porch steps, he straightened up and reached out his hand as if to steal some candy from the trick-or-treat bag of a small girl dressed as an angel. The girl jumped back in shock, then giggled when she realized she wasn't being attacked by a human corpse. Dad roared with laughter, slipped his head out of the noose, and took a quick swig of Buckeye Beer from the case he had stashed under the porch where mother couldn't see it. Mollie and I laughed at the sight.

Dad moved back into his routine again as another group of children approached the porch steps. But the barrel collapsed under his weight, and the noose pulled tight up against his neck. Dad dangled there stomping his feet in search of a footing on the remains of the barrel. The only thing he accomplished by his stomping was to break off more pieces of the barrel. Soon his toes swung in open air and he began to choke as the full weight of his body pulled the noose tighter against his neck. Mollie screamed, which brought Mother to the door. She ran to Dad, wrapping her arms around his legs, trying to hold him up and stop the choking. I dropped Mollie's hand and ran toward the two of them as fast as I could.

"Cut him down, Charlie!" Mother shouted. "Get a knife!"

I pulled my Boy Scout knife from my pocket, climbed up on the porch railing and, still wearing the Lone Ranger mask, leaned way over to reach the rope, holding on to a post with my left arm while I began slicing away at the rope with the knife in my right hand. Fortunately, the rope was only a clothesline that would not be too difficult to cut. But I was off balance and couldn't get full leverage on the knife. In the meantime, Dad's chest was heaving as he gasped for breath. Finally, I cut through the rope, and it dropped to the ground. With Dad's full weight suddenly in her arms, Mother also collapsed, and Dad fell on top of her. She sniffed his breath and looked around with suspicion until she saw the half-empty case of Buckeye Beer hidden by the porch. But she didn't say anything. She just sat there for a moment and held him in her arms.

By now, a dozen kids had gathered in a circle, staring at my parents sitting on the hard, cold ground, and the circle grew as more kids came by to see what had happened. I suddenly felt humiliated as everyone stared at Dad. I picked up the basket of treats, took them down to the circle of kids, and shooed them away by handing out the candies one-by-one. "Move along now. Everything's okay. Here's your treat. Move along."

Dad disentangled himself from Mother, slipped the noose off his neck, and tried to reclaim his dignity by helping me shoo away the gawkers. Mother moved the basket of candies to the porch, where she took over the task of handing them out. Dad picked up the case of beer and retreated into the house, rubbing the red circle the rope had made around his neck.

I went out in search of a friend. However, I had lost my desire for trick-or-treating. I went to the phone booth in front of the Norwood Avenue Drugstore and dialed Mr. Jackson's number. When he said, "Hello?" I let the phone dangle from is cord. Then I just wandered aimlessly through the streets and watched the small children in their costumes hurry along from house to house.

CHAPTER 25

On the first Friday of November, I found myself embarrassed again, just as I had been embarrassed on the first Friday of October. And, unless I did something soon, I could expect to be embarrassed on all the first Fridays for the rest of the school year.

"What's your mother doing here?" Billy Byrne nudged me in the ribs as we knelt at the mass all the kids at St. Matthew's attended each morning before school. There was Mother, up front in a side pew, huddled over, her hands folded in prayer on the back of the railing in front of her, and her head covered with a babushka, making her look like one of those war refugees who used to show up in old newsreels. Displaced persons, or DeePees, if you wanted to be nasty.

"She's doing the nine first Fridays," I said. "She's done two so far and she'll have six more after today."

A person who received Holy Communion on the first Friday of nine consecutive months was promised by the Sacred Heart of Jesus that he would not die in a state of mortal sin. A person who died without repenting his mortal sins was condemned to the everlasting fire of hell. However, with the protection of the nine first Fridays, you had the promise of Jesus you would not go straight to hell. You would always have a last chance to repent and have your sins forgiven.

I had already done my nine first Fridays. And Danny should have done his when he had Mrs. Hanratty for a teacher. She made you do them. Poor Danny forgot one of the first Fridays, and I'll never forget him crying at home that night and screaming that he would never go back to Mrs. Hanratty's class again. Since it was so rare to see Danny cry, every detail of that night stood out in my memory.

If you wanted to receive Holy Communion in the morning, you had to fast from the previous midnight. But Danny ate a slice of toast that morning which broke his fast and made him ineligible to receive communion. Mrs. Hanratty became so angry at this carelessness she grew red in the face, Danny told us when he got home. "Don't you understand that you will burn in the everlasting fire of hell if you die with a mortal sin on your soul?" She took him to the coatroom to get on his knees and make an Act of Contrition. "I would let you do it out in the classroom, but I don't want you to embarrass yourself in front of the class," she told him.

After the few moments it took to say the prayer, Danny came back into the room, and she asked, "Was it an act of perfect contrition?" When Danny hesitated to answer, Mrs. Hanratty sent him back to the cloakroom to make his act one of perfect contrition.

This distinction was very important. In an act of perfect contrition, you expressed sincere remorse for having offended God, contrasted to an act of imperfect contrition in which you were sorry only because you did not want to burn in the everlasting fire of hell. Normally, you could wipe a mortal sin off your soul with an act of imperfect contrition only if you made it while confessing your sins in the Sacrament of Penance. Otherwise, you needed an act of perfect contrition, which was very hard to do. Suppose you had been good all week and then you suffered a heart attack just as you were working up a hard-on thinking about a tan-colored girl walking around in shiny, white nylon underpants? Or worse yet, this vision led you to start committing an impure act? How could you possibly have sincere remorse about these offenses to God just at that moment when you were only seconds away from both finishing your impure act and being sent to the everlasting fire of hell? That was the beauty of the nine first Fridays. No matter how many times you gave in to the temptation of impure acts, you never had to worry whether your final Act of Contrition was perfect or not. As long as you repented, Jesus had promised he would save you.

Of course, if Danny didn't have any mortal sins on his soul that day, he didn't have to make any act of contrition in the first place. Maybe Mrs. Hanratty assumed that there had to be a mortal sin on the soul of a boy who had stood up in her class one day to show a picture of an artist who'd cut off his own ear and given it to a prostitute.

Dad did not believe in the nine first Fridays. "It's a lot of hocus," he told Mother when she started doing them. She got angry and walked out of the room. Dad got another bottle of Buckeye Beer from the refrigerator and told me, "It's hogwash, Charlie. You either believe in an all-loving God or you believe in hell. But you can't believe in both."

None of us understood why Mother had started doing the first Fridays, because she had already done them before. But there she was kneeling in a side pew. As Billy Byrne and I filed out of church with the rest of the eighth-graders, I glanced at her and hoped that nobody else had noticed.

Unfortunately, Butch Bower noticed, and he came up to me in the schoolyard at lunchtime. He had a menacing grin as he towered above me. Well, he didn't really tower over me, since he was only an inch or two taller. But he had such powerful shoulders and such a ferocious reputation as a fighter, he seemed to tower over me.

"What's your mother doing in church all dressed up like a DeePee?" he challenged me, the smirk on his face growing wider. He looked around to see who was watching. "Hey everybody! Parnell's old lady is a DeePee." He gave a forced laugh as he bent over and slapped his knee for emphasis. A circle of kids started to gather around us.

I still hadn't forgotten his calling me a cripple that first day of class, and I shook with anger at him calling my mother a DeePee. Before thinking, I said, "Well, at least I got a mother, which is more than anybody can say for you!" Butch lived alone with his dad. His mother had packed up and left the two of them three years earlier, and no one had seen her since then. I stiffened my arms to get ready for the blows I expected Butch to rain down on me any second. But instead of beating me to the ground, he just stared at me. His lip quivered for a second. Then he turned on his heels and walked away.

For a moment, I felt elated. I had stood up to Butch Bower, and with just a few words, I had sent him slinking away. Once again, Danny was right; look for the weak spot. Just as I was starting to bask in this newly discovered power, however, Carl Broda, the Hungarian, shook his head at me and said, "That was mean, Charlie. That was hitting below the belt."

The circle of kids that had formed around Butch and me began to break up. Sister FAH tee mah had run over to stop any trouble the minute she saw the circle form. She gave me a disapproving look just as the bell rang and we all headed inside to the classroom.

When school let out at 3:15, Sister FAH tee mah kept me waiting at my desk until the floor was swept, the chalkboard was washed, and the erasers were cleaned. It wasn't until the last kid left the room that she came over to me. I stood up.

"I heard what you said to Butch Bower."

She paused, waiting for a reply, but I didn't know what to say and kept quiet. How could it be that she seem to be staring down at you even though she was quite short and looking up.

"I am disappointed in you, Charlie," she said, still pronouncing my name Sharlie. "That was a very mean thing to say."

"Well, you should have heard what he said about my mother. That wasn't very nice either."

"We're not talking about what he said to you. We are talking about what you said to him."

"Sister, Butch Bower is a bully. If you don't get even with him, he'll just push you all over the place and get away with it."

"Get even? That is a bad idea. 'Vengeance is mine, sayeth the Lord.' Vengeance poisons the soul, Sharlie. Don't let me hear any more talk about getting even."

"But Sister," I said. "You're a nun and people are polite to you. What would you do if you weren't a nun and they insulted you any time they wanted? What'd you do when you were a kid?"

This was not a wise thing to say, because I wasn't supposed to have eavesdropped on her telling Father Stan in September about being called a Dago, and I wasn't supposed to know that she had slapped Butch Bower. She got a very hard look in her eye for an instant, as if she suspected me of something, and then the look softened.

"But I am not a little girl anymore, Sharlie. I am a nun responsible for teaching you and the other children what is right and what is wrong. And you are not just a run of the mill child. You have been given a special gift and you cannot let it be poisoned by vengeance."

A special gift? I had no idea what she meant.

"Don't look so innocent. You know what I am talking about. Of all the children I have taught, you are one of the few who has a chance to do something special in life. What that gift is or why God gave it to you, I don't know. But I saw it in the way you bore your pain that day on the football field when everyone turned away from you. I saw something in the face of that pretty little colored girl who is so fond of you. I've never met a white boy before who could bring colored people into his life the way you do. I see it in your confidence when you come up to the blackboard and solve a problem before anybody else can do it. But you will lose it all if you strive after vengeance. Vengeance poisons the soul, Charlie! Remember that. Vengeance poisons the soul!"

She stared at me for a long moment, then stepped aside so I could leave.

I fumed the rest of the afternoon. What a crock! Butch insults anybody he wants anytime he wants, beats them up if he thinks they're worth the trouble, and nobody says anything. I put him in his place and suddenly I'm the bad guy getting a lecture. And what's all this crap about a special gift? Sister FAH tee mah's a very nice person, but this turning the other cheek stuff doesn't work with guys like Butch Bower. And she didn't exactly turn the other cheek herself that day she slapped the daylights out of him.

However, none of my fuming would get Mother to stop doing her first Fridays. And that was the important thing I had to address. So at supper that night, I raised the question, "Mother, why are you doing the first Fridays? You only need to do them once, and you've already done that. Doing more of them won't do you any good."

"I'm doing them for Danny," she said.

"For Danny?" I passed a quizzical look over to Mollie and Dad, but they didn't seem to understand any better than I did.

"Yes, for Danny." She smiled and shook her head up and down once. "If you remember, he never finished them. Mrs. Hanratty did the best she could for him, but he never finished."

That floored me. Mother actually thought Mrs. Hanratty had been helping Danny when she humiliated him in front of the class and sent him home in tears.

"He can't do the first Fridays himself now that he's in Korea," she said. "So I'm doing them for him. We have to be realistic. With all that booze and gambling and what not around a Marine camp, there's no chance for Danny to keep a pure soul. He needs the nine first Fridays."

I wondered if she had overheard Danny during his leave telling me he hoped there would be a whorehouse when he got to Korea. But I didn't interrupt, and she went on talking.

"So I make the first Fridays and ask the Sacred Heart to credit them to Danny."

I shook my head in wonderment. In case Danny got killed in the war, the nine first Fridays would keep him from being plunged into the everlasting fire of hell. Even if his death came in a sneak mortar attack just as he was walking out of the whorehouse. She beamed as she told us of this good deed she was doing.

Oh my God! If she really believes this, she'll come to church and embarrass me every first Friday for the rest of the year.

"I don't think that's possible," I said cautiously and looked over to Dad for support as Mother's proud grin turned to a scowl. "Can you do that Da? Can you do the first Fridays for somebody else? Or does each person have to do his own?" Of course, asking Dad a question like that was a wild shot. I might just as well have asked him something about atomic energy. He'd have just as much chance of knowing the answer. Probably a better chance. At least he believed in atomic energy. Whether he believed in God I was never quite sure.

Dad just shrugged his shoulders, while Mother looked back and forth between the two of us. "Well, I'll just find out," she said. "I'll ask Father Stan at confession tomorrow."

So at 4:00 o'clock Saturday afternoon, Mother threw a thick shawl over her shoulders and headed out the front door for the church. I pulled out a jigsaw puzzle and spread it on the coffee table, challenging myself to finish it before she got back.

I was good at jigsaw puzzles. Last year I had won a $5 prize in a puzzle contest at the Boys Club downtown. I beat out a couple of high school kids, but they got jealous and beat me up afterwards and stole the $5 bill. I never went back to the Boys Club. Who'd want to fit in with guys like that? Mollie came over to help me with the puzzle and Dad sat on the sofa reading a book about World War II, *From Here to Eternity*. The house was quiet, except for the noise from the bus when it rumbled down Oakwood Street in front of our house. I put the last puzzle piece into place just as Mother came back in through the front door. We all looked up at her, eager to hear Father Stan's verdict.

"That man's an imposter!" she declared as she hung her shawl in the front closet. "Do you know what he said?" Her eyes scanned Dad, Mollie, and me as she walked over to the easy chair and sat down. None of us interrupted her. "We don't really know if there is a fire in hell," he said. "The true pain of hell is the absence of God. The fire of hell is just a semaphore."

Dad squinted at her in puzzlement. "A semaphore?"

"Yes, a semaphore. You know. A word that's a symbol for something. Look it up in the dictionary."

"A metaphor!" said Dad. He pushed his head back and laughed, then sent me to get him a bottle of Buckeye Beer from the kitchen.

"Hmph," said Mother. She never liked it when we laughed at her word mixups. "You're missing the point. That man doesn't even know the teachings of the church. What kind of priests are they putting out these days? Imagine, the fire of hell is just a semaphore."

She never went back to Father Stan after that; she

always joined the line of old ladies waiting outside Father Doyle's confessional. How could she trust a priest who did not uphold the teachings of the church? To my distress, she clearly didn't intend to give up the first Fridays.

CHAPTER 26

Clarice and I met at the library the week after Thanksgiving, and I told her about the incident of the nine first Fridays. Of course, there were some things I left out. Such as the parts about Butch Bower and getting beat up at the Boys Club. It was bad enough I had to hide my limp when I was with her. I certainly didn't want her knowing that other kids pushed me around.

"You do jigsaw puzzles?" she asked. Her focus on that part of the story surprised me. I thought she would laugh at Mother's word mix up or she'd say something about hell or communion or something. Instead, she just asked if I really did jigsaw puzzles.

"Yeah," I said. "What's wrong with that?"

"Nothing," she said with a slight chuckle. "I just never thought of you as the jigsaw puzzle type."

I must have frowned, because she added, as if to show she wasn't insulting me. "I just thought of you as a great trumpet player or a math teacher or maybe a leader like you're doing with the band."

"But it's all the same," I said. I tapped my toes on the floor under the table at the chance to tell her something good about myself. "What I like is putting things together and seeing how all the pieces fit."

"What's that got to do with the trumpet?"

"When you play music, you fit all the notes together. It's like that hymn you sang at your church that day. You did a great job, but everything fit together. There you were singing and James tapping that triangle and the choir humming and the hush that was over the people and then Sister Sheila bringing the church out of the hush when she started preaching."

I threw up my hands in a stop gesture. "Now don't get me wrong. I'm not taking anything away from you, because without your singing the whole thing would have fallen flat. But it took all those pieces fitting together that made it so great. That's why it's like a jigsaw puzzle. And that's what I like, putting things together."

She got a funny look on her face, almost as though she had stopped hearing me and was off in a bit of a trance. Her eyes gazed in an unfocused look at the wall behind me. Then she looked me in the eye and flashed a big grin.

"Oh, Charlie! I can't tell you how great that felt. It was the best moment of my life. There I was singing, and everybody was hanging on every note. I felt like I had the whole congregation in the palm of my hand." She unconsciously lifted her brown hands–the pale palms up–a few inches off the library table.

"You did!" I said. But she was so engrossed in the memory of that moment, with that unfocused look in her eye, that I don't think she heard me. We just sat quiet for a moment, not talking, which was probably a relief to Mrs. Nordstrom.

Then she looked at me again with a satisfied smile

on her face, like she was enjoying the taste of a delicious piece of candy I'd just given her and like her smile was thanking me for it. Or maybe that was just the way I was feeling, and her smile didn't mean anything of the sort. Then she broke the dreamy look and changed the subject.

"What are you gonna be in life, Charlie?"

"I don't know," I said. "I haven't even gone to high school yet."

"James and I are going to go to Scott High. Where are you going?"

"Albertus Magnus," I said. I half twisted so she could see the big red letters AM on the scarlet and gray letter jacket Danny had left behind when he went off to the Marines.

"That's a funny name for a school."

"No, it's not. It's named after Albert the Great. He's the patron saint of scientists."

"Then your grade school must be named after St. Matthew's. What's he the patron saint of?"

"Bankers and bookkeepers."

She laughed and tossed her head back, her hair bobbing back and forth with the movement of her head. "That fits. The way James says you're always making bets with kids and taking their money, it makes sense that you go to the patron saint of bookkeepers."

I laughed. "No. A person who makes bets is a bookmaker. A bookkeeper is a guy who keeps records for a company."

Her smile turned to an angry pout. "Why you laughing at me? That's not nice."

"Well, you laughed at me."

"You got a point," she said and went back to her question. "What are you gonna do after high school?"

"I don't know. Maybe I'll go to work at the Spark Plug Factory and become a union steward like my Dad. That's important."

"You should go to college, Charlie. That's what I'm gonna do. Momma lets me go to the library at night so I can study and get into college and make something of myself."

I didn't respond.

"Whats the matter? You think a colored girl can't go to college?"

"I didn't say that."

"But you were thinking it. I can tell by that look on your face."

The fact was that I'd never heard of a colored girl going to college. But I surely wasn't going to say that to Clarice. Instead, I said, "What college you gonna go to?"

"Maybe I'll just go right here in Jeeptown."

"What will you study?"

"I don't know. That's the hard part. I want to be a singer, but Momma says I should be a teacher or a nurse. She says a colored girl needs a job with a lot of security."

"Why does a girl need a job? Won't your husband have a job?"

She brought her eyebrows together in a frown. "Of course he'll have a job! You think I'm gonna marry some shiftless guy who won't work? But Momma says you can't count on a colored man being allowed to keep a job. They get fired all the time. So a woman needs a job for a backup when that happens."

"My mother worries about my dad going on strike."

"Why's he gonna do that?"

"The union's mad at the company. Like I told you

before, they're making money hand over fist, but they don't want to give anybody a raise."

"So why do you want to go work in a factory where they don't pay you enough and you gotta go out on strike all the time?"

"I don't know. I never thought of it that way."

"You should go to college, Charlie. You got a head for numbers. You shouldn't join the Marines. People like you and me should go to college."

CHAPTER 27

Ever since that night with Mr. Jackson, I had put off going to confession. Not because I feared dying with a mortal sin on my soul and being sent to the everlasting fire of hell. My nine first Fridays guaranteed me a lastminute repentance that protected from that. But Mother had started to nag me about not taking communion at the Sunday mass. With Christmas coming up, her nagging was bound to get worse. The problem was that you couldn't take communion with a mortal sin on your soul. So as much as I dreaded it, I couldn't put off much longer confessing what I'd done with Mr. Jackson and telling about those images that kept popping into my mind of Tony Morelli in his jockey shorts.

I knelt on the hard wooden kneeler, my hands folded together on the back of the pew in front of me, in the Church of St. Martin de Porres. This was the church established for Negro Catholics, who would not be welcomed at the regular parishes in Jeeptown. It was a cold, drafty, old building a few blocks from Clarice's house. I decided on St. Martin de Porres for my confession because I could not risk being recognized by Father Stanislaus at my home parish of St. Matthew's.

Each confession had to be preceded by an examination of conscience in which you reflected on what sins you'd committed. Whatever sins I'd committed were dwarfed by what happened that night with Mr. Jackson. Even with over two months to think about it, I still couldn't decide on the words to confess my sin.

My knees were getting sore from kneeling so long at St. Martin de Porres. Finally, there was no one left in front of me, and I couldn't put it off any longer. The priest might poke his head through the curtain in hopes that nobody would be waiting and he could leave the drafty confessional box and go home to a warm dinner. I did not want to be spotted and identified when this happened. I rose and limped toward the confessional booth.

"How did this happen? How did you get into such a situation?" he asked after I confessed what had taken place.

I explained about the pictures of Tony, the camping trip, and the doubling up in sleeping bags because of the cold. He didn't say anything for a second. It seemed like an hour. Then he replied.

"You are not the sinner here, my son. The true sinner is the man who did this to you. You did not crawl into that sleeping bag expecting this to happen. Did you?"

"No, Father."

"Then it's not your sin. It's only a sin if you intended it to happen."

"But Father." I hesitated and shifted weight from one knee to the other. "Once it started, I didn't want it to stop. And I can't get those pictures of my friend in his jockey shorts out of my mind. What does that mean?"

"It doesn't mean anything. You are not the one who caused this, and you are not guilty for things you didn't cause. What you must do is to end all contact with that man."

"I already have, Father."

"Good. God forgives whatever sins you may have had. Now make the Act of Contrition, then go in peace. And for your penance say one 'Hail Mary.'"

Amazing! This was the worst sin I could think of, and I had just received the lightest penance of my life. I didn't even stop to kneel in the pews to say the penance. I just said the prayer in my mind as I walked toward the door. And it was a good thing, because the priest stepped out of the confessional before I reached the end of the aisle.

Not wanting to be identified by my limp, I walked as properly as possible. I pulled on my gloves as I stepped into the cold.

It had started raining. Using a glove to wipe the bike seat dry, I stepped on the pedal, swung my other leg over the seat and headed home, the icy rain stinging my forehead as I pedaled into the wind. I pulled my stocking cap down almost to my eyes and continued home.

As I tucked my head down to shield my face from the rain, I thought about what had happened. It doesn't mean anything, the priest had said. And he gave me a penance so light it almost seemed like I hadn't sinned at all. But I still felt humiliated from having to confess it. I was still shut out of the Boy Scouts. And I still cringed at the memory of that big prick pressed against the crack of my butt.

I screamed into the wind. "I'm gonna get that son-of-a-bitch!"

CHAPTER 28

Two Saturdays before Christmas, I finished my newspaper collections early and heard Dad on the telephone as I came through the back door into the kitchen. He had left his pay envelope in his locker at the Jeeptown Spark Plug Company, and he wanted a ride back to the plant so he could get it. He had already made three calls and was sounding frustrated. "Maybe after my pay raise we should think about getting a car," he muttered as he saw me come into the house. Finally, he set the black telephone down in its cradle sitting on top of the china cabinet just below the plaster patch from where he had almost blown off Mother's head two months earlier. "It's all set up," he said with his cocky grin. "Ned Delaney will pick me up in half an hour."

"Good," said Mother. "But don't stop off for a drink on the way home. We've got a lot of Christmas shopping to do today."

"Can I go?" I asked, rushing over to him by the telephone. "I won't get in the way or anything."

Dad looked like he was about to say no, but after pausing for a second he surprised me. "That might not be a bad idea," he said.

When Ned Delaney pulled up front with his old Plymouth four door, I sprinted through the cold December wind and climbed into the back seat, excited for this chance to see the mysterious plant where Dad disappeared every morning to make spark plugs. As we drove, the two men talked about the union's preparations for a strike. They were both union stewards who would be strike captains if a strike took place, and I felt important to be on the inside of these discussions. I didn't even mind that Mr. Delaney, who had coached St. Matthew's football team, took no notice of me, just as he had never missed me after I quit the team. The car moved out Dorr Street, then south on Upton until it came to the Spark Plug Company, pulling into the parking lot under a sign that was topped off with two giant spark plugs standing like exclamation points on both sides of the company's motto, "the plugs that move the world."

Despite being Saturday, the plant was running full blast as it stockpiled spark plugs in case the union called a strike. Stacked up on the loading dock by a railroad track were cases of spark plugs for a range of vehicles. Spark plugs for jeeps, trucks, airplanes, Fords, Plymouths, Chevies, Studebakers, and even Cadillacs. Each type of plug required its own specifications, Dad proudly told me. His job was to hone out the metal base for these plugs with exact precision. As we walked through the parking lot to the employee entrance, I bent forward into the wind and zipped my jacket up tight.

A blast of heat and noise stopped me in my tracks as we passed through the door, but Dad and Mr. Delaney just walked in as though the noise never bothered them. They pulled little wads of cotton from their pockets to stuff in their ears. Dad gave some to me and motioned for me to plug my ears as well. That brought a great relief from the noise, but I could barely hear him speak.

He motioned to a strange looking clock on the wall and shouted, "This is the time clock." He had to shout to make his voice rise above the noise of the plant. He showed me how the workers pulled a card from a slot in the out rack, slid it under a stamp, which punched the time on the card, and then placed the card in a rack on the opposite side of the clock. At the end of the shift, the process was reversed. If a worker showed up as little as one minute late, his pay envelope was docked by a minute's worth of pay. However, Dad grumbled, he did not earn any extra minutes of pay if something came up at the last minute that delayed his getting out of the plant.

We walked down an aisle between two rows of loud, clanking machines to an area at the back, where Dad went to his locker. Next to the lockers stood a huge semicircular sink with faucets operated by a foot pedal. The sink was big enough that half a dozen men could wash their hands at once. Dad spun the combination lock on his locker, opened it, and retrieved the envelope containing his weekly pay. The din was lower back in this area, and we did not have to shout quite so loud.

"I'll show you my machine," he said.

He headed us back down the aisle between the two rows of big, noisy, dirty machines. "These are automatic screw machines," shouted Dad. "This is the most automated part of the factory." He proudly explained how they worked. In front of the machine was a hexagon device. It held six long steel rods and fed them into the machine. As each rod entered the machine it was attacked by a combination of diamond tipped drills and blades that bored a hole through the middle, shaped a spark plug base, carved out a set of threads on the bottom so the plug could screw into the proper engine head, and sliced off the spark plug base so it could fall into a collecting bin. One by one the plugs dropped into the bin as the steel rod disappeared into the machine. When the rod was completely gone, the hexagonal device twisted one-sixth of a turn, and the machine operator shoved a new rod into the slot to start its journey into the teeth of the hungry machine. Dad pointed out a constant stream of brown oil pouring over the drills and blades to keep them cool, and a mist of oily air floated in the air surrounding the machine. A film of oil had already formed on Mr. Delaney's glasses.

"My job," shouted Dad, "is to set up the machine so it shapes the exact spark plug being called for. Here comes an inspector." He pointed to a stout man moving along the row of machines. The man was not quite as sweaty and dirty as the machine operators were. He picked two or three spark plugs from each machine's collection bin, measured them with an instrument, and made some markings on a card hanging from the front of the machine to indicate that the plugs met specifications.

"Hey!" shouted a voice behind me. Dad grabbed my arm and pulled me aside so a man pushing a cart could move down the aisle. He was collecting buckets of scrap from each machine. All the boring, slicing, and cutting produced an enormous amount of metal shavings that collected under the machine. Dad showed how the machine operator used a long rake every half hour to pull the oil soaked shavings into the buckets that the cart pusher loaded onto his cart. We followed the cart pusher to the area where he dumped the shavings into a hole in the floor. No sooner did he empty his bucket than a huge piston in the hole compressed the shavings into a block of steel the size of a brick. An automatic arm ejected the compacted blocks from the piston chamber and they slid to a collecting area where a man with big, insulated gloves piled them onto wooden pallets. From there a forklift picked them up and moved them to the loading dock where they would be put in a railroad car and shipped back to the steel mill to be reused. Dad motioned for me to touch one of the metal blocks that had just been ejected from the compactor. I put my finger on it, then jumped back in shock.

"Get's hot, doesn't it?" laughed Dad at the trick he had played on me. "That's why that guy wears those big gloves."

Before we left the building, Mr. Delaney walked back to the big sink, soaped up his horn-rimmed glasses and slipped them under the water to wash off the oil film that had collected on them. Watching him made me realize for the first time why Dad's work clothes were always so filthy when he'd get home from work and dump his clothes in a pile by the washing machine in the basement. Mother wouldn't let him put them in the hamper with the other dirty clothes.

As we turned toward the exit, a very agitated man rushed up to us. He was much better dressed than anybody else on the floor. His slacks were pressed, and he wore a dark-colored shirt with a necktie.

"Parnell, what the hell are you doing?" he shouted. "You're not supposed to be here today."

"Just came in to get my pay envelope. You passed

them out so late yesterday I forgot it," shouted Dad, with a grin.

"Why is that kid in here? You know you can't bring a kid in here."

"This is my son Charlie. Charlie, meet Mr. Schultz. He's the day shift foreman."

"Why is he limping? Did he get hurt?"

"No," said Dad. "He just has a limp."

"This is no place for a kid. Get him out of here before he gets hurt. I've got a mind to write you up for this."

Dad scowled. "You do that and you'll have a union grievance on your hands. If you'd handed out our pay envelopes on time yesterday, I wouldn't have left mine behind. The union's not going to like it if the company screws around with our pay envelopes."

"Just get out of here," repeated the foreman, "before that kid gets hurt."

As we stepped outside, I felt an enormous relief to be out of the noise and heat and oily air. My chest felt damp as my shirt began to cool in the outdoor air. I wiped my hands over the gray colored jacket to wipe off any of the oil that might have settled on it.

"Well, that's my job," Dad said as he pulled the pieces of cotton from his ears and dropped them into a nearby trash basket. "Mr. Delaney's, too. From seven to three o'clock every day, with a half hour off for lunch. We make the plugs that move the world." He grinned as he said the company motto, and I couldn't tell if he was being proud of the work he did or being sarcastic because the company wasn't giving any raises.

I said nothing. I struggled to absorb the idea that Dad could put up with the noise and the heat and the dirty air and the nasty foreman eight hours every day. We got out of the car when Mr. Delaney pulled up in front of our house on Oakwood Street. As we reached the steps to the front porch, Dad grabbed my arm and stopped me.

"Charlie, I took you there on purpose. You need to see what it's like to work in a factory. You can do better than this, but you can't do better unless you finish high school and go to college."

Dad was taller than I was, and standing one step above me on the porch stairs, he looked like a giant. He continued, "If I had used that GI Bill to take college classes at night school when I got out of the Army, I'd have some nice cushy office job today. I tried to make Danny understand that, too, but he wouldn't listen and he dropped out of school to join the Marines. Maybe I should have taken him to see the factory. It's no place for a boy to spend his life." Dad's eyes seemed to mist when he mentioned Danny.

"Don't get me wrong, it's been a steady job," he said, then added, "as long as we've got the union. But it's no good for you. Promise me you'll go all the way through high school and to college." Dad stared hard at me, and his unusual frankness dazed me.

"I will," I said.

"That's my boy." He slapped me hard on the shoulder and brightened his mood. "Let's see if your mother still wants to go Christmas shopping. Maybe we should look at cars so we know what to get when the contract's settled. If they force us to go on strike, we'll hold out for back pay as well. Add on to that what I made at the Sports Arena and we'll have enough for a really good car."

"How about a TV?" I asked.

"Yeah, we'll take a look at TVs, too."

We walked into the house and Mother had the radio

on. Johnny Mercer was singing, "Accentuate the Positive."

CHAPTER 29

Before my Wednesday trip to see Clarice at the library, I stopped at the drugstore, slipped into the phone booth, closed the door behind me and dialed Mr. Jackson's number. When he said, "Hello?" I held the phone up to my mouth, making loud breathing sounds, sucking in and blowing out, just like a panting dog. I kept doing that until he shouted, "What the fuck is this?" Then I dropped the phone and let it dangle from the cord while I stepped out of the booth and headed toward the Lucretia Mott Branch Public Library.

What would Clarice think of me if she knew of my plans to get even with the scoutmaster? I would have to make sure she didn't find out.

As I slid into my chair across the table from her, she handed me a package and motioned with her eyes for me to open it.

I tore open the package and found a brass music holder for my trumpet.

"You never bring one when we practice, and you'll need one when you play in your high school band next year." She beamed with pride as she looked at me.

"I got you something, too." I reached into the bag I'd brought and pulled out a flat package. "Hold this side up when you open it."

With careful neatness, she slowly unfolded the tissue paper, sticking her little finger out in the air while she unwrapped the paper with thumb and pointing finger. It was a record of Peggy Lee singing the song Clarice had played at the Old North End Café, "Golden Earrings." In the big hole of the forty-five rpm record, I had put a small box containing a pair of yellow earrings I had bought at the North End Dime Store. They were just brass, but they looked like gold.

She grinned brightly at the record but she looked puzzled when she saw the earrings. She frowned as though something was wrong, but she managed a smile as she lifted the record and said, "Charlie, that's sweet. That's the nicest gift I ever got."

However, she didn't show the same enthusiasm for the earrings she had for the record. Something was wrong about the earrings, but I couldn't tell what it was. Girls are weird.

Louis invited me to his family's Hanukkah party. "It's gonna be a great party, Charlie. You're gonna love it. But whatever you do, don't say anything about Father Coughlin."

"Who's he?"

'I don't know, but my parents can't stand him. They say he used to say bad things about Jews on the radio."

Except for Louis and his parents, I didn't know anyone at the party. Before the party began, the men put on little black skullcaps for the prayer. "That's a yarmulka," explained Louis as he gave one to me. "We wear it when we pray." Louis's dad read in Hebrew from a big missal. Then we took off our yarmulkas, and Louis led me through a buffet line that had been set up on the dining room table. I loaded my plate with fish, salad, and strange looking breads. Louis handed me a Coke, and we went to a corner of the living room, where Louis introduced me to a group of teens and younger children. Some of the kids were curious about me, and that felt strangely good. It's not that they didn't know any Christians. However, they had never seen one at a Hannukkah party, and they wanted to know what made me tick.

"What did you think of the reading?" a boy asked.

"I couldn't understand it," I replied.

"Neither could I," he admitted with a giggle.

Louis's mother passed out a small present to each child. I got a dreidel, which confused me until a cute girl with black hair and a thin face showed me how to use it. Then Louis's mother organized a sing-a-long. Louis went to the piano. A boy with a clarinet stood to his left and a man with a violin to his right. Louis's dad passed out sheet music, which was a good thing. Otherwise, I never would have been able to join the sing-a-long of "The Dreidel Song."

Finally, I got up to leave. The black-haired girl who taught me the dreidel game slipped me a piece of paper with her name and telephone number. I thanked Mr. and Mrs. Rubenstein for inviting me and headed home. Should I invite Louis over for Christmas? If so, how could I make sure no one said anything insulting? I pondered that as I trudged home through the crisp December evening, my boots crunching in the snow.

CHAPTER 30

C hristmas passed without any family fights. Not that we lacked for opportunities. Mollie got on Mother's nerves when she complained about Christmas Eve dinner.

"Macaroni and cheese?" she squealed, her nose turned up. "Couldn't we have something better, especially with Grandma and Grandpa coming over?"

Mother pulled her big wooden spoon out of the pot and snapped her arms down to her sides in exasperation. Melted cheese from the spoon dribbled down to the floor.

"The vigil of Christmas is a day of abstention. You should know that by now." Then she paused and smiled. "You'll get a nice big feast tomorrow."

I was sure that Dad and Grandpa Parnell would start arguing about Ike, who had won the election and kept his campaign promise to visit Korea. However, Grandpa kept quiet about Eisenhower, Mother didn't mention her fear that the union was planning a strike, and Dad didn't tell her the union had already decided to put a strike vote before the membership after the New Year. For the past week, he had been talking about it on the phone with other strike captains just about every time Mother was out of the house.

Mother put Grandma and Grandpa on the side of the table where they wouldn't have to see the bulge in the paint above the china cabinet where their son just three months earlier had blown a hole in the wall with his shotgun. We said a prayer for Danny in the Marines in Korea, and the adults talked about the old days, avoiding any controversial topics. Grandpa Parnell said children were much better behaved in his day. "All my da had to do was look at me and I would behave," he said. Grandma Parnell looked at the ceiling and rolled her eyes. After dinner, we gathered around the green, short-needled Christmas tree. Each person got to open one gift. The rest would be opened in the morning along with the gifts left by Santa Claus.

"I don't believe in Santa Claus anymore," Mollie told me as we headed upstairs to bed.

"Well, don't tell Mother," I replied. "She'll be disappointed. Give her another year to get used to the idea."

Late that afternoon, we went over to Grandma and Grandpa O'Rourke's for Grandma's dinner of baked ham, potatoes, cranberries, and mincemeat pie. This posed another chance for a family fight, since Mother would get irritated if Grandpa O'Rourke talked about the union with Dad, and Dad would get irritated when eventually Uncle Jim would spout off on some topic. It wouldn't matter what the topic was; almost anything he said would irritate Dad. However, none of these things happened. Grandpa waited for Mother to go to the kitchen before he peppered Dad with questions about the union's contract negotiations. Grandpa spent most of the time talking about his role in the famous sit-down strike at General Motors before World War II. He and a bunch of other workers locked themselves inside the factory in Flint, Michigan, and didn't come out, even when the police threw tear gas grenades into the building. I had trouble getting interested in anything that far back in the past, but I enjoyed seeing Grandpa so excited. He must have been a tough bird when he was young. Best of all, Dad and Big Jim behaved themselves, refused to say anything negative, and even clinked their Buckeye Beer bottles together in a toast to the New Year.

Over the next few days, I stopped by my friends' houses to check out what they got. James was testing a new cymbal he had gotten for his drum set, and Clarice showed off a new beret and knee length dove-white cloth coat. They made a brilliant contrast with her smiling brown face and black hair. Bernie Karolak boasted of some new attachments to his already impressive accordion collection. Tony Morelli was out in the alley shooting baskets at a hoop on his garage with a new basketball he had received. After repeated dribbles in the slushy cinders, the ball was already losing that leathery smell and shiny luster it had when it came out of the box. I had barely arrived when Tony's seventh-grade sister, Carmelita, came out, twirled around in front of me, opening up her long overcoat to flash a new blouse and skirt she was wearing. I wondered if I dared visit Roberta Quinn, but decided against it.

All in all, it had been a great Christmas, from the moment I'd exchanged presents with Clarice to the moment Dad and Big Jim clinked their beer bottles together. Mr. Jackson had barely entered my mind. But I remembered that last year at this time I had been busy organizing my gear for the Boy Scout overnight camp-out that we always did after Christmas. However, I sure wasn't going to camp out with Mr. Jackson again. Something was going to have to be done about that pervert.

CHAPTER 31

Clarice waited for me at the old, wooden table in the library. She leaned stiffly on her elbows, and on the chair behind her, she'd draped the new dove white coat she'd gotten for Christmas. I set a notebook and pen on the table and hung my brother's letter jacket on the back of the chair across from her. Before I even sat down, she challenged me.

"Did Old Schmidt really say it?"

"Say what?"

"What James said he said."

"I don't know what James said he said."

Her eyes flashed. "You know what he said, Charlie. You were there. Did he call my brother James a nigger?"

I stiffened, and she noticed.

"Don't look so shocked. You've heard that word before. You probably say it yourself."

She was right, and she was wrong. I heard it every day, but the more I became friends with James and Clarice, the more I hated that word. I swallowed before saying anything. "Yeah, he said it. He was trying to cheat James, and James wouldn't let him."

"James said you were the one who caught him cheating."

"I'm just good at numbers, Clarice. You know that." I doodled some figures on the notebook I'd set on the tabletop. "I saw him add up the numbers wrong, so I told James, and James refused to pay the extra money. That's when he yelled at James and told him to go back to Africa and I called Old Schmidt a bigot."

"Then Old Schmidt called you a nigger-lovin' cripple."

"Why're you smiling? You think it's funny to call a guy a cripple just because he's got a limp?"

"No. That's not funny. What's funny is you callin' Old Schmidt a bigot. James said you got guts."

"That's not what he said at the time. He said he didn't need no white boy's help."

"He was just mad because of Old Schmidt. Later on, he cooled off. He said you got guts."

I sneered. "Old Schmidt's an asshole."

She stiffened. "Don't talk that way, Charlie. Jesus don't want that."

"Well, he is. He shouldn't have said what he did."

"You look mad. You're gritting your teeth."

"I am mad." I forced my jaw to relax, but then my hand started moving up and down hitting the table, and I raised my voice. "He's got no cause to call James and me names like that. I deliver my papers just as good as anybody there, and I pay my bills on time."

She put her hand on my fist to stop it from hitting the table. "Don't talk so loud. Mrs. Nordstrom's looking at us."

"She can't see us. Her desk is out of sight behind that big pillar."

"She's walking around, and I see her over your

shoulder. So, she can see us, too. Lean closer so we don't have to talk so loud. You got a funny look, Charlie."

"It's what we're talking about. I feel funny talking about this with you."

"Me too. But we've got to talk about it. I've heard that word before."

"I still don't like him calling James that. I don't like what he called me either. Just cuz I got a limp, why do people call me names?"

"You're looking look mad again."

"You'd be mad, too. Old Schmidt sent me to the back of the line, and that made me late delivering my papers."

"You talkin' too loud again. Talk softer, or Mrs. Nordstrom's gonna look over here."

"Let her look. I don't care."

"Does it hurt?"

"What?"

"Your limp?"

"No, that doesn't hurt. The left leg's just shorter than the right one, that's all. It didn't grow proper after I had polio when I was a kid."

"You had polio?"

"Yeah. That's why I'm behind you at school. I missed so much of the second grade that I had to repeat it."

"What was that like?"

"The polio?"

"Yes."

"It was so long ago I don't remember much, except for the chills and the aches from the fever. And the iron lung going whoosh—whoosh—whoosh."

"What was that like, being in an iron lung?"

"Why are you asking me all this, Clarice?"

"I don't know. You're just different, and you're nice. Don't you want to talk about it?"

"I don't mind. It's just that nobody cares to hear about it anymore. I know I'm lucky I didn't end up paralyzed like a lot of kids. But when I was in that iron lung, I couldn't move my leg, and I was terrified by the idea that it might be like that forever. Mother cried all the time. But afterwards, when I got home, nobody wanted to talk about it anymore. I think she and my Dad are afraid that if they let me talk about it, I'll forget how lucky I am and start feeling sorry for myself. Why do you want to hear about it?"

"It's just that I can talk to you. I can't tell anybody else how it hurts being looked down on and being called names. I tell Daddy and he just says, 'Get over it and learn to deal with it.' But Daddy's mad all the time."

"He doesn't look mad when I see him."

"He's not gonna let no white boy know he's mad. But he's mad, believe me."

"Are you mad?"

"No, I'm not mad. The world's changing, and things are going to get better. But I wish I had someone to talk to besides you. I like talking to you, Charlie. Most boys I can't talk to."

"So why can you talk to me? Why do you keep meeting me here in the library to talk?—Say something, Clarice. Why are you looking down at the table?"

"I just like talking with you and being your friend."

"Well, why do you want to be friends with me?—Say something, Clarice. You're looking down at the table again."

"It's your limp."

"You're grinning. You laughing at me?"

"No, I'm not laughing at you. But it's your limp."

"Clarice, I don't need nobody feeling sorry for me."

"I don't feel sorry for you, Charlie. You got guts, like James says. But you got something more. Can't you see? Kids give you a bad time because of your limp. Maybe that gives you some feel for what it's like for me to be looked down on for being colored. Maybe I can trust you.—Say something, Charlie. Don't just sit there looking like a bump on a log."

"I don't know what to say. You're pretty smart, Clarice."

"So are you; you just don't know it. Lean closer."

"I lean any closer, and we're gonna be kissing."

"Is that bad?" She tilted her head and looked at me from the corners of her eyes.

"Mrs. Nordstrom won't let us sit together anymore, and she'll tell on us."

"What would your daddy do if you kissed a colored girl?"

"I don't know, but he wouldn't like it. What would your dad do?"

"If I kissed a white boy? My daddy'd whoop me somethin' fierce."

"Don't lean so close. She's gonna see us."

"No, she's not. She went to the back room, through that wood door."

"Your hands feel cool."

"Move away. She just came back."

"Oh, shit."

"Don't talk that way, Charlie. Jesus don't want that."

"Let's go outside."

CHAPTER 32

I was so delighted that I skipped down the street on my way home. I'd finally kissed a girl. And that pushed the scoutmaster out of my mind for the first time in a long while. We left the warm library and into the cold outdoors, down the steps to the sidewalk and back into the shadow of the steps. She leaned forward and brushed her lips against mine. Before I knew what was happening, we wrapped our arms around each other. I pressed as tight as I could against her, but the thick winter coats kept us pretty much apart. The kiss only lasted an instant before Clarice pulled away, looking a little sheepish. Holding hands, we walked together up to Fernwood, where we split and she headed down the street to her house. I happily watched her walk away. Her dove white overcoat seemed to glow in the light from the moon and the streetlamps. That was when I started skipping. I didn't even mind the bitter cold, with the temperature slated to drop below zero that night. I just skipped on home.

Even more overwhelming than the kiss was what we had talked about. Never had anybody told me anything as personal as she had said about herself. And never had anybody seen my limp as something positive. If she thought that the grief I got because of my limp made me more sensitive to grief she got, I would have to be careful not to disappoint her.

For the next several days, I floated on a wave of happiness. Schoolwork was a breeze. For the first time I played high C on my trumpet without any special effort. Mother's cooking got better, it seemed, and Dad stayed sober for the weekend.

It was on Monday that I came back earth. When James picked up his newspaper from Old Schmidt, he did not come over by me to fold them. He carried them to the opposite end of the bench. I came up to him and said, "Do you want to go now?"

He gave me a sullen, icy look, unfolded one of his papers and spread it flat on the counter. "You go ahead. I want to read the paper first."

Rebuffed, I mounted my sack of newspapers on the basket of my bicycle and rode off. James also failed to stop by the drugstore where we usually drank cherry Cokes. The same thing happened Tuesday and Wednesday. I decided to ask Clarice about her brother's strange behavior when we met on Wednesday at the Lucretia Mott Branch Public Library.

That night I rushed through the dishes again, eager to see Clarice, but a little anxious about how she would react after the kiss we had shared the week before. Not knowing quite what to expect, I left Mollie complaining about all the dishes I had piled up in the drain tray, grabbed my math book, and walked rapidly to the library.

When I got there, Clarice had not yet arrived, and I

was annoyed to find that two high school white girls sat at our table and whispered together. I went to the magazine rack and saw the next monthly issue of *Ebony* sitting there. I picked it up from the rack and brought it over to an empty table to wait for her. I flipped through the magazine, but the pictures had no meaning for me. The stories were all about Negroes, and I recognized none of them. One story told about a segregation case coming up before something called the Supreme Court, but that didn't interest me either. I opened my math book to do some homework exercises while I waited, but I couldn't concentrate. I glanced over at Mrs. Nordstrom and shifted my gaze back from her to the big clock over her head to the wooden doors behind the circulation desk, to the giant oak doors leading outside, to the magazine rack, and to the two high school girls gabbing at the table where I normally sat with Clarice.

After an hour, I realized she was not going to show up. I put the magazine back in its rack, pulled up the zipper on the scarlet-and-gray letter jacket I had inherited from Danny and, wondering what happened, headed out the big oak doors.

I walked down the concrete steps, crossed Dorr Street, passed the North End Tavern, and up the side street which had not yet received the new mercury vapor streetlamps. The street was encased in darkness, broken only by the circles of light thrown out by the old regular streetlights that had not yet been replaced. I stepped out from a cone of light into the darkness at the foot of the alley between Dorr Street and Pinewood Street and suddenly bumped into four Negro teenage boys who came out of the alley.

"Watch your step, motherfucker!" snapped the

biggest one, a very angry looking boy at least two years older than me, with a scar down his left cheek. The boys circled me and a second one said, "It's that piece of white trash that's been making out with colored girls."

"What have you got to say for yourself, white trash?" said the big one with the scar on his cheek.

"Nothing," I sputtered, trying to back away. My heart pounded, and my mind raced for a way to talk myself out of this. One of the boys I recognized as a friend of James who shot baskets at the hoop James's dad had mounted on his garage.

"Nothing?" thundered the big one. "You mess around with our girls, and you got nothing to say about it?"

"What do you mean messing around?" My mind desperately searched for words to slow things down. Where was that damned cop when you really needed him?

"What do I mean messing around? Man, you must be a moron to think that nobody saw you kissing James's sister last week."

"James put you up to this?" I asked in disbelief. "Man, that doesn't sound like James."

"Shut up, motherfucker. James don't have nothin' to do with this. And you better not go talking to him about it either." He pushed the palm of his hand against my chest and shoved me backwards.

I looked over at the boy who had shot baskets in James's back yard. "Shouldn't this be between James and me?" I said to him. "James doesn't want me to do something, he knows how to tell me."

"I told you to shut up," said the big kid as he pushed me back again. The push, I knew, was just a challenge for me to block the push. That would give him a reason to beat me up and claim that I had started the fight by throwing the first punch. "This is between you and me. James ain't got nothin' to do with it."

I froze. I desperately wanted to see Clarice again. But I did not want to get beaten up.

"Say somethin', you little cripple. You gonna let that girl alone?"

I sensed that the danger was easing now that the big boy was talking, but I had to get some help from one of the others. I looked directly at James's basketball friend and said, "You sayin' James's sister can't make up her own mind who she talks to? And you say you gonna do that without letting James know what you've done? James ain't gonna like that." I never used words like "ain't," but this was no time to show off my excellent grammar.

The big boy pushed me back again, but James's basketball friend intervened. "Let him go, Rafer. He got the message. He's practically shitting in his pants. He ain't gonna cause no more trouble."

The four boys moved back, opening a gap for me to leave. "Go on, white trash," said Rafer. "Get the hell out of here and stop poking your nose around where it don't belong."

The boys stepped back further, giving me a wide exit. I stepped slowly toward the gap. Just as I entered it, however, the big boy planted his feet firmly on the ground and swung a hay-maker punch that smashed into my left eye. I staggered backward, tripped over a crack in the sidewalk, and fell onto my ass.

"Just a reminder, little cripple. You don't tell James about this, and you don't kiss any more colored girls." The four boys stepped around me and swaggered down the street toward the library. As I touched my eye, they drifted away, laughing and talking loudly.

Then, out of the shadows stepped Billy Byrne. "Charlie, you okay?"

I was so startled to see him, I didn't know what to say. "You saw that?" I mumbled.

"Yeah, I was coming back from the store, and I saw the whole thing. What were you doing kissing a colored girl?"

"You watched? And you didn't do anything to help me? Didn't even shout so somebody would open a front door and scare them away?"

Billy looked to the ground. "It happened so fast, by the time I thought of that, they were already leaving."

"Well thanks a lot, Billy. I thought we were friends."

"We are, Charlie. Who was the colored girl?"

"None of your business." I turned on my heel and headed home as fast as I could walk. Billy started to accompany me. But when I refused to talk, he dropped back and left me to walk alone.

CHAPTER 33

Mother spotted my black eye the minute I got home. She wrapped a dish rag around some ice cubes and made me hold it against my eye while I sat at the kitchen table.

"You've been up to something, Charlie," she demanded. "What is it?"

"Nothing. I was just shooting baskets with Tony Morelli, and his elbow hit me in the eye when he spun around."

She gave me that squint she has when she doubts what I've been saying. But, to my relief, she didn't press the issue. She just went back to the living room to pick up the tail end of the radio program she'd been listening to.

James broke his silence the next day. Ignoring my black eye, he pulled me aside at the paper station and led me outside. We faced each other as we stood on the hard packed snow in the alley while the wind swirled around us. Neither of us said anything for a moment. Then he blurted out a string of words he must have been bottling up all week.

"Charlie, you got to stay away from Clarice."

"Why?" I said. "Clarice likes talking to me, and I like talking to her. You gonna try and tell us who we can't talk to?"

He looked me squarely in the eye and snarled, "You and Clarice been doing more than just talking. You been holding hands and hugging and kissing right out in public where anybody can see you. Everybody within a mile knows about it, except maybe your momma and daddy."

"That only happened once. All the other times we just talk. You can't stop her from talking to somebody."

"Charlie," said James, exasperated, "My daddy whooped her something fierce for what she did. He took off his belt and beat her until she bawled like a six year old."

I cringed.

"You can't come over to practice at the house for a while," said James. He paused, not sure whether he should say any more. "My daddy's really mad. He called you white trash and a troublemaker. Said you only wanted one thing from her. Once you got it you'd be gone, and she'd be left raising some white kid's baby all by herself."

I felt so numbed I couldn't think of anything to say.

"That's not true, is it, Charlie? You wouldn't do that, would you?"

"No, James. I wouldn't do that," I said slowly and softly, dejected. "I wouldn't do it to anyone, especially not to her."

I'm not sure James believed me, but the hard look on his face softened, and he put his hand on my arm.

"I hate to tell you things like that, Charlie, because

we've been good friends. I don't forget how you stood up for me with Old Schmidt. And I still want to go ahead with our band. But until my daddy calms down, we'll have to do practice without Clarice. Till then, you got to stay away from her. "

I was so overwhelmed I gulped. "James, Clarice and I haven't been doing anything, except for that one time. We just talk. I like talking with her. She makes me feel good." I stared down at the ground. "What does she say?"

"After Daddy was done beating her and she was done bawling, she said, 'You can beat me bloody if you want, but you can't stop me from talking to whoever I want.'"

I was impressed. Clarice had faced her father with more guts than I had faced that big kid Rafer.

"I'll stay away," I muttered, looking down at the ground. "Tell her I'm sorry for the trouble I caused her."

Then, for the first time, James took notice of my black eye. "Where'd you get that shiner?"

"I ran into a fist."

"Man, that's something." James beamed a smile. "You're not the fighting type, Charlie. And here you are showing some real class. Who did that to you?"

"Doesn't matter."

"Yeah, it does. Maybe it was just your little sister swinging a stick or something."

"It wasn't my sister. Just somebody I ran into."

"Somebody got pissed off at you for hustling them out of their money?"

"No, it wasn't that. Some big asshole. Huge son of a bitch."

"White guy?"

"I don't want to talk about it."

"So it wasn't a white guy. A big colored guy? All by himself?"

"No. There were four of them." I couldn't resist adding that. I would look better if I had fought off four kids than if I had gotten beaten up by just one.

"Man, you were ambushed. Where did this happen?"

"I don't want to talk about it."

"Four colored kids? One of them big and huge?" James searched through his memory of kids in the neighborhood. "Light skinned kid? With a knife scar on his cheek?"

I looked down at the ground again. "I said I don't want to talk about it."

"Charlie, you been messing around with Rafer Jones. You're out of your mind. He plays football for Scott High."

I didn't say anything, and James continued his speculations.

"So why is Rafer Jones out to get you?"

"James, you gotta keep this to yourself."

But he was not listening. He was trying to figure out what Rafer Jones had against me. "I got it!" He grinned and slapped his thigh. "Couple of weeks ago Clarice told him to push off. Told him she didn't want no hoodlum in her life. Man, that's what happened. Clarice gives Rafer the kiss-off; then she gives you the kiss. So he gets mad. Man, you're lucky he didn't put you in the hospital."

I grabbed James's arm and shook it hard. "James you got to keep this to yourself. If that Jones kid finds out I been telling you about it, he's gonna come after me."

"Don't worry, man. I keep a wide distance from

Rafer Jones. He's bad news."

At school, the black eye brought me a lot of needling.

"Charlie, you practicing for the Golden Gloves?"

"What happened, Charlie? That girl slug you when she found out what a terrible kisser you are?"

This meant that Billy Byrne had been talking about the incident. He was the only one at school who had seen it.

The heckling was good natured, however. In fact, the shiner brought me a new respect among the eighth-grade boys. Bernie Karolak echoed the same thing James had said. "You're starting to show some class now, Parnell. It's not so bad getting a black eye when you stand up for yourself. That's a lot better than hiding in your house all day banging a piano like that dope Louis you hang out with."

The girls were sneakier. After lunch one day, Brenda Delaney brought a forty-five rpm record player to the classroom, and when I came through the door, the singer Georgia Gibbs began to belt out, "Kiss of Fire."

My new status gave me an opportunity to make a pitch to Roberta Quinn. I bought a bag of candy hearts and presented them to her for Valentine's Day. "There's a great movie playing at the Monroe. Would you want to see it with me?"

Roberta looked puzzled as she stood there in the cold facing me, her girlfriends several paces away walking slowly so she could catch up. She was very pretty up close, with her wide blue eyes and a handful of freckles on her checks. But she looked awkward, standing there with her dark plaid skirt spreading out from under her winter jacket, her hands encased in great big pink soft mittens, her arms crossed as she held her school books tightly up against her chest.

"I've always liked you as a friend, Charlie, but I can't go out on a date with you."

"Do you have a boyfriend?" I asked.

"No, it's not that. It just isn't a good idea for us to go out."

"Why not? We've known each other for years, and we've always gotten along."

"But Charlie, you've been doing some strange things lately."

"What do you mean strange things?"

Roberta shuffled her feet nervously. "Charlie, I don't want to be mean. I've always liked you, but you've been hanging out with some odd people."

"Odd people?" Then I saw the light. "You mean you won't go out with me because I'm friends with a couple of colored kids?"

"But Charlie, I have to think of my reputation. What would people think of me if I dated a boy who kissed colored girls? Any girl would have to think about that."

"Well, I'm not seeing her anymore. So you don't have to worry about that."

Roberta did not reply, but I refused to let her off the hook. There was another reason for her refusal, and I was getting mad enough to force her to say it. "Is there some other reason?"

"Oh, Charlie, don't do this," she said. She almost looked like she was going to start crying. "I don't want to hurt you."

"It's my limp, isn't it? You're not only afraid to be seen with a guy who's got colored friends, you're afraid to be seen with a guy who has a limp."

"Charlie, I've got to go. My friends are waiting." And

with that Roberta Quinn turned sharply on her heels and strode away as fast as she could to catch up with the other girls, the long ponytail on the back of her head bouncing up and down with each step she took.

I watched her walk away, shook my head, and ambled toward home. What a disappointment she is! Who would have expected the beautiful Roberta Quinn to be a bigot? That girl's an embarrassment. She should have given me back the candy. Halfway home it occurred to me that I didn't feel bad about the reference to my limp. I wasn't even unhappy that Roberta had turned me down. Mostly, I just felt disappointed that a girl I thought was so classy had turned out to be so narrow minded. I didn't even try to hide my limp as I walked past some other kids. I just walked on naturally.

CHAPTER 34

In order to keep Mother from finding out I had quit the Boy Scouts, I started spending Monday nights at the North End Café or reading magazines at the library. On the Monday after Valentine's Day, it warmed up enough to do something outside rather than coop myself up in those places, so I headed over to the duplex where Mr. Jackson lived on Fernwood, four blocks west of James's house. The house wasn't so much a real duplex as it was an old two-story house, whose second floor had been made into a small apartment Mr. Jackson rented from a widow who lived by herself on the first floor.

At the sidewalk in front of the house, a row of bushes formed a hedge. The front yard was about three feet higher than the level of the sidewalk, and the yard dropped sharply down at the hedge, making a crevice between the hedge and the downward sloping lawn. I ducked into the crevice so nobody could see me while I kept a watch on at the house.

I didn't know what I hoped to find out from casing the place, but maybe I could find Mr. Jackson's weak spot. As I knelt in the crevice, he and the landlady came out of the house. I peeked out over the top of the crevice to watch while they walked down the steps toward his shiny Ford convertible. When he bent forward to open the door for her, his scoutmaster shirt showed through his unzipped jacket.

"You must really enjoy playing bingo." he said.

"Yep. It's a way to get together with my friends over at St. Theresa's. It's so good of you to give me a ride."

"I'm glad to help out," said Mr. Jackson. "But I'm going someplace after my scout meeting and can't give you a ride home."

"No problem," said the landlady. "I can ride back with somebody else. I'm just grateful for the ride there."

He closed the passenger door behind her as she squeezed stiffly into the front seat.

What a break! The house would be empty for at least two hours. Peering over the top of the crevice to make sure no one was looking, I headed down the sidewalk to the cross street before doubling back and coming up the alley behind the house. I had to hide for a moment behind the garage as a neighbor came out from her kitchen door with garbage wrapped in a newspaper and dropped it into a metal garbage can next to the alley, only a few feet away from me. After waiting for her to go back inside, I walked up to the back of Mr. Jackson's duplex, staying close to a tall wooden fence that hid me from the neighbor's view.

An outdoor stairway led up to a small porch on the second level. I climbed the stairs as quickly as possible, because they were bathed in light from a porch light and a full moon. Once I reached the top, I got out of the light by pressing against the wall of the house.

The kitchen door was locked, but two windows faced

the porch. Maybe they'd be a way to get in. The first, looking into the kitchen, didn't budge when I tried to raise it. The second, however, just a small window with frosted glass, opened when I pushed up on it. I grabbed the inside sill with both hands, pulled my chest up to the sill and wiggled through the opening. Just as I came through the other side, my foot slipped and I fell into a bathtub. A film of water lay on the bottom of the tub, and it got the seat of my pants wet.

"Damn!" I said as the water seeped through the pants.

In case anybody came into the apartment before I finished my business, I needed to plan an escape route. I unlocked the front door so I could run down the front stairs if anybody came up the porch steps. Then, to protect myself in case anybody came in through the front stairs, I went to the kitchen, unlocked the back door, and turned off the porch light. I opened and shut the door once just to make sure I could step out onto the porch any time I needed to.

With an escape route now open, I knew exactly what to look for and figured that it had to be in the bedroom just to the left of the kitchen or in the living room at the front of the house. I tried the bedroom first, looking quickly through each drawer in the dresser. With the bright moonlight coming through the window, I didn't even have to turn on a lamp. The moonlight didn't reach into the closet, however, and I had to turn on the closet light in order to see anything. To keep the neighbors next door from seeing the light, I closed the closet door. However, that made me nervous, because the closed door would block out the noise of steps if anybody came up the stairs. So I pushed the door open a crack and started my search. There were some shoes lined up on the floor and clothes hanging from a pole, pants on the left, shirts on the right, with the shirts arranged from left to right, polo shirts, work shirts, dress shirts, and then Boy Scout shirts. With everything lined up so neatly, he must be a neatness freak. A big box on the floor held a bunch of Boy Scout materials and some other stuff, but not the thing I wanted. By the time I stepped out of the closet, sweat began to drain down my sides from the fear of being caught. "Guess I'd never make a good detective," I whispered aloud just to hear a voice.

In the living room, I struck pay dirt, but it was so much worse than I expected, I almost wished I had never found it. A desk sat in the area where the living room joined the kitchen, and a small lamp sat on top of the desk. It didn't give off much light when I turned it on, but I checked to make sure its cone of light didn't shine on the walls where it could make a shadow of me visible from the upper floors across the street. It didn't, so I left it on and began opening the desk drawers. The wide flat drawer above the spot for a chair, held nothing but a scissors and some other tools. But the big top drawer on the left had a pile of photo envelopes that your pictures come in after you get them developed and pick them up from the drugstore. The first set of photos had nothing but pictures of buildings and trees. I put them carefully back in the envelope and placed it back in the drawer.

Right on top of the second set of photos I spotted what I was looking for, the picture of Tony Morelli standing in his jockey shorts. I took the picture in my fingers and ripped it into little pieces. I started to throw the pieces into the waste basket when I realized Mr. Jackson could just scotch-tape them back together, so

I stuffed the pieces into the pocket of my jacket. A couple of photos down, another picture of Tony showed him with the front of his swim trunks pulled down while he took a piss in the woods. I tore it up, too. Poor Tony! What Mr. Jackson did with us was bad enough, but how could he take such pictures and keep them?

There were pictures of other kids, a few of whom I recognized. Some were in their underwear and some were naked. I tore them all up. One picture showed Mr. Jackson lying naked on a bed with a big hard on. The last picture showed a kid I didn't recognize bending over and sucking Mr. Jackson's dick. I couldn't imagine who he got to take those pictures, and I started to get that gagging feeling you get just before throwing up. I swallowed hard and tore up these pictures as well, relieved that I didn't recognize the kid in the picture as anybody I knew.

Of course, I couldn't leave the negatives behind. He would just use them to make more prints at that photo lab where he worked. I took the scissors out of the top drawer and cut the negatives in pieces. I started sticking them into my pocket when I realized I had no need to do that. There was no possible way he could tape the negatives back together and use them again. I just threw them in the air and let them scatter all over the floor. Being the neatness freak that he was, he would be staggered to see the mess on his floor.

Sometimes when you're tense, it only takes one little sudden movement to trigger a wave of actions you can't control, and that's what happened to me. As soon as the negatives left my hand, I was swamped with the rage I had been stuffing since that night in the sleeping bag. I couldn't even think. I just took the other photos out of their envelopes and threw them all over the floor. I yanked out the desk drawers one by one, dumped out their contents onto the floor, and flung the drawers across the room. One of them hit a picture on the wall and knocked it to the floor. I hit the desk lamp with my fist; it fell on its side and shined up at a weird angle. By the time I finished, my hands shook, I was drenched with sweat, and my knees wobbled. I teetered to the kitchen door.

Just as I stepped out of the kitchen onto the porch, I heard the downstairs front door open and footsteps coming up the stairs. Mr. Jackson had got back early! I headed down the steps but only got halfway down when the next-door neighbor came out of his kitchen door to light a cigarette. This left me trapped in the moonlight! If I stayed where I was, Mr. Jackson would find me. But if I ran down the stairs the neighbor would hear me, look over, and spot me. I lay down on my stomach, slid under the stair railing, and, grabbing the outside edge of the stairs with my hands, I slid myself over the side, just like Dad had slid his way off our deck last summer. Stretched out and hanging by my fingers, my feet were barely a foot above the ground, which let me drop down without any noise. Crouching as low as possible, I ran across to the wood fence to get out of sight of the neighbor puffing on his cigarette. Then, still crouching, I ran along the wood fence until I reached the alley behind the garage.

No sooner did I get there than Mr. Jackson's porch light came back on. His door banged open, and he popped into sight.

"Joe!" he shouted to the neighbor who pulled the cigarette from his lips as he turned toward the voice. "I've been robbed!" screamed Mr. Jackson. "Did you see anybody here?" He sounded louder than I'd ever heard him, and he started down the porch stairs.

I didn't wait to see what happened next. I just walked down the alley past the cross street and halfway up the next block, sticking close to the garages to stay out of sight. When I got to the middle of the block, I looked back in time to see Mr. Jackson and his neighbor poke their heads into the alley and look around. But they couldn't see me in the shadows of the garages. I tossed the ripped up photos into the nearest garbage can, went up two more blocks through the alley, and then headed home. Thinking they would call the police, I kept expecting to hear police sirens any minute, so I stuck to the alleys as much as I could.

Instead of calming down as I got away from the scene, however, I became more and more agitated. By the time I reached the garage behind my house, my knees felt so weak I could barely stand. I sat on the cinders and hung my head between my knees. How could he do those things? At least there would be no more pictures to embarrass Tony or the other kids. But why did he keep the pictures? And who did he show them to? I had to blink back tears when I thought about Tony, one of the nicest kids I knew. All of a sudden I puked my supper right into the cinders of the alley, with my head hanging down between my knees.

"Are you all right?" asked Mother when I came through the door. "You're all pale. You look like you've seen a ghost."

"I'm okay," I said. I sat on the couch, the other end from Dad who had his World War II book, *From Here To Eternity* on his lap. The radio was playing "Duffy's Tavern," and it must have been a good episode, because Mother let out a laugh every few minutes, and Dad had trouble paying attention to his book. But it didn't seem very funny to me, and I didn't laugh at all.

Later, as I lay in bed waiting for sleep, it dawned on me why there had been no police cars cruising through the neighborhood looking for me. If he called the police, they would see all those cut up negatives he had taken of the naked boys. And the moment I realized that, I also realized that, by cutting up the pictures and throwing them out, I'd destroyed the evidence I needed to get Mr. Jackson kicked out of the Boy Scouts. It couldn't be helped, however, because there was no way I could humiliate Tony or those other kids by showing the pictures to anybody.

CHAPTER 35

Waking up the next morning, I half expected Mr. Jackson to show up at the front door screaming at me for breaking into his apartment and leaving it a mess. But he never showed up. Maybe he never suspected that a potential Eagle Scout could do such a thing. Or maybe he just couldn't risk somebody finding out about all those photos if he made any complaints about me. Or maybe he would ambush me someplace when I was alone and get even.

The temperature continued warming up through the day, and it started raining by the time we headed over to Aunt Bridget's house to watch Milton Berle. Then, during the night, the temperature dropped again and the rain began to freeze as it hit the ground, leaving coats of ice the next morning on tree branches, power lines, and sidewalks. It looked so beautiful it lifted me out of the dumps I'd been in for the past few days. I caught up with Tony Morelli on the way to school, and every time we saw an ice patch on the sidewalk we ran toward it, jumped onto it, and slid across to the other side.

Most of the ice had melted by the time I got to my

paper route, but there were still slippery patches on the sidewalks, forcing me at certain points to get off my bicycle and push it along as I flung newspapers onto the porches. When I got to the drugstore to meet James for our daily dose of cherry Coke, I saw Louis waiting for us. He stood outside, his oversized winter jacket hanging down below his waist. He stomped his feet to keep warm, and a broad smile covered his face. He shouted out to James and me before we could park our bicycles.

"We've got a job!"

"What?" we shouted back.

"We've got a job," he repeated, as the three of us entered the drugstore and headed for the soda fountain, unzipping our jackets as we walked. "My cousin's bar mitzvah party, two weeks from Saturday. He knows how good I am at the piano, and they're gonna let us play for an hour. They'll pay us $25."

"$25!" I shouted, and other customers in the store looked over at us. James grabbed my arm and told me to quiet down. Then he asked Louis,

"What's a bar mitzvah?"

He exchanged glances with me as Louis explained the coming-of-age ritual and its purpose. James had nothing like a bar mitzvah in the Pentecostal Evangelic Church of Jesus, and the only comparable thing I had experienced at St. Matthew's was the confirmation ceremony in the sixth grade.

"What time on Saturday?" asked James.

"First we go to the bar mitzvah, which is at noon. Then there's a reception. And the party starts at six o'clock. Normally, the band only goes to the party. But since it's my cousin, it would be rude for us to just show up for the party if we didn't go to the bar mitzvah and the reception first."

"Why is the party so late? Why not have the party at the reception?"

"The adults will all want to go to the reception, but few of them will want to go to the party, so we'll hold the party later. Besides, Saturday is the Shabbat. We can't start the party until the Shabbat ends at sundown. I suppose the Reforms might, but my family is Conservative, so we never do any work until the Shabbat is over."

"Work?" I quizzed him. "It's a party."

"But we're getting paid to play the music, so for us it's work. And as I said, my family is Conservative."

"What's a Conservative?" asked James.

"That's a kind of Jew."

"You mean there are different kinds of Jews?" I asked, a little embarrassed. Everyone except Dad looked down on the Jews, and I did not want to appear snooty to Louis. But Louis had no embarrassment at all. He grew even more excited in his eagerness to tell us about his religion.

"Oh, yes," he said. "There are Orthodox and Reformed and Conservative and Ashkenazy and Hasidic and many more. There are Russian Jews and Polish Jews and German Jews. There are even Italian Jews. Charlie, you'll want to know this. The mayor of Dublin is a Jew."

"Why would Charlie want to know that?" asked James.

"Because Charlie's Irish, and Dublin's the capital of Ireland."

My mind drifted off for a few moments as I pondered all this information while James and Louis were talking. Then James poked me in the ribs.

"Give me a nickel, Charlie. I have to call my momma, but I'm out of change." I put my forefinger on a nickel lying on the wet Formica counter and pushed it toward him. He ambled over to the telephone booth at the front of the store. "I gotta go," he said when he came back. "My momma wants me to do something. However, she said we can hold a planning session at my house on Thursday to figure out what we're gonna play and what we're gonna call ourselves. She's so happy we got the job she said she will cook dinner for us."

"James, how are we going to meet at your house? Your father will hit the roof if he sees me there."

"Momma said she'll settle him down and get him out of the house so he doesn't have to see you."

"How's she gonna do that?"

"Maybe she'll send him to a meeting at the church or something. I don't know. But when she really wants Daddy to do something, he does it."

That sounded very much the same as what Clarice had told me two months ago about her mother controlling her father's drinking. Their mother was a very small, thin woman. Almost as small as Louis. What source of power did she have over James's father, a huge, big shouldered hulk of a man? And why could my mother not get the same devotion from Dad?

"Is Clarice going to be at our meeting?"

James frowned. "I told you, Charlie. You got to forget about Clarice. You've already caused that girl enough trouble."

James and Louis walked out of the drugstore, while I stayed behind to skim a comic book on the magazine rack. Then I zipped up my red and gray athletic jacket and stepped from the warm drugstore into the cold February air. James and Louis headed off toward their own houses, and I found Dirty George standing there, leaning against a tree, smoking a cigarette.

"What are you and James and Louis doing together?" he asked.

"We got a band," I said.

"A band!" said George with a skeptical ring to his voice. "You three are a band? Man, that must be some band. Two weird guys and a cripple. Whatta band!"

My shoulders tightened. "Yeah, well our band is gonna get $25 for a job, which is $25 more than you're gonna get walking around talking like a bigot. And James's mother is going to cook a dinner for us, too."

From the look on George's face, I could see he was stung by being called a bigot and by me gloating over our upcoming $25 payday.

He retorted, "You're gonna let James's mother cook you dinner? Man, she's gonna feed you chitlins." He laughed loudly, but it sounded like a faked laugh. "Two weird guys and a cripple, all eating chitlins together."

I took a deep breath. George was obviously trying to provoke a fight. He was probably still mad from when I'd knocked him over and called him a pig last fall. I swung my right leg over the seat of the bicycle and began to peddle away. George shouted after me, "Two weird guys and a cripple." I glanced over my shoulder at him. A woman came out of the drugstore and looked curiously at George shouting and pointing at me with the cigarette between the fingers of his right hand. She shook her head in disgust as she walked away.

I asked myself, "What are chitlins?"

CHAPTER 36

fter Billy Byrne gleefully explained chitlins to me, I spent the rest of the week worrying. The mere idea of eating pig's intestines made me gag, but I didn't want to insult James's mother, which I surely would do if I refused the chitlins. And I'd insult her even more if I ate them and threw up on her dining room floor. Louis had an easy out. As a Jew, he couldn't eat pig meat under any circumstances, so he would gain respect when he turned down the chitlins. He would be showing that he lived up to what he believed. If I refused to eat chitlins, however, it wouldn't be a sign of anything. Why couldn't we have set this meeting up for a Friday? As a Catholic who isn't supposed to eat any meat on Friday, I could have gained just as much respect as Louis.

To take my mind off the issue, I turned back to Mr. Jackson. I'd been so obsessed about what he did to me, it took me a long time to realize what his collection of photos really meant. He was doing it with all the kids. Doing worse things. I thought of the picture of the kid sucking his cock, and I cringed. If I hadn't been determined to stay away from him, he would have been pressuring me to do that.

I felt stronger than ever about getting him kicked out of the Boy Scouts. Not only would that be my way to get even with him, it would help all the scouts as well. Tony Morelli and the other scouts could come back to the troop. And nobody would have to do anything with him anymore.

But how could I do this without telling somebody about the pictures and exposing Tony to humiliation? Maybe a strong letter would do the job.

So I sat down at my desk, under the ugly sketch Danny had drawn of the artist with a missing ear, to write a letter to the Boy Scouts office downtown. I felt uneasy about not putting my name down, but I sure didn't want anybody coming around asking questions about it. After finishing the letter, I realized that even my handwriting might give me away. Some Boy Scout official might be so eager to get the story behind the letter he'd go around showing the handwritten envelope and maybe even a piece of the letter to each parent until my unsuspecting mother would proudly announce, "That's my boy!"

So I borrowed a trick from detective movies and cut out enough letters from the newspaper to spell out what I had in mind. "Mr. Jackson has sex with the scouts in his troop. Kick him out of the Scouts." I cut out letters for the Boy Scout address, taped them to an envelope, and licked the back of a six cent stamp to paste onto the envelope. Then I walked down to the corner and dropped it in a mailbox.

Taking care of Mr. Jackson, of course, did not take care of my chitlin problem, and I thought of it that night when Mother cooked pork chops for supper. I worried about it in school the next day, and Sister FAH tee mah criticized me for not paying attention. I worried about it in the schoolyard and did not even hear Sally Quinn sneak up behind me until she shouted "Boo!" in my ear. I worried about it delivering newspapers and dropped a sackful of papers on the sidewalk when I failed to spot a patch of ice and my front wheel slid out of control. It still weighed on my mind at 4:30 Thursday afternoon as Louis and I trudged up the driveway into James's back yard. I still didn't know what to do when James's mother put that plate of pig guts in front of me.

We sat down in the three chairs James had pulled close together in the living room. Clarice came in, sat up straight in one of the easy chairs and gave me the same shy smile she had given me the day we had met. She wore tight, gold-colored pedal pusher pants that were becoming popular with the teenage girls, and her breasts pushing out against a tight white blouse caught my eye. Embarrassed, I forced my eyes away from her breasts and returned her smile.

"Get out of here," said James.

"This is my house, and I'll sit wherever I want. You guys need someone to keep track of what you decide about the music and the job." She raised a spiral notebook for us to see. "Isn't that right, Charlie?"

"Leave Charlie out of it," said James. "We don't need no secretary."

Then Louis piped in. "Maybe she's right, James. And she is a very good singer. We gotta figure out a way to keep her in the band." I smiled thankfully at Louis for helping out. Being very short and shy, Louis did not have much chance to hang out with girls. And being Jewish, maybe he didn't know that white boys weren't supposed to admire Negro girls. So not only me, but Louis as well, liked having Clarice in the room. James grimaced in disgust, but once again Clarice had outmaneuvered him.

"What are we gonna call ourselves? Let's decide that first."

"How about 'The Shades of Gray' or something like that," I said, "to show we're an integrated band."

James sighed. "They'll know we're integrated when they see us. So that name doesn't help much."

"How about 'Scheherazade,'" said Louis. "It's an exotic piece of music about the Middle East and all the different people there." He fidgeted excitedly at the chance to put his knowledge of classical music to practical use. James shot a skeptical glance at me, then he let Louis down gently. "That has a nice ring," he said. "I like it. But let's face it. Most kids won't have the foggiest idea of what it means."

We brainstormed a dozen other suggestions, but each one had a flaw. Clarice began squirming in frustration. Finally, she blurted, "How about the ding dongs? That's what you guys sound like yammering back and forth."

"Shut up, Clarice, and mind your own business," said James. "You're supposed to be the secretary, not the chief buttinsky."

"Let her alone, James," said Louis. "Until we can think of something better, let's just call ourselves the North End Dance Band. In the meantime, we have to decide what we're going to play. Clarice, you got any ideas?"

This new assertiveness in Louis impressed me.

"You got time for about a dozen songs," said Clarice. "And you got to play things that are popular. But I've never heard you play. What are you good at?"

"Louis is very good," I said. "He can play any kind of music." Louis smiled proudly at my recognition of his talents.

"Well, if you have time for a dozen songs, let's each pick four of our favorites and put them up to the group for a vote."

After a little bickering, we ended up with a list that came directly from the Hit Parade of the preceding several years.

"You know what else we need?" said Louis.

"What?"

"We need a singer for some of these songs. Now I heard Clarice at the church, and we need her singing for us."

"Louis," James explained patiently, "I agree. My sister is a great singer, even if she is a pain in the neck. But our daddy is never going to let her sing for us. It's a miracle Momma figured out a way to let her be in the same room with us here."

"Why not?" said Louis.

I smiled at how little Louis seemed to know about the kids in his neighborhood. I felt as though everyone in the world had heard by now of the kiss that had brought so much trouble to Clarice and so much heckling to me. Maybe you get out of touch when you spend so much time playing classical music.

Clarice interjected, "He'd let me go if Momma came along as a chaperone."

James rolled his eyes in disgust. "Chaperone! That'd make us look like a bunch of little kids."

"Think about it James," she said. "How you gonna get those drums of yours to the party? Louis, where is this party?"

"Ottawa Hills."

"See. You need a driver to carry the equipment. Momma can drive the car to help us out and be the chaperone to help Daddy stay calm. Louis, there gonna be other chaperones there?"

"There'll be some mothers and maybe some fathers sitting around."

"Colored woman like Momma gonna feel out of place?"

I marveled at the bluntness of Clarice. Then Louis replied with equal bluntness.

"Probably, but nobody's gonna treat her bad."

"All right," said James, hanging his head down in resignation. "Go ask Momma."

She went to the kitchen and came back a few minutes later with a big grin on her face, the broad grin that pushed her cheeks up into little bumps under her eyes. She looked so pleased she didn't even have to tell us what had happened. James groaned.

"Oh, man! Now we gotta split that $25 four ways. Means I'm only gonna get—what? Five to ten dollars?"

"Six dollars and twenty-five cents," I said.

They all looked at me in amazement. "How'd you figure that out so fast?" asked Louis.

"Charlie's just good at numbers, that's all," said James. "Everybody's good at something. Like you're good at the piano and Clarice is good at wrapping everybody around her little finger."

Before she could retort and start another argument with James, I asked her, "What are you going to sing?"

"I like that new Kay Starr song, "'The Man

Upstairs.'"

"Great song," said Louis, "but it won't work. It's too Christian for a bunch of Jewish kids."

"You know what you'd be good at?" I said. "'My Melancholy Baby.'"

She didn't respond. She just sat there with a thoughtful look on her face.

"Remember that movie we saw? I told you that Doris Day should have sung it."

"And I told you I didn't want to be no Doris Day."

"Think about it for a minute," I said. "It would fit your voice perfectly, and it has a great melody."

I started humming the tune. She listened, turned it over in her mind, began humming it herself and said, "That might work." Then to salvage her pride, she retorted, "You've got getter taste in music than I thought you had, Charlie."

I frowned. Sometimes Clarice gets a little too edgy. But she laughed when she saw the frown.

"Oh, Charlie. When are you going to learn to see when people are teasing you? I know you got good taste." We all chuckled at that, including me.

"One more thing," said James. "Most of these songs are slow songs. We need something with pep to start with. Louis, can you play a honky tonk piano?"

"Oh, yeah!" he said. "I love that. But my momma hates it."

"Your momma?" asked James, squinting and looking at Louis with amusement. "Jewish people say, 'My momma?'"

A sheepish look came over Louis. "Not really," he said. "I just wanted to fit in."

James got up and clapped Louis on the shoulder. "Don't we all?" he said, and the four of us laughed loudly.

Just at that moment, James's mother poked her head through the archway and called us into the dining room for dinner. My heart must have skipped a beat, because I still did not know what to do about the chitlins. I stared at the table. A charred roast beef sat on a big platter, the marks showing where the string had held it together while roasting. A dish of mashed potatoes sat next to the roast, along with a bowl of gravy and a serving dish of something that looked like spinach but was actually collard greens. A small dessert sat by each plate.

Mrs. Washington pointed to the desserts. "You boys are going to love this sweet potato pie. Clarice baked it herself."

Clarice smiled, and we all loaded up our plates, but Louis passed up the mashed potatoes. When James's mother urged him to try them, he explained.

"Please don't be offended, Mrs. Washington. But I'm kosher, and I'm not allowed to mix meat with dairy products."

"So you had to choose between the roast beef and the mashed potatoes with the milk and butter?" she asked.

"Yes, ma'am," said Louis. I'd never seen any kid as polite as him. Nobody else I knew would have said 'ma'am.'

"Well, you made the right choice," she smiled.

Just as I had thought, Louis gained respect for acting on his beliefs. But best of all, there were no chitlins in sight. All that agonizing over the chitlins, and they were not even served! Sometimes you can worry too much, I concluded.

James's mother came in with a camera and took several pictures of us at the table. The big blue flash bulbs popped each time she snapped the shutter. She removed them one by one after each snapshot, shaking her fingers as she did so, because the flash bulbs were very hot. Later on, Clarice gave me one of the photos. I taped it to the wall above the desk in my bedroom, right next to Danny's crummy sketch of the painter who'd cut off his own ear.

CHAPTER 37

I felt anxious when it came time to tell Mother and Dad about the band's upcoming job playing at the bar mitzvah party. I thought she would object to me going to a synagogue. Instead, they surprised me by greeting the news with glowing smiles. Dad clapped me on the shoulder, and she gave me a rare hug. "Charlie, I knew all that effort you put into the trumpet would work out." They didn't even object to my spending several afternoons each week practicing with the band at Louis's house.

On the appointed day, we rode to the bar mitzvah party in the battered old Ford James's dad had been working on the day I biked up the driveway and met Clarice. I sat in back with the drums while Clarice and James sat up front next to their mother. She dropped us off but said she didn't want to sit around making small talk with a bunch of women she would never see again. Instead, she would do some errands and then find a place to read her Bible. We should be packed and waiting by 9:00 o'clock sharp. She pulled James and Clarice aside and warned them. "Your daddy expects you two to behave yourselves. Clarice, you so much as shake hands with Charlie and I'll whoop the both of you myself."

"That's cool," laughed James. "Mamma's gonna whoop Charlie."

Pent up as we all were with nervous energy, Clarice scowled at James, "She meant you, dimwit."

It helped ease our nervous energy when Louis came out to help us carry our equipment to the community room to set up for the party. He introduced us to the mother and father of the boy having the bar mitzvah, then gave James and me a yarmulka to wear inside the synagogue sanctuary. At first, I felt almost as awkward in the synagogue as I had when Louis and I went to James's church. But I soon got intrigued with the rituals, especially the ritual of bringing the scrolls out of the ark at the start of the service and returning them at the end. However, I didn't understand much in between. Louis's cousin sang in Hebrew from the scroll as he stood before the altar. How such a young kid could read from such a weird looking alphabet and sing with no musical notes to guide him mystified me. He must have studied for a year. Men strolled around the sanctuary with sashes over their shoulders, muttering prayers in Hebrew and rocking back and forth as they prayed. The service dragged on, however, as church services tended to do, and my mind kept going over the songs we planned to play that evening. I ran a finger between my neck and the starched collar of the white shirt that scratched my neck. White shirts and neckties were the easiest things that James, Louis, and I could think of to make it look as though our band had a uniform.

When we got to the party, I spotted a few teens from the Hanukkah party at Louis's house. I started things going with a trumpet fanfare to gain the attention of the audience, then introduced the group, starting with Louis. "Ladies and Gentlemen, the North End Dance Band presents Louis at the ivories." Louis pounded out a honky talk piano version of "Won't You Come Home Bill Bailey?"

After Louis ran through the song, Clarice sang the lyrics, trying hard to sound like Lena Horne, and when she came to the final line, she did not just sing, "Won't you come home." Rather, she trilled the word "home" and dragged it out as though it had three or four syllables.

She looked stunning, wearing a close fitting pink dress, buttoned up tight against her neck, like some kind of Chinese outfit, the hem dropping down to the knees, and the bottom of her legs covered with white stockings. She had so much zest she looked like she might explode. When she finished singing, she pulled a tambourine from somewhere, waved it in the air, its bells jingling, and pointed it at me as a signal for my trumpet solo. James came next with a solo on the drums. Then the three instruments came back in for one last stanza together. This became the pattern we followed for the rest of the night, except that Clarice did not sing every song.

In between her songs, she danced back and forth in front of the band, waving her arms up and down like a conductor. She retrieved the tambourine with bells around the edge, held it in her left hand and clapped it with her right in rhythm with the music. James frowned in disgust, trying to get her to calm down, but the audience gave her a big ovation twice. She worked so hard that little beads of sweat glimmered on the back of her neck. Finally, we came to our last song. Clarice put down the tambourine and stood demurely in front of us as she began to sing "My Melancholy Baby."

For me, this was the best part of the show. I did a solo to introduce the song, then put a mute on my trumpet to back up Clarice softly as she started to sing. Louis added to the backup with some great piano chords. I felt like Kirk Douglas playing the trumpet along with Doris Day in the movie we had all seen several months earlier. If you could picture Clarice as a tan-colored Doris Day and me as the cool Kirk Douglas. When Clarice reached the last stanza, she half turned and gazed directly at me as she wailed:

Come to me my melancholy baby.
Cuddle up and don't be blue.

One girl at the edge of the dance floor stuck her tongue out at Clarice. It was the girl who had slipped me her telephone number at the Hannukkah party; I had never phoned her. The slow, dreamy music brought the dancers together, and when the music stopped, it took a few seconds for them to disentangle. They gave us a rousing ovation and clapped loudly for Clarice as she made her bow, bending at the waist and bowing so low that her forehead almost touched the floor.

All of a sudden, the show ended. Louis's uncle handed us an envelope containing our money. We carted our instruments out to the car where Mrs. Washington waited. I sat in the front bench seat next to James, while Clarice took her turn in the back, bumping up against the drum equipment. When she sat down in the back seat, her dress rode up her thighs and showed off the garter belt strap attached to the hem of her shiny white nylons. Her mother yanked the dress down hard and got behind the wheel. Nobody talked. I looked over my shoulder and watched Clarice sitting with the same dreamy look on her face that she had the night in the library when she'd told me how good it felt to sing in front of the church and hold the audience in the palm of her hands. When she saw me looking at her, she flashed that big smile that pushed up the bumps under her eyes. I must have blushed or something, because all at once her mother said, "Keep your eyes to the front, Charlie."

It was one of the best days of my life.

CHAPTER 38

O n Strike!" said the headline of the *Jeeptown Gazette*, as I took my papers from Old Schmidt and carried them to the side counter. So that's what got Mother so mad this morning.

On the first day of the strike, a worker on the picket line stood in front of a supervisor's car and tried to block it from entering the factory parking lot. The car inched slowly through the picket line and its front fender edged the worker aside. With a slight push from Dad, the picketer fell down, screaming in mock pain, while Dad and the other fellow picketers yelled in protest at the supervisor, pounded dents into the hood of the car, and screamed that the supervisor had deliberately run over the striker. A company big shot ran outside to inspect the man's injury, but the strikers pushed him away and wouldn't let him near the man on the ground. Finally, an ambulance moved the man to the hospital, and the evening news showed the angry union president kneeling next to the fallen worker while he shouted at the TV camera, accusing the Spark Plug Company of violence and attempted murder. A hospital spokesman refused to comment in front of the television cameras. At midnight, Dad and Mr. Delaney drove the union president to the hospital to pick up the injured picketer who walked unassisted out of the hospital to Mr. Delaney's car.

Dad chortled with glee when he told us about it the next day. "Great job!" the union president told the man. "Stay at home for a while. If anybody calls, you're in bed recuperating from your injuries. Don't come back to the picket line for a week."

A week later, to the day, the man returned to the picket line, amid a flurry of cheers among the strikers. The union tried to get the television cameras to record the event, but by then the TV station realized it had been tricked earlier and refused to show up.

The company threatened to retaliate if the strikers refused to return to work. A company vice president showed up on the evening news. "We have the best paid workers in the industry," said the grim-looking man, with strands of hair pasted down on his head. "We've offered them a very generous wage boost. But they don't want to work. They just want time off to go ice fishing before the ice melts. Well, if they want to keep their jobs, they'd better forget about fishing and get back to work!"

"Gone Fishing!" said the editorial in the *Jeeptown Gazette*. It blamed the lazy workers for turning down the company's lavish offer. Jeeptown could not afford to go back to the old days when it had the image of a bad labor town. The workers and their union must be responsible and understand that no other companies will build plants in Jeeptown if they face labor conflict. The Spark Plug Company might be forced to call up non-union workers from the South or maybe even close down. How will it help the cause of the good workers if a few agitators cause honest people to lose their jobs?

Dad threw the paper in the garbage as soon as he saw the editorial. "The least they could do would be to put in an article showing the other side. What a piece of crap." But Mother hadn't read the paper yet, so she pulled it out of the garbage can, and when she saw the editorial, she hit the ceiling.

"I told you not to strike," she yelled at Dad. "You guys have to stop this and go back to work before you lose your jobs."

"Just scare tactics," said Dad. "Don't fall for them. If they kill my job, I'll start driving a bulldozer for some construction company, just like you've always wanted me to."

Mother had no retort for that. She tossed the paper back into the garbage and began to bang dishes around in the kitchen.

Dad gloried in his new role as strike captain. He gave me a union song to practice on the trumpet. Someone had typed the lyrics on a big blue stencil, and then one afternoon he brought me down to the union hall and showed me how to run the stencil through the mimeograph machine. You had to turn a crank on the machine to run the copies through it. By the time I finished, I had blue ink all over my hands. Dad looked over one of the copies I'd run off and wrapped his arm tight around my shoulder. "Great job!" he said.

On the first Saturday of the strike, he brought Mollie and me to walk the picket line. As we shuffled along with the picketers in a big oval pattern in front of the plant entrance, a photographer took a picture of little Mollie raising a sign that said, "My daddy needs a fair wage!" The photo was so touching that *The Union Advocate* ran it on page one, and even the *Jeeptown*

Gazette carried it. Not on page one, however.

At first, I felt self-conscious on the picket line, surrounded by grown men, and I got embarrassed when the sole of my left shoe came loose and flapped against the ground with each step. There was no chance of getting it re-soled as long as the strike continued. And as I got caught up in the excitement of the moment, I soon forgot about my shoe. The union men shook their fists and chanted slogans when they saw anybody go into or leave the plant. "Scab!" shouted the picketers when a temporary maintenance worker walked toward the picket line. "Scab!" I shouted, wondering what a scab was. The company had taken advantage of the strike by hiring temporary workers to make equipment repairs and do maintenance during the shutdown.

As the temporary worker reached the picket line, I got a better look. It was Mr. Jackson, the scoutmaster, who had come to make some extra money replacing the striking janitors. He passed within a few yards of me. "Scab! Scab! Scab!" I shouted, pressing forward to the front of the picket line, my shoe flapping on the ground as I stepped up. "Scab! Scab!" I screamed so loud one of the picketers put his hand on my shoulder. "Hold on, my boy," he said. "The scab is gone now."

Just then, Channel 13's truck drove up with a portable TV camera. Dad had me open my trumpet case and start playing "Solidarity Forever." He shouted, "Sing, everybody! Sing!" as he hopped along the picket line, passing out the mimeographed copies of the song's lyrics. You could feel the surge of excitement in the crowd when my trumpet began belting out the lively melody, and all the picketers joined in the singing. Our sad, slow shuffle speeded up into a proud march. We must have made quite a spectacle, because the television camera panned across us.

Eventually, the camera stopped filming and the workers stopped singing. They went back to shuffling in silence just outside the plant gate. Dad led Mollie and me to a refreshment table where we each got a donut and a cup of hot chocolate. The union president smiled as he patted us both on the shoulder. "Great job!" he said. Then Dad pushed us into a car that whisked us back home. Once the photographers and television cameras were gone, our job was done.

I found it all very exciting, especially the part about yelling "Scab!" at Mr. Jackson. However, the more I thought about it, the more I could see the viewpoint of one disgruntled picketer in front of me who had turned to me and said, "This sucks, kid."

After the excitement of the picket line, the house seemed dull, and Mollie was restless. She badgered Mother as she prepared supper in the kitchen. "Charlie," she called. "Take Mollie out and do something with her. She's driving me nuts."

I took her to the basement where we found an old kite. I cut a piece of cloth for a tail and then took her to the little park two blocks from our house where Oakwood Street splits around a small grassy park space. I showed her how to feed out the string as I ran into the wind to launch the kite. Once she got it into the air, I sat on the ground with my back resting against the weeping willow tree at one end of the park.

Eventually, she got bored with the kite. She let go of the string, and ran over to me by the swing, letting the kite sag to the ground

"Why did you shout at that man at the strike?"

"He's a bad man," I said. "A very bad man."

"He looked scared when you shouted at him."

She looked up proudly at me as she said that, and it made me realize that I now had a certain power over the scoutmaster. As long as he never caught me alone where he could break my neck as he had threatened to do, I could do whatever I wanted to him, and he would never dare get even. He couldn't retaliate against me in front of the picketers, and he must be dying of fear that I would expose his secret. For all he knew, I still had the pictures of the naked kids and could turn them over to the Boy Scouts any time I wanted. That was his weak spot.

CHAPTER 39

On Monday I told Mother I was going to study at the library. By now I had stopped pretending to be going to the Boy Scout meeting on Monday evenings. The strike preoccupied her so much she couldn't pay much attention to where I went. She just shook her head back and forth as she gave me a sad look. She didn't even notice I didn't take any school books with me.

When I walked into the warm building, I naturally looked to my left, half expecting to see Clarice seated at our table. But, of course, she wasn't there. Mrs. Nordstrom looked up when I came through the door.

"I haven't seen you for a while," she said with a warm smile.

"I've been busy."

"I haven't seen your little girlfriend either," she said.

Why did adults keep calling Clarice a little girl? She wasn't little at all. I looked closely at Mrs. Nordstrom's face to see if I could figure out any hidden meaning to what she said. But she just looked normal. Almost as though she had no objections to a white boy sitting in her library with a colored girlfriend.

"She's not really my girlfriend," I said. "At least, not anymore."

"That's too bad. She seemed like such a nice girl." Her smile turned down at the corners of her lips.

As soon as it got late enough for the Boy Scout meeting to be over, I left the library and headed toward Mr. Jackson's duplex, where I hid in the small crevice between the embankment and the hedge, just like I had the night I had broken into his place. I peeked over the hedge as Mr. Jackson's red Ford convertible came up the street, made its u-turn, and pulled to a stop right in front of the duplex. Once he walked past the crevice where I crouched, I peered over the top of the hill in time to see him take his last drag on a cigarette. He flicked it away with his forefinger, just as he had flicked the cigarette butt into the fireplace at Camp Miakonda.

After he entered the house and closed the door, I ran to his car, took a bar of Ivory soap from my pocket and wrote "Pervert" on the windshield and side windows. The soap would be tough to get off in the morning after it had spent the cold night hardening. He would have to scrape it off with a razor blade, and I grinned as I thought of this.

Looking over my shoulder to make sure nobody was watching, I stooped down by the left front tire and took from my pocket a notched tire valve cap I had picked up from Dad's tool box. I inserted the notched end of the cap into the air valve and slowly turned the valve stem to the left until it came out of the tire. The stale air made a nice hiss as it leaked out of the tire, and the tire became completely flat within minutes. I ran across the street, around the corner, and into the safety of a dark alley, being careful to run on the ball of my left foot and the heel of my right one. That would even out my limp so nobody could identify me in case they were watching. When I reached the alley, I sat down on the cold cinders and chuckled to myself.

Serves him right. And I would not even need to confess any of this. I had not done any damage to his car, so I had no need to make restitution. The tire could easily be pumped up as soon as Mr. Jackson went to a gas station to replace the valve stem I'd thrown in the gutter. I had even left two nickels on the hood of the car to reimburse him for it. Writing pervert on the window where everyone could see might have been mean, but it wouldn't be a sin unless it violated the Ten Commandments' rule not to bear false witness against your neighbor. Since Mr. Jackson really was a pervert, I was not bearing false witness by calling him one. I was bearing the truth. I clicked off the rest of the Ten Commandments and could not find a single one I had violated. My only regret was that I would not be there in the morning to see the look on his face when he came outside and saw how he had been exposed.

Something Sister FAH tee mah had told me that day last fall when I had put Butch Bower in his place popped into my mind. "Vengeance poisons the soul!" But I didn't feel poisoned at all. "Vengeance is sweet," I told myself as I got to my feet and ambled home.

CHAPTER 40

The strike put a lot of pressure on the family. "How can you continue that strike when your own son needs those spark plugs in Korea?" Mother challenged Dad.

"The Marines have all the spark plugs they need. We've been working overtime for months putting out the damn things."

'Don't use that language with me!"

That's the way it went as the strike dragged on longer than anyone had expected. The company had stockpiled tens of thousands of spark plugs, so many in fact that the company was barely affected by the strike. The son of the company president was an amateur tennis player, and the sports page showed a picture of him at a tournament down in Florida. The strike certainly didn't hurt him.

For us, however, the money problems began to pinch. Normally, I don't know anything about the family's money. Mother is in charge of that. But even a blind person could see the signs. We hadn't gotten any coal delivered in weeks even though the pile in the coal bin kept getting smaller. Instead of buying new socks when our old ones got holes, she stuck the old socks in her big purse and took them with her to Aunt Bridget's house on Tuesday nights. As we sat there watching Milton Berle, she darned the socks, sticking a burned out light bulb into the sock, pushing the fat part of the bulb to the toe or heel or wherever the hole was, then using a needle to stitch a covering of thread over the hole. We were eating a lot more leftovers, and a lot of suppers were just pancakes. When pieces of bread went stale, instead of throwing them out, Mother saved them until she got enough of them stored up to make a supper of French toast. When I complained that French toast wasn't a very good supper, she said. "Be glad you've got it. Some starving little kid in India would feel lucky to have it."

One morning before I went to school, Mother was so out of sorts she was banging pots and pans around in the kitchen. She had to go downtown that day to empty her savings account at the Jeeptown Trust Company. Her mood got worse when that money ran out and she had to dip into the old hat box in her closet where she hid her personal cash, unknown to Dad.

On Ash Wednesday, she told me to come home from school at lunchtime. When I got there, she shocked me as she led me by the arm to the Oakwood Street bus, which took us downtown to the Jeeptown Trust Company. I had wrapped adhesive tape around the toe of my shoe to stop the loose sole from flapping, and I stared bleakly at the tape as we sat on the bus. Then I remembered I had forgotten to wash the Ash Wednesday ashes off my forehead, and I felt as though all the other bus riders were staring at me. Pretending to scratch my head, I raised my arm to wipe off the ashes with my sleeve. But when I saw my reflection in the window of the bank, I had spread the small spot of ashes into a huge blob.

Normally, I loved visiting the Jeeptown Trust Company with its stone pillars out front, making it look like one of those Greek temples you see in history books. The quiet hush inside always intrigued me, with peoples' heels clicking on the shiny marble floor, guards standing stiff in their blue uniforms with pistols on their belts, and tellers stationed behind the iron grates where the customers talked to them in soft voices as they came up to ask for their own money. A lot different than the foreman shouting at Dad at the Spark Plug Plant. I imagined myself as a teller confronting a bank robber pointing a gun through the iron grate, and me becoming a hero by setting off the burglar alarm would be the robber's downfall. One time Grandpa Parnell had taken me down to the vault in the basement. He sat me quietly in a green leather chair while he passed through the thick metal door and went over to the safe deposit boxes that could not be opened unless there were two keys. Afterwards he bought me a milkshake at one of those new drive-in restaurants. But there wouldn't be any milkshakes today.

"It's only a loan," said Mother. "We'll pay you back as soon as the strike is over and your da gets his pay raise." I was skeptical. Hadn't Dad already promised that pay raise to buying a television set, a car, a house in the suburbs, and who knows what else? Even if the union got its entire demand for a ten cents per hour raise and Dad used it all to repay me, it would take an entire year to earn back the $200 that was being cleaned out of my savings account. And I was not convinced Mother had totally emptied her hat box.

Some afternoon when I had the house to myself, I would check that out.

However, it wasn't for nothing that I had watched Mother build up her private stockpile of cash in her hatbox and the Company build up its huge stockpile of spark plugs. Down in the coal bin, I had my own stockpile of cash nobody knew about. Nobody but me ventured into the coal bin, since I was the guy charged with shoveling coal into the furnace. There, hidden under a pile of coal in one corner, sat a small locked metal box into which I had laid ten crisp, clean ten-dollar bills. I had personally washed them in the bathroom sink and dried them out to give them that crisp feel of new money. This was the best hiding spot in the entire house. Thank God Dad hadn't yet converted to a gas furnace, I thought, as we sat on the bus and headed home.

"What are you smiling at?" Mother asked suspiciously.

"Oh, nothing," I said. "I'm just glad I could help out."

"That's my goy," she said. She meant boy, but I didn't say anything. She glanced at her watch. She wanted to get back home in time to visit the church. She had not yet gotten her ashes. And she wanted to start a Novena to the Sacred Heart of Jesus, offering the prayers for the safety of Danny in Korea.

CHAPTER 41

Maybe Mr. Jackson really did fear me, as Mollie had said, but I felt wary about him. At some point he would realize I was the one harassing him. And one day, as I rode my bicycle down the sidewalk delivering my newspapers, Mr. Jackson stepped out from behind a huge elm tree and grabbed the handlebars of my bike. I was off balance because I had just tossed a paper onto the Rubenstein porch. With my forward motion stopped, I struggled to keep the bike from falling.

"How come you're not screaming 'Scab' at me now, you little turd? You don't feel quite so tough when you don't have those union goons around. Do you?"

I stood there with my legs straddling the bar of the bicycle and didn't say anything. Mr. Jackson was a powerful man, and there was no telling how badly he could hurt me if he wanted to. But I also knew from my experience with Butch Bower, Dirty George, and the union picketers that it would be a big mistake to let him see how scared I was.

"Say something, you little rat. You're the one who's been harassing me, aren't you?"

"I don't know what you're talking about," I said.

He pushed hard on the handlebar of the bike, and I lost control of it. It fell to the pavement, and my remaining papers spilled onto the sidewalk.

"You don't know what I'm talking about! Like hell you don't! You think you can disguise your voice when you talk on the phone, but you can't." He was getting angrier as he talked, and his voice got louder. "You been screwing around with my car, and you're the one who trashed my apartment. I'm warning you. You keep this up and you're going to get hurt. Bad!"

So this was just a warning. He didn't have any intention of smashing me to the ground right here in the middle of the afternoon. He was just trying to scare me.

"I don't know what you're talking about," I repeated. "But if you think I did something wrong, why don't you just call the police?"

"You little smart-mouth! I should teach you a lesson!"

He pushed me back with the palm of his hand, just as that fat cop had once done. Then he grabbed my jacket where it was open at the collar. In the background, I heard the Rubinstein porch door open, and when my eyes glanced in that direction, Mr. Jackson also looked there. Seeing Mrs. Rubinstein staring at us, he let go of my jacket and used the palm of his hands to smooth it out. Then he bent over to help me pick up the newspapers. Just before he walked off, he gave me a pat on the back and a big smile. Despite the smile, his voice was nasty.

"I can get you anytime I want, Charlie. I know where you live, where you go to school, where you peddle your papers, when you go to the library, and when you go to your trumpet lessons. I even know about your little girlfriend. So watch your step, or you're going to be sorry."

Then he walked off. Mrs. Rubenstein came down to the sidewalk.

"Charlie, who was that? Are you okay?"

"I'm okay, Mrs. Rubenstein. He's just my scoutmaster, and it's a game of catch me if you can that we play."

"I never heard of that game."

Neither had I. I just made it up on the spur of the moment. Still looking skeptical, she nevertheless walked back to her porch, picked up the newspaper, and went inside the house.

CHAPTER 42

The conflict at the Spark Plug Plant started to get wild. The demand from Korea for plugs was so great that the company's huge stockpile started to run down. Instead of giving in to the union, however, the company announced it intended to bring up men from the South to work the machines. Dad was fuming.

"That's what happens," he said one night when he got back from picketing. "We let them get away with hiring scab janitors to clean up and now they're hiring scab machine operators to take my job. We never should have let those fucking scab janitors through the picket line."

"Watch your mouth," said Mother. "We have children here." But she didn't have the usual anger she flashed when the union came up for discussion. If the company could get away with hiring scabs to operate the machines, they could destroy the union, and the strike leaders like Dad would never get his job back. Even I could see that.

The Friday after Ash Wednesday, Dad didn't come back from the picketing, and after supper Mother sent me on my bike to find him. It was hard to get through to the plant, because the police had closed off Upton Street. I had to ride around the block, lean my bike against a tree, and walk through somebody's backyard to get around the barricade of sawhorses that had been put up.

The cops had pushed the picketers back from the plant gate and stood around the entrance to keep anyone from going in or out. It was starting to get dark, but the cops had set up a huge set of lights that made it look as bright as day.

Union workers had invaded the plant. A hundred or more of them had walked around the site to the railroad tracks behind the plant. Unseen by the police, they snuck along the railroad tracks until they reached the loading dock. When the scab maintenance workers filed out of the plant at 3:30 on Friday, the union men pushed aside the guard at the loading dock door and streamed into the factory. Dad was now somewhere inside the building.

"Illegal Strike!"

That was the headline on the *Jeeptown Gazette* when I did my paper route on Saturday. A big picture on the front page showed the union president and the company president glaring at each other.

"Get those goons out of our building," the company president was quoted as saying. "You know that sit-down strikes are illegal."

"They went in on their own, so it's not a sit-down strike. They're just mad because you gave their jobs to scabs," replied the union president. "Since we didn't send them in, we don't have any way to get them out. If you want them out, get rid of those scabs. But if you force them out and somebody gets hurt, you'll be the one with blood on your hands. There will be hell to pay."

I'd never seen the word hell in the paper before.

The radio said that women were holed up in the building with the men, and a company spokesman said, "We will not permit any immoral behavior in our plant."

I thought Mother would explode when she heard that, but she said, "Don't pay any attention, Charlie. They're just trying to turn the women against the men so the wives will make their husbands come home."

The Spark Plug Plant had now become the most exciting spot in the Old North End, with the cops lined up outside the building, the workers inside leaning out the windows jeering the cops, and picketers cheering their buddies in the building. Alongside the picketers was a scattering of women scanning the faces of the men leaning out the windows of the plant. When someone would spot her man, she would shout to him.

One blond-haired woman spotted her man leaning out of a window. "Wendell!" she shouted. She pushed herself right up to the front of the picketers and pulled open her coat so Wendell could see her dressed in a very short skirt and a pair of black stockings. The skirt was so short you could see the garter snaps attached to the hems of the stockings. I had never seen a young woman wear black stockings before, except in the movies, but she sure looked sexy, standing there with her long blond hair blowing in the breeze. I found it impossible not to stare as she cocked her hip and showed off her legs in those shiny black stockings. Several men whistled.

"Wendell! Is that the kind of men you hang around

with?" she shouted. Everyone looked at her now. "Men who whistle at your wife?" She pulled her overcoat closed, shutting out that delightful sight of her figure. "If you want me there when you get back, you'd better get out of that building now."

Wendell had a torn look on his face. First he looked to his wife, that pretty young woman in the overcoat and black stockings, then he glanced over his shoulder at the dirty faces of the men crowded around him, then back at his wife, who pulled her coat open again. He started to climb out the window. The men tried to pull him back, but Wendell moved too quickly. He tumbled out the window to the ground. Two big cops helped him to his feet, dragged him to his wife on the other side of the barricade, and ushered the two of them through the striking picketers, who shoved against the cops and screamed at the poor guy.

"Coward!"

"Pussy whipped!"

"Traitor!"

"Henpecked!"

If Mother was right that the company was trying to turn the wives against their husbands, the plan had sure worked with Wendell's wife. But the union moved fast. Some guy leaned out the window, shouting through a bullhorn that the company was spreading dirty rumors. To stop the rumors, he said they were going to move all the women out of the plant. And fifteen minutes later, a dozen women filed triumphantly out the building's main entrance. All the picketers in front and the workers in the building clapped and cheered as the women raised their hands in the air and strutted past the police.

On Monday, when I finished my paper route, Mother was gone. She'd taped a note to the refrigerator. She had dropped Mollie off at Aunt Bridget's house and had gone to the union hall on Monroe Street to help form a Women's Auxiliary Corps to cook food for the men locked inside the building. I hurried to the plant and got there just in time to see Mother and a bunch of other women unloading food packets from a truck. The cops refused to let them near the main entrance, but there weren't enough cops to stop them, and the women charged around the barricades, where they handed the food packets through the windows to the men inside.

"Anarchy!" screamed the next day's newspaper headline. The paper ran a picture of the wives scampering around the police. Sit-down strikes were illegal, explained the story, and something had to be done to preserve law and order. The governor called in the National Guard, and by nightfall their soldiers had not only blocked off the main entrance, but they had mounted a machine gun on a flatbed truck. Two men stood by the machine gun and pointed it toward the picketers beyond the barricades.

In contrast to the turmoil in front of the plant, everything was quiet at home that night. I sat at the kitchen table catching up on my homework, while Mother stuffed marbles and stones tightly inside a small burlap sack she had sewn. She sewed on a leather strap that she could loop over her wrist. Jesus, I thought, as I stared at her.

"That's a blackjack!"

"They showed us how to make these at the Auxiliary," she beamed. Putting on a jacket with loose sleeves to hide the blackjack, she practiced flicking her arm to make the hidden blackjack snap into her hand ready for use. After a few practice strokes, she got the movement down perfectly. She then got a big red Women's Auxiliary Corps armband, which she tacked to the sleeve of the jacket.

I just stared at her. I looked over at Mollie, but she didn't understand anything about blackjacks. She laughed at Mother's trick of flicking the blackjack from her sleeves to the palm of her hand and she asked for the blackjack so that she could try the trick herself. What was happening to Mother? For as long as I could remember, she had badmouthed the union every chance she got. And now she was making weapons for them.

"Mother!" I demanded. "The plant is surrounded by soldiers, and they have a machine gun down there. What good is that blackjack going to be against a machine gun?"

"You worry too much, Charlie," she said. "Just keep doing your homework."

CHAPTER 43

Things stayed quiet for the next few days, and on Friday, Sister FAH tee mah asked the class for advice.

"I promised to go to Calvary Cemetery with Sister Paulette to say prayers at her mother's gravesite tomorrow. But we have lost our ride. Does anybody know how to get there by bus?"

Billy Byrne raised his hand. "That's easy, Sister. Just walk down to Dorr Street and take the bus out to the cemetery." He beamed with pride at the chance to show off his knowledge. Billy didn't get that chance very often.

She repeated the instructions and cocked her head down, looking for confirmation from Billy that she had the correct directions. Billy nodded back, and Carl Broda piped in, "But make sure you take the bus going west. Otherwise, you'll end up downtown."

As the day wore on, I got a bright idea. The nuns didn't get out much. They couldn't just walk around town like the rest of us, and when they did go out, they always went in pairs. Sister FAH tee mah usually went with Sister Paulette, the nun who had gone with her to the football game last September where she had met Clarice and watched me embarrass myself by dropping that punt return. Since the two nuns were going to the cemetery tomorrow, this would give them a chance to see a little bit of the town. So when school let out at 3:15, and I had finished off my part of the clean-up chores, I went to her desk.

"Do you know what you ought to do, Sister?"

She smiled, "Yes?"

"Since you and Sister Paulette will be at the cemetery tomorrow, when you come back, you should get off the bus at Upton Street and walk up to the spark plug plant to see the strike."

"Why would I want to do that, Sharlie?"

That stumped me. The turmoil at the Spark Plug Factory fascinated me so much I just assumed that it fascinated everyone else as well.

"It would just give you a chance to see something different."

"But I am a nun. I am not supposed to get involved in politics."

"You're not getting involved, Sister. You're just seeing what's going on, a slice of life, as they say. It might be a chance to see another side of the kids in our class, especially those whose dads are on strike." I made it sound as though half the class had dads on strike. But this was not as big an exaggeration as it sounded. True, only Brenda Delaney and I had dads on strike, but half the class had dads who worked at other plants that could just as easily go on strike some day.

Sally Quinn came over from where she had been pinning decorations on the bulletin board. She had taken a great liking to Sister FAH tee mah and helped her out whenever possible. Sally said, "I don't think that's a good idea, Charlie. My da says that this strike is illegal and those strikers are dangerous."

Sister got a frown on her face. But Sally's objection only gave me fresh ammunition for my argument. "See, Sister. You'll get to see both sides. Sally's side and my side."

"It's a nice idea. But it is out of the question. We will only have enough money for two bus rides, and if we do what you say, we will need to take a third bus to get from the factory back to the convent."

I dug into my pocket and pulled out a quarter. I had no idea what two adult bus fares would cost, but a quarter should cover them. I held out the coin for her.

"Sharlie, I cannot take your money. Teachers don't take money from their pupils."

'It's not my money, Sister. I won a bet, and I promised Jesus I would give half of my winnings to a charitable cause. Helping you and Sister Paulette get to know us kids better is the best cause I can think of."

She frowned in a doubtful way, but she took the quarter. Sally and I walked out of the building together. When we got down the stone steps to the ground, she poked me in the ribs with her knuckles, as she had done to Butch Bower that day at the blackboard.

"Ouch," I said.

"Charlie, you're a con man," she laughed. "It's a bad idea, but I wish I could be there tomorrow to see those two nuns right in the middle of all those strikers."

"Why don't you just get on your bike and go? It's not that far."

"Oh, my God! If my da found out about that, he'd ground me for a week."

Funny, I thought as I headed home. Clarice does something wrong and she gets beat with a belt. Sally does something wrong and she gets grounded. I do something wrong and Da just tells me not to do it again. Mother, on the other hand, screams up a storm.

CHAPTER 44

O ut!" screamed the headline of the *Jeeptown Gazette* when I picked up my papers. The paper called for the National Guard to kick the strikers out of the building so law and order could be restored. I rushed through my deliveries and pedaled toward the Spark Plug Company as fast as I could.

It was bedlam. There must have been 300 women and children lined up like a parade in front of the barricade, with Mother in the very front row. Oh Jesus! Right next to her, standing in the cold was little Mollie in her bright red coat. She looked happy in the midst of all this excitement, and she held up the same sign she had held that day when Dad had let us join the picketing. "My Daddy needs a fair wage!" And slowly coming up toward Mother were Sister FAH tee mah and Sister Paulette. Their arrival was such an extraordinary sight that people opened a path for them as they edged forward. With each step they took toward the barricade, the crowd closed in behind them, and in no time they were pushed right up front next to the police line. Their heads swiveled as they looked around the crowd, and Sister FAH tee mah had that frown she gets when she looks puzzled or anxious.

Just as the nuns reached the sawhorses that had been put up as the barricade, the National Guard sent two soldiers in gas masks up to the flatbed truck with the machine gun. One of the soldiers squatted by the side of the gun where he could feed in the belt of ammunition. The other one knelt down behind the gun, put his fists on the handles behind the trigger and aimed the gun out toward the people. A gasp spread through the crowd. Then we all went completely silent as we watched, and I could feel pressure on my chest as the people in front of me pushed backward.

However, it wasn't the machine gunner that the National Guard planned to use. While our eyes were riveted on him, a bunch of soldiers ran to the doors of the building and tossed in can after can of tear gas. The women broke ranks when they saw this, pushed through the barricade, and charged the building. Mother flicked her blackjack into her hand and ran along the building, using the blackjack to smash open windows and let in some fresh air for the men who were being gassed. The other women did the same thing, and those blackjacks seemed to appear out of nowhere. Not wanting to be left out of the excitement, I pushed my way to the sawhorses and joined other people picking up stones to throw at the windows. The soldiers threw tear gas grenades at us, while the cops raised their nightsticks and began chasing after the women. The two nuns dropped to their knees right inside the barricade, clasped their hands together and looked up to the sky as they said some prayer. They were right in front of me now, half-turned in my direction, and for a second I made eye contact with Sister FAH tee mah as her lips moved in prayer.

A policeman came up to her, and I recognized him at once. It was the fat cop with the mean eyes who had pushed me around that day Rafer Jones had robbed the grocery store.

"No!" I screamed as the cop raised his billy club over Sister FAH tee mah's head, and she turned to see the billy club poised to come down on her at any second. "She's a nun!" I screamed. Startled by my shout, the cop glanced past my shoulder, then turned away from Sister FAH tee mah and clubbed somebody else instead.

"Good work, kid!" I heard from behind me. A tall man pushed me aside. He had a press card stuck in the brim of his hat and one of those great big, black cameras that the newspaper photographers use. "You saved the nun and you got me one hell of a good picture."

The women with their blackjacks were no match for the cops with their nightsticks, however, and the riot did not last long. My eyes and nose stung from the awful smell and the irritants of the tear gas. Everyone without a gas mask rubbed their eyes as tears ran down their cheeks. The soldiers regained control of the barricades. The machine gunner hadn't pulled his trigger. He was still kneeling there, looking out at us through his gas mask. The workers were still inside the building, sticking their heads out of the broken windows as they gasped to suck in some fresh air. They looked a little sick, but they shouted at the soldiers.

"Cowards!"

"Women beaters!"

"Thugs!"

Mother, some other women, and even the two nuns, were hustled into nearby paddy wagons. There looked to be a bloody spot on top of Mother's head. All of a sudden I remembered Mollie and searched around frantically until I found her sitting in her red coat on a curb across the street, crying, trying to rub the tear gas out of her eyes. She had lost her sign, and she looked terrified. When she saw me, she jumped up and wrapped her arms around my legs.

"Charlie, what happened?" she asked. "What are we gonna do?"

I took her hand and led her over to where I had left my bike, trying to settle her down. "It's all over," I said as calmly as I could. "Let's get you home."

I put her on the cross bar of my bike and rode over to Grandpa Parnell's house. He was the only one I could think of who would know how to get Mother and the nuns out of jail. He didn't say a word when I told him what happened. He just muttered to himself while he shook his head back and forth. "The damned fools," it sounded like. Nevertheless, he phoned St. Matthew's to warn Father Doyle about the nuns, then drove his car downtown to see if he could get Mother out of jail.

He turned to Grandma, "We should get Charlie and Mollie home. I'll drop all three of you there so you can keep an eye on them until I get back."

He ordered Mollie and me into the backseat of his car, while he and Grandma sat in front. She rolled down the car window. "You two stink to high heavens," she said.

"It's the tear gas," I said.

"When we get you home, I'm going to put Mollie in the bathtub. You can go in afterwards. And take those smelly clothes down to the basement. I don't want you smelling like this when your mother gets back."

Grandma made pancakes for supper, and we had

finished eating by the time Grandpa got Mother back home. She had a small bandage on the crown of her head where she had been grazed by a cop's nightstick.

"Why did you do it?" asked Grandma Parnell.

"I guess I just had to," Mother answered. She had a sheepish grin on her face. "I hate that damned union as much as you do. They're a bunch of troublemakers. But he's my husband. And if he had the guts to stay in that building with all that tear gas I had a duty to help him."

None of us said anything. Then Mother's sheepish grin turned into a big smile. It was the brightest smile she'd shown in weeks. "But I have to say this. It was a lot more fun than listening to the radio."

Grandpa Parnell shook his head in puzzlement.

CHAPTER 45

Sally Quinn ambushed me at church that Sunday. As I stepped out through the huge church doors, she stepped boldly in front of me and blocked my path. She pushed the morning newspaper right into my face and pointed at the big, front page photo of Sister FAH tee mah looking up wide-eyed at the billy club held over her head by the cop with the fat face.

"I told you that was a bad idea!" she shouted. She was so mad she practically spit the words at me. I had forgotten how devoted she had become to Sister FAH tee mah, and I should have guessed how mad she would get at the photo making it look like Sister was getting clubbed. Too bad I didn't go to mass at St. Martin de Porres where Sally wouldn't show up.

"She didn't get hit," I protested. "The picture just makes it look that way."

"She shouldn't have been there in the first place, and if it hadn't been for you, none of this would have happened."

Her face got redder and redder the more she argued, and she waved the paper in front of my nose.

"What can I say?" I shrugged. "All I wanted was to

give her a chance to see a slice of life."

"Slice of life!" Sally shouted. "When my da heard about it he stormed over to see Father Doyle. He wants Sister FAH tee mah to be fired. He says that nuns shouldn't be hanging around labor goons."

"Goons?" I shot back. "It wasn't the strikers that beat people over the head. It was the cops. You think my da's a goon? And Brenda Delaney's?"

I was really steamed, and it must have showed, because Sally backed off.

"Of course not. I didn't mean to call your dad a goon. That's just the way my da talks."

"What did Father Doyle say?"

"I don't know. It's confusing, and Da wasn't very clear. Something about Leo the Thirteenth and the rights of the workers."

"The what?" I said. "I've never heard of that."

"Me neither," she said. "But Da was fit to be tied. You should have seen him." As she recalled the sight, she started to grin. The nice thing about Sally was that she never stayed mad very long. She lowered her voice an octave to mimic her father. "What's this world coming to? Even the popes are communists."

Sally and I both laughed. Her dad sounded like Mother when she came back from Father Stan after he'd questioned the everlasting fires of hell.

"But, Charlie, it really isn't funny," said Sally. "Sister FAH tee mah's in deep trouble. And it's all your fault. The bishop's called everybody over for a meeting this afternoon to figure out what to do about her."

"Your dad's going to meet with the bishop?" That impressed me.

What happened at that meeting with the bishop, I don't know, but there was no teacher standing by the front desk the next morning when we filed into the classroom. Since this could easily be a sign that Mrs. Hanratty was coming back, we speculated about that in very shaky voices. This possibility depressed us so much that we lapsed into total silence when we heard footsteps in the hallway coming toward the classroom door, fully expecting to see Mrs. Hanratty step through the opening. But it wasn't Mrs. Hanratty, because whoever was coming through the door wore a nun's habit. An instant later, when we saw that it was Sister FAH tee mah, we were so relieved that we all started clapping.

"You mustn't cheer," she said, raising her hand for silence. "The bishop is very mad at me. And if you want me to continue teaching here, you must be perfect pupils and not get me into any more trouble." She looked at me as she said that. But she had that twinkle in her eye that she gets when she's teasing, and I couldn't figure out what she was thinking. At lunch hour, she pulled me aside.

"You have caused me much trouble, Sharlie."

But she didn't seem angry about it.

"However, you also saved me from getting clubbed by that policeman, and I want to thank you for that."

The word "saved" came out in two syllables, "save ed." And I marveled that even after all this time at St. Matthew's, she still said my name wrong and often mispronounced words in the past tense. Instead of thinking about that, however, I should have admitted that I wasn't the one who had saved her from being clubbed by the cop. What had saved her was the cop's fear of being photographed while doing it.

But sometimes it's better not to admit to everything you know.

"Also," she said. "I must give this back to you." She pulled a quarter from some hidden pocket in her habit and held it out. "I never got a chance to use it."

"Oh, I don't need that," I said. "You can keep it, or give it to a charity."

"No. It's yours," she said as she reached out, lifted my hand, and put the quarter into my palm. "And there is one other thing."

"What's that," I asked, warily.

A huge smile came onto her face. "Thank you for showing me a slice of life."

The newspaper that afternoon contained a long letter from the bishop. He vowed to keep the nuns out of politics. However, they had as much right as any other citizen to get down on their knees and pray for peace. He could not sit by in silence while the police threatened his nuns and clubbed innocent women.

What happened next seemed unbelievable to me. The bishop's letter started a flood of criticism of the company, the police, and the National Guard. The strikers held up posters with the picture of Sister FAH tee mah looking like she was about to get clubbed by the fat-faced cop. I had never heard anyone criticize the police before, much less the National Guard. But people were upset that the women had been clubbed and tear gassed, and everyone thought this had happened to the two nuns as well. The union took advantage of the situation by offering to ask the workers to vacate the building if the company would stop using strike breakers. With all the bad publicity it was getting, the company had little choice but to agree. The strike would go on, but at least Mr. Jackson and the other scabs wouldn't be able to take the union's jobs. Dad and the other strikers marched out of the building in triumph. A huge crowd of friends and family members greeted them. Grandma and Grandpa O'Rourke and even Grandpa Parnell came down with us to see the event, and everybody except Grandpa Parnell sang "Solidarity Forever!" as the workers passed through the police barricades.

However, no picture of this showed up in the *Jeeptown Gazette*, and the strike continued. Our pile of coal in the basement kept getting smaller, but my cash box was still out of sight. How much longer could this go on?

CHAPTER 46

The strike was still in full force when I got the idea for the sock hop. The North End Dance Band kept practicing once a week. We practiced at Louis's house now, since he had the piano. After the good impression we had made performing at the bar mitzvah party, his parents did not seem to mind his once-a-week diversion from serious music. But we hadn't had a job since the bar mitzvah party, and we were getting demoralized. One day, I skimmed the newspaper while I waited for James and saw a picture of teen-age girls in oversized sweat socks dancing at a sock hop in California.

"I've got it!" I said.

"Got what?" said James as he continued folding his papers and putting them inside his paper sack.

"We don't have to wait for a job. We'll put on our own show. Let's put on a sock hop like they're doing in California."

I held up the picture for him to see. He stared longer than he should have at a girl whose skirt had swirled up to her thighs as she spun.

"That's an idea," he said, smiling. "Where would we

do it?"

"The union hall on Monroe Street," I said. "Dad's in good with the president right now, and we'll get him to give it to us for free."

Dad furrowed his eyebrows. "You're going to put on an integrated dance? Where white girls and Negro boys will dance together?" Since using a strong anti-bigotry stance as his excuse to resign from the Knights of Columbus, Dad had become careful to use the word Negro instead of some offensive words he would have used a few months earlier. I don't think he had really changed his racial opinions. He just didn't want to get caught using the same language he had said marked the Knights as bigots.

"This is not a good idea," he said. "Would you want your sister to have a colored boyfriend?"

Dad must never have realized how much I liked Clarice. Nevertheless, this was the question that hampered all discussions of integration. It was one thing to be for integration in principle. But would you want your sister to marry a Negro? If you said "Yes," you looked like a fool or at the very least like some inconsiderate slob who didn't care about his sister. If you said "No," you looked like a hypocrite. I wisely kept silent as Dad continued.

"I don't know, Charlie. I'd like to help out your band, especially after your work on the picket line and getting those nuns to come down to the plant. If it hadn't been for the reaction to that picture of your teacher getting clubbed, we'd still be holed up in that building, fighting off the scabs." I didn't interrupt him and remind him that it only looked like she was going to get clubbed.

"But I don't like the idea of white girls dancing with Negro boys."

"But only ones with white blood," I said quickly.

So what was Dad to do? He himself had made so many selective exceptions for Negroes with white blood that he could hardly criticize me for doing the same.

"I'll check with the union to see if you can use the hall. But you know what they're like, so don't expect too much from them."

Obviously, Dad hoped to get the best of both worlds. He would show support for my band while at the same time expect that the union president would let him off the hook by rejecting the idea outright. I steeled myself to the idea that we'd never get the union hall for our sock hop.

To everyone's astonishment, the union president agreed. "By all means, yes. The NAACP is always bitching about us. This might help us show a good side that will get them off our back. But I tell you, Parnell," Dad reported the union president saying, "Those black kids better not cause any trouble, or your ass will be in a sling."

Something about the way the union president said that got under my skin. The best things going on in my life at the moment came out of my friendship with James and Clarice. Why shouldn't they be allowed to walk around with their heads up and proud without being put down by the union president? Why shouldn't we be allowed to stage an integrated dance if that's what we wanted? How was that going to hurt anybody? Something had to change.

But the bottom line for my immediate concern was that we got the union hall from six to ten on the second Saturday in May.

"However," Dad said, "You'll have to make enough money to hire a janitor to clean up."

"No problem, Da. We'll keep the heat turned up, and everybody will get so thirsty we'll make a fortune selling soda pop."

There were other hurdles to clear as well. It seemed like the narrow-mindedness of the union president affected everybody. When Louis tried to sell tickets to the Jewish kids from the bar mitzvah, his mother got a complaint. "We're going to let our Jewish girls dance with those goys? I don't like that," Louis's mother was told.

But Louis remembered me telling him how I had turned the tables on Dad by using Dad's own crazy white blood theory. So he adapted it. "But they'll only be the bad Christians, Mom. We won't invite any good Christians."

James, Clarice, and I were appalled that Louis thought we were bad Christians, and he explained.

"I don't really mean that you aren't good Christians," he said. "It's just that when my mother thinks of good Christians, she doesn't think of you guys. She thinks of the Christians who wouldn't let my Uncle Moe, the dentist, into the country club. So for her, a bad Christian would be better than a good Christian."

This weird logic prepared Clarice for her mother's objection to the integrated sock hop and her remembrance of Clarice kissing me. "But Momma," Clarice said, "They won't be real white people. They'll be mostly Jews and Catholics."

Between the four of us, we refined this tactic to counter almost any objection. When Clarice's father complained, "A Negro should not sing with a white band," she shot back, "It's only half white. Besides,

Billie Holiday worked with white musicians."

When Father Stan heard the kids at St. Matthew's talking about the sock hop, he called me to the rectory. "I don't like this idea of Catholic kids dancing with Protestants. This could be as bad as a public school dance."

"But we won't invite any good Protestants," I replied. "We'll only invite the ones who might be open to conversion." He scrunched his eyes together in a look which said he was not impressed. Nevertheless, since the dance would take place at the union hall rather than St. Matthew's, he couldn't stop it.

The four of us sat in my living room to brainstorm. Mother prepared hot chocolate for us, even though the strike had caused our food supplies to run short. She was very nice to James and Clarice, almost as though she forgot what she had said about Clarice just a few months earlier. Then she ran off to St. Matthew's to start another novena for the safety of Danny in Korea. Clarice turned out to be an unexpected source of great ideas.

"We'll have prizes," she said. "A prize for the biggest socks. A prize for the ugliest socks. The best boy and girl matching socks."

"The smelliest socks," said Louis.

We all laughed and James asked, "Where we gonna get all these prizes?"

"Simple," I said. "We'll do just like my mother does with the Altar and Rosary Society. We'll get the North End Dime Store store to donate them."

"Why will they do that?"

"Good publicity. They're right in the neighborhood.

If they run a sock hop special, the money they make selling socks to all the kids will more than make up for what they'll give away in prizes."

The sock hop idea started to grow. Not only did the Dime Store donate socks for prizes, the North End Music Store donated some 45-rpm records that could be played while we were taking breaks and that we could raffle off. The North End Café even donated two free lunches.

The best sign that we had a success on our hands came when Carl Broda, the Hungarian, approached me. "Your band needs a saxophone." I still resented his having snubbed us last fall, but he was right about the sax. It would give us some spice. So, I brought him to a practice session at Louis's house. Louis's mother beamed with pleasure at all these new friends showing up for her son, even if we weren't Jewish.

However, adding a saxophone to the band made the music too complicated for us. I asked for advice from my music teacher, Mr. Kneusel, and he told me to bring everybody with me to my next music lesson. So the following Monday found the five of us riding in the elevator up to the Eighth Floor of the Fine Arts building. Clarice slunk to the back of the elevator when she saw that the operator wasn't going to close the brass gate, but James stood right up front and put his finger through the opening to see what it felt like to trace a line through the dust on the wall of the elevator shaft as we sped upward. In response, the operator stopped the elevator, closed the gate, and ordered us to move to the rear. As I stepped back, I could feel Clarice's breath on my neck, and the warmth of her body just inches from me. I pressed back a little closer.

Mr. Kneusel dug out some dance band

arrangements and took us to the big rehearsal hall. "I have to charge you for this sheet music," he said. "It is very expensive, and I cannot afford to just give it away."

He gave us tips on how to meld our instruments together and play differently when we were backing up the singer than when we played solo. "At that point, Charlie, you need to play softly," he said and told me to buy a special mute so that my trumpet wouldn't overpower Clarice's voice. "And James, do you have a pair of brushes for your drums?" James shook his head. "Try these," said Mr. Kneusel, handing him a set of brushes. "They'll help you smooth out the sound. You especially want to use them when Clarice is singing. Normally keep them at a forty-five degree angle. From there you can lower the angle when you want a smooth legato sound and raise it when you want a more staccato sound."

Then he recorded us as Clarice ran through her first song. "Oh, I sound terrible," she complained when Mr. Kneusel played back the song. She put her face in her hands and refused to look up. Never having heard her own voice before, she was shocked to hear it on tape, even though the rest of us told her she sounded great.

"You are actually very good," said Mr. Kneusel. "You've got a nice gospel quality in your voice that comes out great. But you're doing the song too upbeat. This is what we call a torch song, a song where the singer is pining for a lover she can't have. Do it again, and this time I want you to sing it as though you really mean it. Feel in your mind the same emotions you're singing about. Pretend there was some boy you couldn't have but whom you really wanted to put your arms around."

James, Louis, and Carl burst out laughing, and

Clarice buried her face in her hands again. But she stood up and followed his directions. She turned toward me, put a sad smile on her face as she looked me directly in the eye, and lifted her hands as though she was inviting me into her arms.

> Come to me my melancholy baby.
> Cuddle up and don't be blue.

Mr. Kneusel interrupted her, stood up and looked at her, then at me, then shifted his eyes back and forth.

"Oh my God! The two of you ARE the melancholy babies."

He paused while both Clarice and I looked down at the floor.

"Two great, gutsy kids, the salt of the earth. And you're playing with dynamite."

Then he looked her in the eye. "Are you sure that this is the song you want to sing?"

Decisively, she nodded yes.

I had never put as much energy into anything as I put into the sock hop. I had become the manager, setting up the prizes, getting the tickets printed, collecting free records to be raffled off, and keeping track of our expenses and ticket sales. I still missed the Wednesday night meetings with Clarice at the library. Despite rehearsing together and discussing business together, we no longer had the personal conversations that had meant so much to me in the fall. But it felt good to be in the same room with her, and everything else was moving along great. A dance. Colored and white. Christians and Jews. Protestants and Catholics.

The kids in the neighborhood all dancing together. And the North End Dance Band providing the music.

At the paper station one day, waiting for the paper truck to arrive, James and I stood watching a circle of boys playing marbles. I shuffled my feet nervously, not knowing quite how to bring up a delicate subject.

"James, we gotta talk about something difficult."

He looked suspicious. "What?"

"Well, most white kids and colored kids can get along okay. But what are we gonna do about the ones who can't?"

"Like who?"

"Well, you never know what Bernie Karolak and Billy Byrne are going to say. If they say it to the wrong guy, there could be a problem. And then there are the kids who are always looking for trouble. Butch Bower is like that, and so is Rafer Jones."

James rubbed his chin. "We'll get chaperones. I'll get my dad and the pastor. They're big enough and tough enough to keep the colored kids in line."

"Will they do that?"

"Course they'll do it. They don't want to see any fights that the colored kids will get blamed for. Who you gonna get?"

I got Father Stan, and Dad promised to get a union member who moonlighted as a bouncer.

I found it amusing that none of our five chaperones liked the idea of the integrated sock hop. But each had his own reasons for making sure everything stayed peaceful. Mr. Washington wanted to make sure that Clarice didn't flirt with any white boys, especially me. James's pastor did not want any fights to be blamed on the Negroes. Dad wanted to avoid any troubles that would put him on the bad side of the union president. Father Stan wanted to tone down any boy-girl contact, especially between Catholics and Protestants. And the bouncer just wanted to make an easy five dollars.

For decorations, we relied on the girls. Clarice set up a decorations committee, and I recruited Carmelita Morelli and Sally Quinn to help out. I marveled that the two Quinn sisters could be so different. Sally was open and friendly, while Roberta was snooty. Too bad Sally was not as pretty. I loved the whole business of finding people to do things and fitting everything together. I even got Bernie Karolak to borrow some sheet music from his father's band. "But just the normal songs, not the polkas."

"How about the 'Beer Barrel Polka?'"

I mulled it over. That one might work. "Okay, the 'Beer Barrel Polka.'"

"And I get to play my accordion."

"Only if you sell ten tickets."

"How many songs do I get to play?"

"The 'Beer Barrel Polka,' not the normal songs."

"Why not?"

James and Clarice would hit the ceiling if Bernie joined the band, and I didn't want any more people in on the profits, so I made up an excuse that was partly true. "We're having trouble putting all our instruments together, and one more right now would just make it too hard."

Bernie looked dejected.

"But you doing a solo of the 'Beer Barrel Polka' would add a lot of spice."

For some strange reason, that satisfied Bernie, and he didn't even demand to be paid for doing his solo.

To keep track of these assignments, I taped a big chart on my bedroom wall. Each time somebody completed a task, I used a pen to put a big check mark by that task.

I never remembered anything else in my life ever making me so excited. The only sad thing was the huge wall between Clarice and me. If the sock hop went well, maybe her parents would let me see her more often. And if that happened, I could work on converting her to be a Catholic. Except for the strike, everything was moving right.

Then we got the telegram.

CHAPTER 47

I lifted the black handset from its cradle and dialed Prospect 4 6501. If a man answered, I would hang up. But a cheery "Hello" came into my ear.

"I got to talk to somebody. Can you see me?"

"Charlie, you know I can't be seen alone with you. I shouldn't even be talking with you on the phone."

"I know, but this is an emergency."

"What kind of emergency?"

"I'll tell you when I see you."

"Just tell me what's going on."

"I've got to see you. I got to talk to someone."

She paused. "You don't sound very good."

"I'm not. I've gotta see you."

"Right now?"

"Yes, right now."

"Where? I can't go to the library. Somebody will see us there."

"You know where Oakwood Street splits in two and there's a little park in the middle."

"Yes."

"At the end of the park there's a weeping willow tree. Meet me under the branches, and no one will see you."

"Okay, but I can only stay for a few minutes."

When I hung up the phone and reached for my jacket, Mollie cried, "Take me with you, Charlie."

"No," I said.

"Yes," she screamed. "You can't leave me here."

I looked at her face all twisted in misery. "All right, but you've got to keep quiet. Get your coat."

Clarice got to the willow tree before we did, and when we climbed through the branches, she was sitting on the ground, wearing James's coat.

"This is my little sister, Mollie," I said.

Clarice gave Mollie a big smile. "I know Mollie," she said. "We played cards together, remember?"

Then she looked at me. "So why did you drag me out here to sit on the ground under some dumb tree?"

I swallowed hard. "I don't know how to say it. There was a telegram—Danny's dead."

Once the words were out, I lost control of myself. I bent over toward the ground and began to sob. So did Mollie. It seemed that this went on for a long time, and when I finally stopped crying, I was too ashamed to lift my eyes up from the ground.

"Oh, God. I'm so embarrassed," I mumbled.

"There's nothing to be embarrassed about," said Clarice. She reached out with both hands, putting one on Mollie's shoulder and one on mine.

"Why did he have to do it? Why did he join the Marines?"

"I don't know," she said. But I really didn't expect an answer.

"Why didn't he just stay home and finish school?"

"I don't know," she said again as she withdrew her hands.

Mollie and I rubbed our faces on our sleeves as the

three of us sat quietly under the tree branches. "Charlie," said Clarice. "You and Mollie got to talk with your Momma and Daddy."

"Mother shut herself in her bedroom. And Da went out. Probably for a drink." I spat out the word with more bitterness than I intended. "That's why I called you and why Mollie came. We just had to talk to somebody."

"I'm proud that you called me and that Mollie came." She looked down at Mollie and patted her head. "You got to talk to your parents." She put her hands in her lap, where she rubbed them together as though they were chilly. Mollie had cuddled up next to me, and the three of us sat staring at the ground. Then Clarice said, "Charlie?" I looked at her.

"I've got to go in a minute or I'll get in trouble. But there's one thing."

"What?"

"I'm ashamed to say it."

"What?"

"You won't drop the dance band and the sock hop, will you?"

"Oh, Clarice, I can't even think about that now." That was the most polite thing I could think of. What I really wanted to say was, "Fuck the sock hop! Why should I play for a bunch of kids who don't care about my brother?"

"I'm ashamed for asking it. It's gonna make me look selfish. But we need you."

"No, you don't. You've got a saxophone now. You can find another trumpet."

"It's too late to find another one. It's only a few weeks from now."

"Then just go ahead without me. We made it without

a sax, and you'll survive without a trumpet."

"It's not just your trumpet. It's you. You're the glue that holds us together."

"That's not true. We're partners."

"But you're the glue, Charlie. If you go, everything will fall apart. I won't have an excuse to see you anymore. Carmelita and Sally will go, and I'll lose two new friends I've just made. You know that Carl won't have the guts to play by himself with two colored kids and a Jew. We need you; don't you understand?"

"Clarice, I can't do that now. I can barely think."

"Charlie, think about what we're doing. Nobody's ever done it before in Jeeptown. We started something that gets colored kids and white kids together. We can't just let it die." She bit her lip the instant she said "die."

But I didn't say anything. I just sat there feeling torn apart as I stared at the ground.

"If you can't do it, I understand. And I can't blame you." Her voice was very soft now, and I had to strain to hear her. "But think about this. Danny would want it. He didn't quit in what he was doing, and he wouldn't want you to quit, either. Would he Mollie?"

My head snapped up. "Clarice, don't pull that shit on me."

Her head jerked back at my language, but she didn't rebuke me as she usually did if I swore. And after a pause she continued.

"I'm sorry, for saying that. But answer me. I can't stay any longer or my daddy's gonna find out and whoop me again. Please say you'll try."

I still didn't say anything.

"If you can't do it for our cause, can you do it just for me?"

"I'll try," I said. I barely got the words out.

"Oh, thank you, Charlie. I feel so bad for you and Mollie." She was on her feet now. "You shouldn't be alone. I want to stay and sit with you, but I can't."

"I know," I said. "We'll be okay. You'd better go. It helped us just to see you."

She bent over and kissed Mollie on the forehead. Then she took my face in her hands, looked me in my eyes, kissed me full on the lips, and let the kiss linger. I relished the touch of her lips and the smell of the perfume in her hair, but just as I started feeling good about that, the picture of Danny came into my mind and I felt worse than I'd ever felt in my life. How could I enjoy that with Danny now dead? I felt like I'd betrayed him. I pulled my head back, and she withdrew. Tears beaded in her eyes, and the eye whites were now streaked with red. She flashed Mollie and me a weak smile before she ducked through the tree branches and disappeared. I waited a few moments, then took Mollie by the hand and led her home. We passed four boys playing together. Two boys rode piggyback on two others who charged at each other, seeing which pair could knock over the other. The four tumbled to the ground amid a burst of laughter. I got angry at the laughter and swore at them under my breath.

When we got back home, Mother and Dad were in the living room, sitting at opposite ends of the sofa. Dad had turned back before reaching the North End Tavern. "I couldn't stand the thought of going inside with a bunch of strangers," he said. Mollie ran to Mother's lap, crying. "Mother, I feel so terrible."

"I know," said Mother as she stroked Mollie's hair.

"We all do."

Aunt Bridget knocked on the front door and came in without waiting for an answer. She brought in a casserole dish that she set on the dining room table. She led Mother to the table, and the rest of us followed. But we just picked at the food. Grandma O'Rourke came with celery and carrots and cherry tomatoes and a dip. Uncle Benny appeared with a platter. Uncle Jim lugged in a case of cola. Mother sent me to the kitchen to get some ice and glasses. I pulled the metal trays from the small freezer in the top of the refrigerator, tugged at the lever to loosen up the ice cubes, and dropped the cubes into a bowl, which I set out for the Coke drinkers. Grandma Parnell brought soda bread and a big bowl of Irish mashed potatoes with cabbage leaves mixed in. Soon the living room was filled with relatives speaking in hushed tones and snacking at the huge potluck of food that they had placed on the dining room table. Dad got a case of Buckeye Beer from the garage and set it out for the company, but he didn't drink any himself. Eventually they all left, and the house became emptier than I could ever remember.

I was absolutely unprepared for the impact Danny's death would have on us. I missed a couple days of school, and after Sister FAH tee mah read Mother's note explaining my absence, she pulled me aside.

"I will say prayers for your brother," she said. "But are you all right?"

"I don't know," I said. "My mother's all torn up. She feels guilty because she never finished the nine first Fridays she was offering up for Danny. And she just mopes around."

Sister waited in silence for a moment before replying. "Tell her not to worry about that. God is merciful, and he will give Danny his reward in heaven. Especially since his sacrifice came at the hands of the godless communists."

Mother lost interest in all the things she had loved so much before. She dropped out of the block rosary, stopped doing her novenas, and did not do any more stations of the cross. She went to the Holy Thursday services, but they gave her no comfort. She started crying halfway through, and we led her out as Father Doyle walked up the center aisle swinging the silver container that clinked against its chain and spread the smell of incense throughout the church. She barely got the Easter baskets out for Easter, and I had to take over the job of helping Mollie color the Easter eggs.

After a week of this, Mother was suddenly overpowered by a need to keep busy. She scrubbed the kitchen floor, washed windows inside and out, and hung the rugs out on the clothesline so she could pound the dust out of them with the rug beater.

I took a break from the North End Dance Band. It was so hard to concentrate that my schoolwork was turning shoddy. I had no idea how I would be able to keep my promise to Clarice. I went for a long bicycle ride to the park on the South Side, where I sat for a long time on the top of the hill overlooking the river. A sailboat tilted far over to its side as it turned to avoid a pile of debris in the water. And watching it reminded me of the day last fall when Danny was here with me and telling me, "Whoever told you it was fresh water never saw all the crap flowing down this river." It was nice to remember a pleasant thought about Danny. That was what I liked about sitting up on the hill overlooking the river. It helped me think pleasant thoughts.

But the river's magic didn't last long. As I came back Detroit Avenue from the park, I stopped at the bottom of the dip where the street passes under the railroad yards, and I looked at the huge, dirty, old concrete bridge holding up the railroad tracks above my head. I let the bike drop to the cracked sidewalk and stared at the ugly concrete structure. How could something this ugly still be standing while Danny was dead? I picked up some rocks and one at a time hurled them as hard as I could at the massive bridge. "God damn you! God damn you! God damn you!" I screamed.

CHAPTER 48

What brought me back to my senses, as much as anything, was getting knocked to the ground by Billy Byrne. Of course, if I'd stayed home that night, it wouldn't have happened, but I went out walking around because evenings at home had become unbearable. Mother kept up a whirlwind of activity that helped keep her mind off Danny, and Dad just moped. He gave up the union and the strike, which up till then had kept him so busy. The union president said he understood. He praised Dad's work as a union steward said Dad could have that job back any time he wanted. To make Mother happy, he stopped hanging around the VFW. And resigning from the Knights of Columbus took another activity away from him. The strike only made things worse, because he had no job to occupy him during the day. He didn't even read his World War II books anymore. He just sat out in the garage reading my collection of old Hardy Boys books.

He no longer stashed cases of Buckeye Beer in the garage, however. One afternoon, I went looking for a pliers in the garage and spied an empty pint wine bottle hidden at the bottom of his toolbox.

Why would Da hide an empty wine bottle? As I sat down on his sofa to unscrew the pieces of a bicycle axle, I landed on a hard lump. Three empty wine bottles were tucked under the cushion. I got up and went to the old dresser that served as a storage chest. In the bottom drawer I found a collection of empty wine bottles, lined up neatly, one after another, just like the crosses in a soldiers' cemetery.

This was puzzling. Why would Da drink so much wine when he always drank beer? Why did he keep the empty bottles? Why did he hide them? Why did he line them up so neat and orderly in the drawer? Why not just dump them in the trash? I had no idea what it all meant, but it didn't look good. And I knew enough not to tell Mother.

Mollie's birthday came during this period, and Mother put on a party that relieved the tension for a while. Grandma Parnell came over early in the day to put a roast beef in the oven. Mother baked a chocolate cake, placed six yellow candles on top, and put it on top of the china cabinet to sit until suppertime. Everyone tried to get along. Grandpas Parnell and O'Rourke didn't argue about the union or the strike, and Mother didn't mention Danny. Mollie bounced up and down in her chair in glee. She got some dolls and other toys for presents. She blew out the six candles in one breath.

"What'd you wish for?" I asked.

"Don't tell him!" cautioned Grandma O'Rourke. "If you tell anyone, you won't get your wish."

The roast beef and cake were delicious, but Dad barely picked at his food.

"The least you can do is eat that delicious roast your

mother made," said Mother.

"I'm just not hungry," said Dad.

That night, I woke up at 4:00 a.m. at the sound of his walking around the house and opening doors. He was still awake when I got up to go to school.

"I had insomnia," he said, his breath smelling of wine.

When I got home from school that afternoon, he was fast asleep on the living room sofa. I dropped my books on the kitchen table and slammed the cupboard door a little too loud as I took out a glass.

"Quiet down out there," Dad roared from the sofa. "I'm trying to take a nap."

The days and nights were like that. We all tiptoed on eggshells so we wouldn't set Dad off, and in the evenings I had a powerful urge to escape the house. Like Dad, however, I had no place to go. I had quit the Boy Scouts. Clarice no longer came to the library. The art museum was closed evenings. Lent was over, so there were no evening programs at the church. My homework took little time, because I just went through the motions of doing it. If I didn't immediately know the answer to a math question, I would just write down whatever came to mind. Except for Tuesday night with Milton Berle at Aunt Bridget's house, I had nothing to do in the evenings.

So I took to wandering the streets. And on a Monday night, I found Billy Byrne also wandering the streets.

"What are you doing out here?" I said. "How come you're not at the Boy Scout meeting?"

"I quit that chickenshit troop. It's just a bunch of little kids now."

I was stunned. "That pervert is at it again," I said without thinking. This was the closest I had ever come to telling any of the kids what Mr. Jackson had done with me, and it scared me a little that I had let the cat out of the bag.

Without warning, Billy pushed me in the chest and punched me in the jaw. My heel caught on a crack in the sidewalk as I fell back from the assault, and I went sprawling on the ground. He towered over me, his fists clenched in rage.

"Who are you calling a pervert? Nobody calls me a pervert and gets away with it."

I looked up. Billy didn't understand.

"Bill, nobody thinks you're a pervert. I know you're not."

"Why'd you call me one?"

"It's not you. It's Mr. Jackson."

"I'm no pervert, you creep. Keep your mouth shut." He kicked me in the side and went stomping off. I waited for the pain in my side to go away and then boosted myself to a sitting position. All I wanted was to do something about Mr. Jackson. But Billy didn't understand.

"Why is that kid so stupid?"

Billy's reaction to Mr. Jackson seemed stronger than Tony Morelli's or mine. Other than quitting the Scouts, Tony didn't seem bothered by it, at least as far as I could tell. Billy, on the other hand, seemed to think that he was the one who was the pervert. The more I thought about it, the more the details of that moment in Mr. Jackson's sleeping bag came back to me and the madder I got. Not only did he humiliate me and cheat me out of the chance to be an Eagle Scout, but now he'd pulled Billy Byrnes into his web. And probably the rest of the scouts as well. I'd bet a hundred dollars that he was still getting them to jack him off, and, from the pictures I'd seen probably, give him blow jobs. Nothing I'd done to stop him had worked. Danny would never have let him get away with all this.

CHAPTER 49

B efore I could do something about Mr. Jackson, however, I had to do something about Mollie. The excitement of her birthday party didn't last long. With Mother throwing herself into a frenzy of activity, Dad drinking wine in the garage, and me wandering the streets each night, Mollie was being ignored. I could see it the minute I got back home from getting knocked down by Billy. She sat on the living room floor as she moved her dolls back and forth in silence. With Mother and Dad so withdrawn, she wasn't even getting to sleep on time. At 9:30 I led her upstairs and helped her get ready for bed.

The next day, after completing my paper route, I took her to The Norwood Drugstore for a cherry Coke. We ran into James who discussed the upcoming sock hop with me while Mollie sipped her drink.

One day I put her sidesaddle on the bar of my bicycle and rode her to the art museum. We looked at the four-hundred-year-old Swiss family room. It had been one of my favorite exhibits when I was little. We sat in the quiet on a nearby bench and stared at the little room with its woodcarvings and the dummies dressed up like sixteenth century people at peace with the world. I read from the placard to tell her the story of the room, but she didn't listen. It seemed to be enough for her just to be getting some attention.

We went to the Lucretia Mott Branch Public Library for the Saturday morning story hour, and she got to pick out some storybooks. Each evening I read her a different story. I promised to take her to a movie on Sunday if she went to bed by 8:30 each night. "Bambi's back in town," I said.

My efforts worked. By week's end, Mollie began showing more life. She went out to ride her scooter on the sidewalk. And she went across the street to jump rope with the Fontenell sisters.

Near the end of April, the strike finally ended, and Dad went back to work. Since the union held out for back pay for the time on strike, he got an enormous back pay envelope. He celebrated by taking us all out to supper at the North End Café. True to his word, he bought a television set. Nobody said anything about the money Mother and Dad had borrowed from my savings account. But I didn't mind. My lost $200 was a small price to pay, especially if the family could get better again.

My seething anguish over Mr. Jackson, however, just got worse. Seeing Billy's reaction had opened up my old grievance. But I didn't know what more to do about him. If I kept breaking into his apartment and soaping his car windows, I was sure to get caught eventually. Of course, when that happened, everyone would want to know why I did those things. Everyone would find out what I'd done with him, and the guys would be calling me a queer forever. They would never stop teasing me. And I dreaded what Clarice would think.

I needed someone to talk to, someone who could help me think about what I might do without me having to tell exactly what happened. So on a Thursday afternoon I stayed after school to see Sister FAH tee mah. It was one of those beautiful April days when the sun is so warm you take off your sweater and sit in your shirtsleeves. Narrow shafts of sunlight came into the classroom through the windows and little threads of dust floated in the sunbeams.

"Sister, what do you do when somebody has done something really bad?"

"Sharlie, I told you once before, you must forget about getting even. You have enough to worry about without getting back at Butch Bower."

"It's not Butch, Sister. It's somebody else. An adult. Somebody you don't know."

"It doesn't matter who it is. Vengeance poisons the soul. Whatever he did to you, you must overcome it and move on with your life."

"But he's still doing it. And if I don't stop him, he'll do it to everyone."

"Sharlie, I don't even know what you are talking about. It is not our place to judge everything that happens. That is God's place."

"But Sister, it's bad!"

"Is it a crime?"

"I don't know. But if it's not, it should be."

"Then you must tell the police."

Tell the police? I stood in front of her astonished for a second. Two weeks ago, the police had almost split her skull open, and now she wanted me to march downtown and tell them about what Mr. Jackson had done with me.

"I can't do that, Sister."

"Well, you must make up your mind, Sharlie. If you know a crime is about to be committed, you have a responsibility to tell the police so they can stop it. But if all you have is an old grudge against this person, then you must ask Our Lady of Fatima to help you forget it."

I left and delivered my papers. Then I sat on the front porch pondering my situation as I waited for Mother to make supper. While I sat there, Grandpa Parnell came over in his big red Pontiac, and as he drove up, a loud rattle came from the right front wheel. I could hear it half a block away.

"What's that noise, Grandpa?"

"Damned if I know," said Grandpa. "Something's banging around in the hubcap. Run inside and get me a big screwdriver, Charlie."

I came back with the biggest screwdriver in Dad's toolbox, and Grandpa Parnell used it to pry off the hubcap. Inside, one of the lug nuts had come off, and its banging against the hubcap was what had made all the noise. This gave me a brilliant idea. There's more than one way to send a message.

CHAPTER 50

Luckily, most of the planning for the sock hop had been finished by the time we heard the news about Danny. I had given out various jobs to Clarice, James, Louis, Carl, Sally and Carmelita. Interest continued to build, and kids were still asking for more tickets. One afternoon, about a month after Danny's death, I took my trumpet to Louis's house to see what the band rehearsals were like. Once we started playing, I realized I should have come back earlier. The rehearsals became a big help. They required so much concentration that they distracted my mind from Danny and the family. Sometimes I felt guilty about that, as though I was somehow betraying Danny by doing something I enjoyed. But it helped me understand Mother, who also had a powerful need to keep busy. And I really wanted the sock hop to succeed.

It was raining the night before the sock hop as James and I went to make a final check of the dance floor at the union hall on Monroe Street. The stands for the sheet music were set up around the piano, which Louis had come over and tuned himself. We didn't want to eat into our profits by hiring a real piano tuner. The girls had hung purple and red and green streamers of crepe paper through the banquet room that served as the dance floor. The table next to the musical instruments held a phonograph and the stack of 45-rpm records that had been donated by the North End Music Store. We planned to raffle off the records when we took breaks between sets. We would play half a minute of the record, then have Sheila Quinn or Carmelita Morelli pick the winning ticket from a big bowl. We had sold more than a hundred tickets, and we hoped for more sales at the door. James pranced back and forth with the excitement and nervous energy of a football player just before the championship game. "Let's get a Coke to take with us," James said as he guided me toward the soda pop machine.

I put my hand into my pocket for a coin. When I pulled it out, several glass marbles fell to the floor. Big marbles. Boulders. Not just small marbles. But boulders. I scampered after them.

"What'ya got all those marbles for," he asked.

"Nothing," I said, feeling a little self-conscious. "Just something I've got to do tonight."

"Tonight? You're supposed to come over to my house so we can finish the planning."

Clarice and the girls on the social committee were going to be there for one last check of the program for the next evening. I marveled that Sally and Carmelita would be there. To get them to come, I had had to agree to walk each of them home after the meeting, since it would be dark by that time, and they were anxious about walking alone in a colored neighborhood. Even so, it would have been unthinkable six months earlier that the two white girls from St. Matthew's would go into a colored neighborhood to spend an hour at a

Negro's house.

"I'll be there," I said. "It's just that I have to run an errand first."

"I'll go with you," said James. "Then we can go over to my house together. I don't want to be stuck by myself with a bunch of girls."

"No. I need to do this myself."

James squinted at me with suspicion. "What's going on, Charlie? There's something strange going on. You got to do something with marbles? That doesn't make any sense."

I looked at him pleadingly. "If I tell you, can you keep it a secret?"

"Sure."

I stared at him for a second without saying anything, and then pulled out two chairs so we could sit down. We sat facing each other, but backward in the chairs, so that our forearms were resting on the backs of the chairs. "There's somebody who's been doing some very nasty things. I've got to stop him, and I got to get even with him."

"Bad idea, Charlie. Getting even with people is only going to bring trouble on your head. That's what my pastor says."

"Don't be so holy, holy, James. You gonna tell me you never wanted to get even with Old Schmidt for some of the nasty things he's done?"

"So, it's Old Schmidt."

"No. It's somebody else."

"What'd he do?"

"I can't tell you. Just believe me. It's nasty."

"What are the marbles for?"

I grinned for the first time. "These go into the hubcap of his car. It'll make such a racket that he'll have to stop to see what's there, and when he takes off the hubcap he'll see this note." I pulled a folded piece of paper from my pocket, holding it out of James's reach.

"Let me see it."

"No."

James slowly lifted his hands palms up, as if to say okay. And just when I relaxed, he shot his right hand out with the speed of a cat and snatched the paper from me. He spread it open, shielding it with his arms as I reached out to grab it back. There he saw in block letters cut out from newspaper headlines, "Quit the Scouts or this won't stop, and I'll tell the police what you're doing."

James handed the paper back to me. "Man! The scoutmaster. He must have done something pretty bad, Charlie. What'd he do?"

"None of your business. Someday I'll tell you. But right now, I can't. Just believe me that what he's doing is nasty."

James said nothing. He just sat there looking at me like I was a stranger he was seeing for the first time.

I said, "James, you got to keep this to yourself. You can't tell anyone. Do you understand? Nobody."

"It's our secret, Charlie. Whatever it is. I don't have the foggiest idea of what's going on with you. But don't worry. My lips are sealed." He drew his index finger across his lips as though he were zipping them shut.

"Then head home," I said, "and I'll be right over as soon as my errand is done."

"Nope. Someone needs to keep an eye on you. I'll just tag along."

"Suit yourself," I said. "It's a free country. You can walk wherever you want. Just keep this to yourself."

CHAPTER 51

The soda pop machine on the back wall made clunking noises as it pushed out two green Coke bottles, one after another.

Leaving the union hall, we locked the door behind us. It was the second Friday in May and the earth was springing back to life from the long winter. The buds on the maple trees had turned into leaves, and they glowed in the light of the streetlamps. The air had a warm, wet smell from the rain, which had stopped. We tossed our empty Coke bottles behind a bush and unzipped our jackets as we began walking to Mr. Jackson's apartment.

Sure enough, he'd parked his red Ford convertible in front of the duplex just as I knew he would. I had cased it on Friday nights and knew that Mr. Jackson never drove off before 8:30 pm. Looking around to make sure the coast was clear, I scurried to the left front wheel and used my screwdriver to pry the hubcap loose, just as Grandpa Parnell had done with his car. The marbles clanked as I dropped them into the hubcap. I dropped in the note, put the hubcap over the axle hub and tried to pound it into place with the palm of my hand as I had seen Grandpa Parnell do. However, the hubcap refused to snap into place. I hit it again as hard as I could, and the sting of the blow ran through my hand and up to my wrist. But the hubcap still failed to snap into place.

"Damn! That stings."

"Let me try," said James. He stooped down, used his left hand to position the hubcap and slammed it hard with his right hand. The hubcap sealed itself into place with a snap.

"Damn, that stings," he said, shaking his hand.

"That's what I just told you," I grinned. I stood up, took a bar of white soap from my pocket and wrote "Pervert" on the driver's window. I had just started writing it on the windshield when James grabbed my arm. "There's a car coming."

"Quick, behind the hedge."

We ducked into the crevice between the hedge and the embankment. "Oh, Jesus! It's a cop."

We huddled behind the hedge as the patrol car drew close. The driver turned on his search light and swept it along the sidewalk. We ducked lower. The beam swept over the bushes and then back to the convertible where it came to rest on the driver's window. The officer got out of his patrol car to inspect the convertible. It was the cop with the fat face and mean eyes, the one who had pushed me around and told me to stay with my own kind. He could see nothing wrong with the car other than the word "Pervert" on the driver's window. However, that was enough to make any cop suspicious. He walked toward the house as if to find out who owned the car and why "Pervert" was written on the window.

The bushes kept us hidden until the cop reached the top step of the stairs going up the embankment.

Precisely at that moment, James said, "Run!"

He tore out of our hiding spot and shot down the sidewalk. I had no choice but to follow, but because of my limp, I couldn't keep up with him. Our sudden movement startled the cop and he shouted at us, "Stop! Or I'll shoot!"

"James, stop!" I shouted.

But James kept running. Aiming to get out of sight by running between two houses into the alley, James sped up the embankment. He reached the top of the hill just as I heard a firecracker pop behind me. Later, at the inquest, the police officer would claim he thought James was the armed burglar who had just hit the North End Café. That he had only fired a warning shot above James's head. And that the only reason James was hit was because he had run up the incline just at that very moment. If James had only stayed on level ground, he never would have been shot said the report from the inquest that cleared the cop.

I watched in horror as James was pitched forward by the big .38 caliber slug that hit him square in the back. He was lying face down in the wet grass and mud when I reached him. He called out as loud as he could, but it came out as a whisper. "Help me, Charlie." Wrapping my arms around his shoulders, I tried to sit him up. But as I moved him, a dark puddle of blood spilled out on his chest, and behind me I heard, "Stop! Or I'll shoot again." Looking over my shoulder, the policeman was barely thirty yards away, pointing his gun directly at James and me.

I panicked and ran as quickly as possible toward a bush to block me from the policeman's aim. Once more, the cop shouted "Stop!" But no bullets came, and I sped as fast as I could between two houses into a backyard and then into the alley between Fernwood and Pinewood. I had never run that fast in my life.

I ran down the alley toward the cross street and checked to see if anybody could spot me. It seemed that every door in the neighborhood opened up and every porch light came on. But nobody looked in my direction, fortunately. All the eyes turned toward the flashing police lights on Fernwood Street. I went through the cross street unspotted and continued up the alley. It seemed that a million sirens were going off. I had never heard so many sirens. I slowed to a walk and kept to the alleys. Blood was splattered on the front of the red and gray letter jacket of Danny that I was wearing. At the sight of it, I sank to the ground and sat down on the wet cinder surface of the alley. "Oh God! Oh God!" was all I could say. I could not even weep. I had just deserted my best friend.

After a few moments I looked at Danny's jacket once again. It was too bloody to be saved. I took it off and held it in my left hand while I limped down the alley until I found a half-full garbage can. I dug out several old newspapers, wrapped the jacket in the papers, then tucked it into the middle of the trash where it couldn't be spotted. Then, sticking to the alleys and cross streets, I slowly limped home through the drizzle.

CHAPTER 52

More than a year passed before I met Clarice again. One afternoon in August, out of the blue, the telephone rang in our new house out in the suburbs. My pulse quickened when I heard her voice.

"Charlie, we have to talk."

"Where?"

"The art museum."

I washed my hair so it would be neat and checked to make certain my fingernails were clean. I brushed my teeth and swirled some of Mother's mouthwash around my teeth. Then I put on a clean, white, freshly ironed polo shirt and rode my bicycle all the way in Monroe Street from the suburbs. I stayed in the shade as much as possible and pedaled slowly so I wouldn't be drenched with sweat when she saw me.

She waited for me inside the huge front doors. She was shorter than me now. I had grown over the previous year, while she had stayed the same height. She wore a pair of blue jean cut-offs and a bright colored pullover, sleeveless knit blouse, but she had a somber look on her face. She looked older than I remembered, as we turned right and ambled toward the Impressionist gallery.

"Did you make the band?" she asked.

"Yeah. The band director wasn't sure at first. He didn't think I'd be able to march because of my limp. But he had to give me a chance, cause I was his best trumpet player. Nobody else can play above high C." I smiled as I thought about that victory. I was babbling, just throwing out thoughts until I found one that would draw a response.

"We had to cancel the sock hop," I said.

"I know," she replied.

"I had to refund all the money. It cost me a fortune."

Abruptly, she stopped walking, stood absolutely still, and snapped at me, "You lost a fortune? I lose my brother and all you can think about is a little bit of money?"

"Oh, I am sorry," I said. "I am so sorry, Clarice. That's not at all what I meant. It was terrible of me to say it that way."

Her eyes narrowed into little slits as she stared at me.

"I did go to the funeral."

"I know." Her voice softened, and she made a stab at a smile, but didn't quite make it. "You and Louis were the only white people there."

We sat on the wooden bench in front of the Renoir, both of us facing the picture on the wall. After a pause she continued.

"You were brave to come. If our positions had been reversed, I don't know if I could have done that." She sounded like she was trying hard to sound like an adult rather than a teen-ager. "I admired you for having the guts to come to the funeral. But at the time I hated you."

That stung. But the truth was I hated myself as well. I couldn't have saved James, but why had I led him there? Why had I run away?

"Charlie, my brother was dead." Her voice quickened, and she turned her face toward me. "You ran away from him while he died. You were his best friend, and you let him die all by himself." I could see tears start to well up in her eyes.

"I'm sorry, Clarice," I finally said. "I tried to call you to say I was sorry. But you just kept hanging up on me."

"Oh, Charlie. It hurt so bad. I just couldn't talk to you. When does it stop hurting? How long did it take after your brother died?"

My shoulders tensed. "I don't know. Maybe it never stops."

We sat quiet again for several moments, staring together at the women and children crossing the street in Renoir's painting. I had never felt this awkward with Clarice before. I never had to grope for things to say. And now I was tongue tied.

"There's something I gotta know," she said. "That's why I called you. It's bothered me all year, and I've got to know."

"What?"

"Why were you and James out there that night?"

My pulse shot up. "Don't ask me that."

"Charlie, you've got to tell me. Because none of it makes any sense. The police said a second boy disappeared. A white boy. You're the only one that could have been. One minute you and James are checking out things at the dance hall. The next minute James is shot dead several blocks out of the way. And you've disappeared. You gotta tell me what happened."

"Why do you have to know? You're better off not knowing."

"I have a right to know!" She snapped her arms down. "My brother's dead, and I want to know why." Her eyes gave me a piercing look that said she wasn't going to give up until she heard what she wanted. She added, "Whatever it was, I'm not gonna tell anybody. I'm not gonna call the police and tell them you were the second boy. If we wanted to do that, we would have done it a year ago. Everyone knew it was you. There was nobody else it could have been. I just need to know what happened. And you're the only one who can tell me."

"You're better off not knowing, Clarice. You're just gonna hate me all over again."

"If that's what you think, then what you're really thinking is that you're the one who'll be better off. Tell me, Charlie. What happened that night?"

"I didn't want him to come with me," I said. "I told him to go home and I would come over later, but he wouldn't do that. Then when the cop told us to stop, I shouted at James to stop, but he just kept running. You've gotta believe me. I tried to stop him."

"I believe you. But why did you and James go there in the first place?"

I looked down and mumbled. "I was getting even with the scoutmaster." I lifted my chin and looked her in the eye. "I wrote stuff on his car window. I put a bunch of marbles in his hubcap to make a lot of noise so everybody would see the writing on the window and he'd have to stop and read the note I put in with the marbles. James helped me snap the hubcap back on."

She shot her arms into the air. "Charlie, this sounds crazy. You were mad at the scoutmaster, so you put marbles and a note in the hubcap? And because of that my brother gets killed? It doesn't make sense. It doesn't make any sense at all. What did you have against the scoutmaster?"

We stared at each other's eyes, and I said coldly. "You don't need to know that. I told you what you wanted to know. And that's all there is."

"No. That's not all there is. My brother's dead, and you can't just tell me that's all there is. What did you have against the scoutmaster that would get you and James to do such an awful thing?"

"Clarice, don't ask me that."

"Whatever you had against him is the reason my brother died. You owe it to me to tell me that."

I gazed at the marble floor again. Half of me wanted to tell her, to tell somebody, to tell anybody. It would be like the relief you get after you prick a boil and all the pus is finally gone. But if I told her, the pus wouldn't really go away. It would be stuck in her mind just as it was stuck in mine. And she'd know what I'd done with the scoutmaster in the sleeping bag. I turned my head to look at her.

"I can't tell you that. There are some things I just can't tell you."

She didn't know what to say, but she wasn't ready to give it up. "What about James? What'd he have against the scoutmaster?"

"Nothing. James had nothing to do with it. He just came along to keep me company, because he didn't want to go home and be the only boy in a roomful of girls."

"Why? Why did you do it? What could the scoutmaster have done that you had to get even?" Her voice got louder and her eyes flashed with more anger than I had ever seen. The guard by the door looked over at us.

"Clarice," I said so softly that she had to bend toward me and strain to hear. I looked at her, my hands resting on my knees, my body bent sideways as I leaned toward her on the bench. "I know you've got a right to know. But I just can't tell you right now. Maybe some day. But not right now."

She looked as though she finally understood that I was not going to tell her. Maybe she was not certain any longer that she really wanted to find out what the scoutmaster had done, because her eyes lost their intense, angry glare. And her head shook slightly back and forth as though she were trying to guess what had happened.

"I hated him, Clarice. I hated him. I've never hated anybody before. But I hated him so much I just had to get even. I did everything I could think of to get even." My eyes drifted down to the marble floor again. "And none of it worked. The only thing I accomplished was I got James killed—and you hate me." I looked up at her again and could see a teardrop come out of her eye and slide down her cheek.

We were alone in the room now, sitting on the wooden bench in front of the Renoir. The guard had gone off to a different room, and all the other people had left. I saw another tear fall out of her eye. Her shoulders quivered, then began to shake as she started sobbing and fell against me. Automatically, my arms went around her shoulders, and she clutched me in return. I could feel her tears against my cheek, and her hair had the same smell of perfume I remembered from the night we kissed at the library. Tears began to well in my own eyes. After a moment, she pulled back.

"What the scoutmaster did was really bad, Clarice. But please don't ask me what it was. It's so hard for me knowing that I let James get into it. If I had just let things alone, James would still be alive. And I feel like a coward for running away while he died. That's what's so hard for me."

We were quiet for a moment.

"Do you despise me?"

"No."

"Do you hate me?"

"I don't know anymore, Charlie. I just don't know. My brother died because of you. You didn't mean for that to happen. But he's dead all the same, and I still don't understand what was going on with you. Why didn't you just listen to the Bible? The Bible would have told you not to do something so stupid."

There was nothing more to say, and we both sat quietly gazing at the picture until she said, "I should go now."

"I know we can never see each other again like we did before? But can we be friends."

"No."

"So you do hate me."

"You're the best friend I ever had, but everything changed for me that night. Everything changed when my brother was killed by a white policeman for no good reason. It's hard for me to be around white people right now. Can't you understand that?"

Oh, God. We'd tried to bring the Black kids and white kids together. And maybe things were as bad as ever. I directed her glance at the Renoir and said, "You know what I always liked about that picture?"

"Why you changing the subject? My brother's dead, and you're talking about a picture. You're just trying to keep me here."

"The colors all flow into each other. The yellows and the greens and all the other colors. There's no border between them. They all just mingle together."

She shifted her eyes from the painting to me, then back to the painting where they rested for a moment.

"No, they don't. The whites are on one side and the darks on the other."

"That's only at the edges. Everyplace else, everything mingles. Like everything's just different shades of one great big color."

"No. The yellows and greens are just one great big wall. It keeps the whites and darks apart."

"That's not true. The yellows and greens are a bridge, bringing everything together. Like our band was a bridge."

"The band is over." She raised her voice, made fists, and snapped her arms down again. "The band is dead, and that white cop killed it. Right now, I can't be around you. Makes no difference if it's a bridge or a wall. I just can't be around you. Let me go. Let me go before I put my arms around you again. That felt so good, Charlie. But it's over. Can't you see that. It's over. Just let me walk out of here alone."

She turned and marched out of the gallery, her brown legs stepping swiftly, her sandals slapping on the floor, and her hips swaying in the cut-offs as she left.

I felt like I'd been kicked in the stomach, and I deserved it. But I also felt like I'd gotten something off my chest. Even though I couldn't tell her about being in the sleeping bag with the scoutmaster, at least I'd let her know why James and I were out there and what had happened once that cop showed up.

Maybe I'd never see her again, but nobody could take away the fact that she'd given me the best year of my life. And someday she would get around to forgiving me. She'd remember how great she'd felt singing at the bar mitzvah, and she'd know that she'd gotten some good things from me as well.

I took one last glance at Renoir's picture as I stood up. The yellows and greens really were a bridge, not a wall. And so was our band. With that, I turned, pushed back my shoulders, and stepped toward the exit.

EPILOGUE: AS TOLD BY CLARICE

Well, that was Charlie's story, and I can see why he couldn't tell me about the scoutmaster. If our roles had been reversed, I wouldn't have told him either.

As he had predicted, it did indeed turn out to be a long story, especially as Mollie and I repeatedly peppered him with questions or clarifications about this point or that point. At dinnertime, Mollie phoned out for pizza. We spent the evening sitting around her living room sipping more wine, reminiscing about the past, and bringing ourselves up to date on what had happened to all the people in his story. This was one of the best parts of the night, because I found out a lot of things about these people that I hadn't known. On two occasions, Mollie made phone calls to friends to find out something about somebody. The wine ran out and at midnight Mollie put on a pot of coffee. When I finally walked out to my car to head home, I felt at peace with Charlie in a way I never had before. The last thing I remember was his tall, lithe form limping out to the porch to wave goodbye as I put my car into gear and pulled away from the curb.

The night had made me nostalgic, so instead of going straight home, I drove through the old neighborhood. Charlie was right; it really was a different world now. The Spark Plug Factory closed a long time ago, but its big empty building hulks over the neighborhood. The Lucretia Mott Branch Public Library still exists, but not in the majestic old building where Charlie and I shared a kiss. That was replaced by a new, antiseptic structure. Many of the streets were torn out to make room for the Interstate Highway, and one of the few things left intact is the art museum. However, even it has a new wing built of big gray, oddly placed concrete blocks that jar the vision (or enhance it, say the artie types).

Dorr Street was the worst. Everything of human scale got ripped out. The paper station where Charlie and James had become friends. The grocery store around the corner. The North End Tavern across from the library. The barber shop where James got his hair cut and the other barber shop where Charlie got his hair cut. The North End Dime Store. The World Theater where we took Louis and the North End Café where we went for treats afterward. The North End Music Store that gave us free records for the sock hop. And all the mom-and-pop stores that had put so much life on the busy street. They're gone now.

In their place is a five-lane highway that speeds you through the ghetto at 40 miles per hour. It was like a nasty joke by an urban planner in a bad mood.

And, of course, the people we knew all changed too, or went away.

Bernie Karolak went on to organize the most

successful Polka band in the history of Jeeptown. With his stronghold of fans, he won election and repeated re-election to the State Senate where he worked his way up to Majority leader, a position he held for more than a decade. He used his influence to send a goodly share of state spending to his district in Jeeptown. Although I never liked Bernie very much, I had to give him credit for helping out so many of my social work clients.

Butch Bower earned a handsome livelihood as a hatchet man who helped local companies save millions of dollars by outsourcing key functions and firing hundreds of workers. Butch bought himself a mansion on River Road where he would not have to look at all the shiftless people in the Old North End who, he said, lacked the initiative to get a job.

Roberta Quinn became a cheerleader, like her big sister, and in her senior year she got knocked up by Tony Morelli. No one was home one night when the two of them returned from a game, and Roberta hiked her skirt well up on her thigh to give Tony as good a view as he wanted of her shiny cheerleader tights. Mr. Quinn advanced the money for them to open a sporting goods store. Tony became a pillar of the community as Little League coach, Lion's Club fundraiser, Knights of Columbus director, and eventually chair of the Jeeptown United Way. He and Roberta had four children. One day, Mollie claimed, he got a vasectomy; Tony and Roberta became even happier than ever.

Sally Quinn continued to be inspired by Sister FAH

tee mah and she became a Maryknoll nun. She was sent to Guatemala, where she worked until she was murdered in 1985.

Billy Byrne also died in 1985—from the AIDS virus.

Mr. Jackson disappeared, and we could only speculate on what had happened to lim. Like everyone else, he must have been drawn outside by the sirens and flashing red lights. The writing on his car window would have made it obvious that he was in trouble. So we surmised that he threw his things into his car and drove off while the police milled around James's body. They were so preoccupied that they would not have even noticed the racket of the marbles clanging around inside the hub cap as his car made a u-turn and drove away.

Rafer Jones got a contract with the Pittsburgh Steelers where he played defensive tackle for a few years before he disappeared from sight.

Louis became a successful anesthesiologist. He married the girl who had stuck out her tongue at me during the bar mitzvah party. They became important patrons of the arts, and Louis played a key role in organizing the Jeeptown Chamber Orchestra. He stayed friends with Charlie and put money into Charlie's hedge fund very early on. That money was multiplied several times over.

Sister FAH tee mah spent her life teaching in Catholic schools. As the number of church schools dwindled, there wasn't much to provide for her retirement. Charlie made a big contribution to the rest home for retired nuns where she spent her last years. When he showed up for the ceremony put on in appreciation of his gift, she still had her mischievous smile, still called him Sharlie, and still pronounced her past tense verbs with two syllables.

Charlie's mother got her house in the suburbs, but the new home was so far away from her relatives that she could no longer just walk down the street and visit whenever she wanted. They eventually stopped the monthly card games that had nourished their spirits so much. She spent her last days living with her daughter Mollie. Charlie set up a trust fund to help Molly pay the bills and give Mother plenty of spending money.

Charlie's dad lost control over his drinking. He just lay around guzzling pint after pint of wine, losing job after job, and just picking at the dinners that his wife set out. His wife finally divorced him and moved in with Mollie. It was only then that he went to treatment and slowly put his life back together. He found another woman to live with, but never remarried.

Mollie fell in love with an Air Force pilot, and they had two children born at two different Air Force bases. She moved back to Jeeptown when he got assigned to

Vietnam, getting a terrific deal on an old Victorian House not far from the art museum. Her husband got killed during his second tour of flying an F-4 fighter-bomber in Vietnam. Her mother moved in to help raise the children while Molly went to college and got licensed as a social worker. Like Louis, she got in on the ground floor of Charlie's hedge fund. He bent some rules to get her in, because she didn't meet the financial requirements. She is now the wealthiest social worker in Jeeptown.

Charlie got an ROTC scholarship to college, which wasn't surprising given his math abilities. After a tour in the Army, he went to Wall Street and eventually got his own hedge fund to manage. He managed the fund successfully, but it stayed relatively small until his big break came in 1971. A friend at the Treasury Department tipped him off that President Nixon was planning to take the U.S. off the gold standard. Although it was illegal at the time for Americans to own gold, Charlie took a vacation in the Bahamas and figured out a way to leverage everything he owned to bet it on gold futures contracts. When the President announced his decision, the price of gold skyrocketed, and Charlie made a fortune overnight.

However, he never forgot the lesson he had learned as a boy about the utility of keeping some cash hidden in the coal bin, and he stashed away a substantial reserve in a numbered Swiss account. Just in case the U. S. authorities got curious about the legality of the gold futures he'd bought or how he had found out what the President was planning. He shot an annoyed glance at Mollie when she brought up this subject and asked her if she was trying to get him jailed for insider trading. However, she assured him that his transgression was so far in the past that the statute of limitations had expired long ago. So he told us about it, flashing that same cocky grin he had once flashed at me when he told me about hustling money away from Dirty George.

His three marriages ended in disaster. However, he doesn't seem unhappy. He keeps in contact with his adult children, goes to dinner with Louis and his wife when they visit New York, and stays with Mollie when he visits Jeeptown. His wealth earned him a large circle of friends in the worlds of politics and art. He has a Renoir original on the wall of his co-op apartment that looks out on Central Park. Not the magnificent Renoir street scene that overlooked our miserable parting that day in the museum. But a Renoir, nonetheless. Deep in his bedroom closet, he said he has a shoe box containing old photographs that he looks at every so often. Right on top is a well fingered picture of fifteen year-old Charlie with a Jew and two Black kids seated at a dining room table.

As for me, I went to college, as my mother advised, and became a social worker along with Mollie at the Jeeptown Department of Human Services. She offered to get Charlie to bend the rules so I could buy into his hedge fund too, but I declined. Getting financially entangled with a childhood sweetheart didn't seem like a good way to start my marriage. It was a fulfilling marriage for thirty years until my husband passed away. But it left me with many fond memories, and today I count myself as happy. I still sing in my church choir, and as a Black professional woman, I'm in great demand for boards and committees that I enjoy, and I often have the pleasure of babysitting with my grandchildren. Every now and then, I must confess, I cast a wistful glance at the bottom of my jewelry box where there still sits that old pair of tarnished brass earrings that Charlie once gave me.

THE END

ABOUT THE AUTHOR

 JJ Harrigan grew up in a place much like Jeeptown. He served with the Army in Germany during the Cold War and later as a U.S. Foreign Service Officer in Latin America. With a PhD from Georgetown University, he taught university level Political Science for many years before turning his hand to writing historical fiction. Currently, he scribbles his tales of intrigue on the banks of the St. Croix River in Minnesota, where he lives happily with his life Sandy.

www.jjharrigan.com

If you enjoyed *Jeeptown*, you might also enjoy JJ's Goodbye Series of historical thrillers.

Army lieutenant Charlie Parnell is sent to Cuba on a covert mission, posing as a reporter from Ireland. Single Mom Isabel Fernandez is assigned to be his watcher. But they fall for each other just as the 1962 Cuban missile crisis erupts. Can they outwit their minders and outrun the threat of nuclear war?
https://amzn.to/47bicOJ

Now a just-widowed businessman, Charlie Parnell puts his stepdaughter Angelita at risk when he takes on a dangerous role tied to 1968 Presidential Candidate Robert F. Kennedy, Sr's intent to end the war in Vietnam.
https://amzn.to/4qkp70I

Now a grown woman, Angelita becomes a Peace Corps Volunteer and marries a U.S. diplomat. Within weeks of their wedding, he is taken captive in the 1979-81 Iranian Hostage Crisis. She must act, but what can she do?

Available on Amazon, April 2026.